Praise for *In the Devi*

"With *In the Devil's Dreams* Felix Blackwell this first-rate novel holds echoes of F. Campbell, with more than a touch of Rod Serling and Richard Matheson thrown in for good measure, but does so in a voice that is all its own: confident, literate, and compelling as hell. Set aside a good chunk of time before opening this one, because it will be glued to your hands until the end — and by then, those hands will be shaking."

  - Gary A. Braunbeck, 7-time Bram Stoker Award-winning author of *To Each Their Darkness*, *In Silent Graves*, and *Rose of Sharon and Other Stories*

"Felix is an up and coming author with a fantastic imagination. One to watch for sure."

  - Layton Green, bestselling author of the *Dominic Grey* series

"*In the Devil's Dreams* distinguishes Felix as a literary juggernaut of terror. Part horror-thriller, part social commentary, this novel is a think piece on fear and inhibition, told with the mastery of a 21st century Poe. Felix shines a light into the darkest corners of your mind and forces you to look."

  - T. Baxter, *Voice of Fear* podcast

"I expected a decent thriller – but this book was ten times bigger than that. It's a page-turner that will have you hanging on the edge of your seat by your fingernails. Riveting... mesmerizing... brilliantly written. *In the Devil's Dreams* is an elaborate puzzle box of dark storytelling."

  - Gail Michael, author of *The Passions of Roxanna*

IN THE
DEVIL'S
DREAMS

FELIX BLACKWELL

illustrations by Rian Saputra

In the Devil's Dreams

Title and drawings by the incredible Rian Saputra.
www.behance.net/Ryannzha

Published in the United States in 2017 with Kindle Direct Publishing.

PREFACE

I'd like to pre-emptively clear up a bit of confusion about this book's authorship.

In the Devil's Dreams was inspired by a particularly disturbing nightmare I had in 2008. In it, I was visiting my mother in her little house by the woods, near a cliff overlooking the sea. A demon visited me in the night, and the conversations that took place between us have haunted me for over a decade. I owe my friend and fellow horror author Collin J. Northwood thanks, both for helping me understand the personal symbolism behind this dream, and for suggesting that I write it down.

It took me six years to finish the story, and not just because of the time I spent hiding Easter eggs throughout its narrative. The plot deals with deeply personal subject matter that was difficult to put into words. So it wasn't until 2014 that the book hit shelves, and four years later, I unpublished it and rewrote the manuscript entirely.

Originally, *In the Devil's Dreams* was attached to a pen name I'd used earlier in my writing career. I had no readership all those years ago, but now many have come to know me (through a series of lucky NoSleep stories that went viral) as Felix Blackwell.

My voice and style have changed dramatically over the years, such that *In the Devil's Dreams* was no longer recognizable to me as my own writing. In short…it wasn't very good. So, I tore it all down and rebuilt it, and now I present to you a work that I feel reflects a better craftsmanship: *In the Devil's Dreams* by Felix Blackwell.

I also want to extend my deepest gratitude to you, the reader, for supporting my work. Your messages, your reviews, and your dollars have a direct effect on indie authors like me, and your support makes the labor of writing a profoundly rewarding experience. Thank you.

— *Felix*

This book is dedicated to Ronan Harris and Mark Jackson
of VNV Nation.

PART **I**

A tide of madness drags me out and steals me from the shore,
and in time my senses warp – I'm stranger than before.

CHAPTER 1

The heavy haze of sleep settled over me. My eyes burned. My body ached. I could hardly follow a train of thought, much less recall where I was coming from. But I knew exactly where I was going, because it was my favorite place as a boy. I was visiting my mother in her little house by the woods, near that cliff overlooking the sea. I vaguely remembered running through those woods at dusk and swimming in the frigid water all those years ago. Or maybe it was just a dream. It didn't matter anymore.

It was a quaint little house – not much more than a few rooms and a kitchenette. No doors separated the main rooms. My mother lived alone now, and had no use for them. There was only a large, sturdy front door, which my father had put in long ago to withstand the whipping winds that often came screaming from offshore. As a child, those winds kept me awake in quiet terror, seeping through the trees like a thousand tormented voices crying from the dark. Or maybe it was all a nightmare. Those memories, like my father, were dim and obscure to me now. I couldn't be sure that either of them really existed at all.

Inside the house there wasn't much in the way of decoration. A few trinkets and knick-knacks lined the tables, mostly statues and candles my mother had collected over the years. There were, however, many shelves of books, which gave the place the ambience of an old wizard's library. It felt like home. It smelled like home. It was a place I could always come back to. But why I was coming back tonight, I struggled to recall.

My mother was a savior to me. I was not born to her, but she raised me into something presentable to the world. I sometimes think of my childhood – that of a lost and dirty orphan swaddled in wet clothes – and I can't imagine why she rescued me. And yet, she loved me at first sight. Now, she was the only one I could turn to.

On this icy evening I particularly looked forward to seeing her. No matter how old I got, I knew my mother would welcome me home with her warm glow. Whenever I was in trouble, she knew what to do. This week-long bout of insomnia deprived me of my ability to recall any specifics, but I was well aware, even though half-awake, that something was very wrong.

I stirred moments before the taxi pulled up, and forced my bleary eyes open. As I shambled out, I tossed the driver an uncounted handful of bills. I can't remember if I thanked him.

The air felt brisk and wet, and no wind rustled the trees. The sky looked like a black canvas smeared with gobs of gray paint. The forest was silent now, and did not herald my return with the joyful birdsongs of my childhood. It was as though a kind of darkness had followed me here, and nature held its breath in fear of my arrival.

My mother opened the door before I could knock and welcomed me into the light and warmth. I instantly felt a flicker of relief. Ancient happy memories awakened in my mind as I stepped inside. She took my coat and hugged me tight. Her smile chased away the doomy feeling I carried with me.

Maybe everything will be okay, I thought.

I have trouble pinpointing exactly how it began. I was resting, perhaps on the second or third evening of my visit. I still hadn't managed to get a full night's sleep. The fireplace threw calming light across the room. I sat quietly in bed with an old book I'd found – something about Merlin or Atlantis I think – and the warm crackle of the radio spilled into the room from elsewhere. My mother was either listening to it intently or already asleep. Her mere presence was comforting to me. I fingered at the rusty old pocket watch my father gave to me all those years ago. It had meant so much to him. When he put it in my hand, he told me, "Son, don't lose this. This is all I got."

I still felt him as I gripped it. He too was not my biological parent, but that hardly mattered. My father was a hero.

What caught my eye I can't say, but I was enticed to gaze up at the little window high on the wall across the room. Through it, I could barely make out the gnarled fingers of the dying trees, grasping at one another and entangling the sky in their embrace. The moon's ghostly glow dripped through the branches and bathed the room in cold silver. It lit up the wisps of fog that lurked across the forest floor outside. That fog was an otherworldly sight to me as a boy; I could still conjure it in my mind, barely, like a memory within a dream. It very well could have been some other forest, or maybe just the setting of some story I read ages ago. I wasn't sure about anything tonight.

I began to drift.

Thoughts swirled and flashed in my head like fireflies. I was unable to catch any of them, and they flitted across my mind for only a moment before dissipating. A strange feeling nagged at me. It was the need to remember why I had come here. But no matter how hard I tried, all I could recall was a murky sensation of dread. I felt my heart sitting in my chest, its stillness an ominous reminder that I was missing something. Where had I been before? What had happened? My brain gave up and my eyes fell shut.

I don't know how long I slept.

I was awakened suddenly by a tremendous banging. At first, I thought lightning had struck a tree outside. The noise thundered throughout the house, rattling the picture frames on the walls. Then it repeated over and over. I looked around, trying to find my bearings, but the house was different.

It looked warped. The room seemed bigger, or maybe I was smaller. The air was stale, and the distinct odor of burnt hair choked me. Bookshelves were tipped over and strewn about. Walls bent, and the bathroom door curled menacingly out of its frame. The house looked like it had melted, but everything felt so cold.

It's a nightmare, I tried to assure myself.

I got up and looked down the hall.

Panic overwhelmed me as my mother started screaming.

He found me.

A white-hot terror washed over me. I stood in the hall, frozen, while my mother barricaded the front door with a bookshelf. She yelled for me to hide, to escape, while she held back the wretched thing that sought me just beyond the frame. Against the instinct to defend my family, I turned and fled. A fear worse than death commanded me like a puppet. It drove me to sink between the bed and rippled wall, making a laughable attempt at hiding from such a monolithic evil.

The door squealed in agony as the creature relentlessly hunted me. Even from the other room, I could feel his lust like a dagger pressed against my neck. I buried my head in my arms and slammed my eyes shut, but I could still see him in my mind. I remembered now. As the door neared the end of its integrity, it budged open a foot or so, and in breached a hideous head. The monster wailed and cackled with hellish malice.

His skin was a patchwork of charred and hairless flesh, pale gray as a corpse in some places and brown like rancid meat in others. It appeared to have been stitched together in a disgusting mockery of a human face. The creature's revolting ugliness instantly made my stomach churn. He was an abomination of nature, a masterwork of the Devil.

He called my name in two simultaneous voices: one a deep and guttural scream, the other a shrill whisper. Both sounds belched forth from a throat as dry as death. I was unsure of whether his voice could be heard by anyone else, if it was actually vocalized or somehow spoken into my mind. But I was certain he existed because of the abrupt change in pitch and terror in my mother's voice as she turned to face him. She screamed like nothing I've ever heard before, and the monster's expression changed the second his serpentine eyes met with hers. I saw now in him what appeared to be a tinge of fear – or hatred. He growled in pain as she peered into him. His cracked lips curled up and exposed his vampiric maw, and he released a deafening shriek. With newfound determination, the monster shattered the door and sent my mother backward, where she crashed into a lifeless heap.

For a moment my fear abated, and I jumped to my feet to help her. As I did, the creature rushed at me with inhuman speed. He clambered over the broken bookshelf that had obstructed his entry and dashed up the hall toward me. With terrifying strength he flipped the bed over, exposing me.

He stopped inches from my body and towered over me menacingly. My face only came up to his chest. I turned my head away but couldn't keep my eyes off his vile form. I stood in the shadow of a burned demon wrapped in dirty rags.

The monster reached out with a meaty arm and grabbed my shirt, ripping me from the ground and pulling me up to his face. I finally screamed after several failed attempts. Sweat ran down my entire body and dripped into my shoes. Every hair on my neck tingled and stood on end; it felt like a thousand tiny spiders scurried over every inch of my skin.

"Say it!" he bellowed, his eyes darkening with glee. A grotesque smile spread across his face.

I couldn't speak. I simply gasped and choked while staring into him. He was hypnotically ugly, and no matter how I tried, I couldn't tear my eyes from his. I don't know how long we stared into each other, but when he dropped me down to the floor again, my paper legs crumpled beneath me and I hit the floor hard. It felt like he stole a part of me with his gaze. It felt like something was gone now. I had been emptied of something important.

The monster crouched down in front of me with his knees spread apart to block any escape. I shut my eyes and turned my head away, expecting him to bite into me with those jagged teeth. He lurched forward and put his face to my cheek. His skin felt taut with death, and no warmth emitted from it. To my surprise, he smelled alluring. It was the scent of a lover's skin.

He smelled familiar.

The thought nauseated me. His foul breath invaded my senses as he brushed his face all over my neck and hair, sniffing me like a wolf. I thought about kicking him in the groin or stabbing him in those pale yellow eyes with my fingers.

"Try it," the creature said into my ear, his voice lively and excited.

With lightning speed, he grabbed my arm and wrenched my hand toward his mouth. I screamed in horror as I waited for him to begin chewing on my fingers, but instead, he licked them with a dog-like tongue. He examined them, as though he were trying to determine what I'd eaten earlier. Sticky drool dripped down my wrist.

"I feel like we've been apart a thousand years," he said. "But I promise, I won't lose you again."

The urge to vomit and pass out washed over me. I wanted to die.

"Gorleth," I muttered.

He shoved his face close to mine and growled,

"That is *not* my name."

The monster pulled away and watched me twitch for a few moments, then patted my head.

"Poor thing," he said with mock sympathy. "I'll take care of you." A gurgling laugh seeped from his throat.

My eyes felt impossibly heavy, and they shut despite my attempts to keep them open. I slumped over, feeling my shoulders and head hit the ground, and then all went black.

I don't know how long I slept.

CHAPTER 2

When I awoke, I was in bed again. Golden sunlight poured through the nearby window, leaving glowing patches on the quilt that covered me. The room was back to normal – nothing bent or warped, nothing out of place. Outside, the birds sang merrily. Relief washed over me, and with it came a wave of nausea. I leaped out of bed and ran to the little bathroom, just barely making it to the toilet. Every muscle in my body ached as though I were sick with a high fever, and my eyes looked red and bleary in the mirror.

I drew a hot bath. I sank to the floor and leaned against the wall as it filled, hoping I was finished throwing up.

What had I dreamed about? I wondered. I could hardly remember.

I shivered in pleasure as I slipped into the hot water. Sleep tried to steal me away there in the tub, but I decided I'd get dressed and go outside instead, to feel the sun on my skin, and to shake off the remnants of a horrible rest. I splashed warm water all over my face and took deep breaths to fill my lungs with the new day.

Why do I feel so strange?

A thick fog settled over my mind. I allowed my eyes to close, and I became lost in thought.

What was I supposed to remember?

I'd been running. I remembered having an argument. I remembered storming out. But I also remembered leaving in fear. I felt like a ghost wandering through an old house, trying to piece together some forgotten tragedy. My skin went cold.

No, it was the water. The temperature suddenly dropped in the tub. I opened my eyes just in time to notice the bathroom light flickering.

"Feeling better?" a hideous voice croaked.

The great being stood beside me. In a split second he grabbed me, snatching me up into the air and slamming me against the cold tile wall. I couldn't even scream. Those lidless eyes burned into mine. A smile crept over his horrid face.

"There's no need to lock the door. It's only me here," he gurgled, and set me back down into the frigid water. The light crackled and dimmed so much that I could barely make anything out. Sunlight no longer seeped through the window above the toilet. It was dark outside now.

The Gorleth sat down onto the toilet with a loud thud and turned to face me. He picked up a towel off the rack nearby and examined it, then wiped his face with it and sighed.

"Why does it run from me?" he asked, then tossed the towel at me.

As I stood up and wrapped it around myself, I kept my eyes on him. He sat quite still, returning my gaze, but occasionally he'd twitch or blink compulsively. His fists, resting on his lap, clenched every now and then. I feared he'd hit me if I upset him.

"I came all this way for you," the creature said, his anger visibly growing. "I *hate* this place." His lips quivered.

"What exactly do you want?" I asked in a gentle voice. My heart hummed in my chest.

The creature jumped to his feet.

"What do I want?!" he shouted.

Every muscle on his body rippled and twitched with rage. Some primal hate overthrew his senses, causing him to thrash his arms around and tear the shower curtain off its old rings. The paint on the walls around him began to bubble and recede, and tiny bits of ice formed on the wet carpet by his feet. The light flickered again.

As the creature calmed down, he hacked now and then, like a cat getting ready to spit up a hairball.

"*Rak! Rak!*"

The foul thing looked over his hands and shot a surprised glance at me, then left the room. He snickered on his way out.

Felix Blackwell

I had no idea what to do. I just sat there, completely still.

"Wake up, wake up," I whispered. My teeth chattered like tiny jackhammers.

This has got to be a dream.

I don't know how long I cowered there in that rancid bathroom, but I was hoping I'd fall back asleep. Or wake up. The floor was stained with unspeakable liquids, and the paint on the walls peeled back to expose rotting wood.

I looked up at the window, at the darkness beyond.

I can fit through that.

I clambered to my feet and put on my clothes.

"Get out here!" the Gorleth screamed, his bellow rattling the walls. The sound jerked me from my scheming and sent icy pins down my back.

Fear commanded me to obey. I grabbed the door handle, took a deep breath, and pushed.

The bedroom was once again warped and decrepit like the bathroom. The creature sat at the edge of the bed, hunched over a toppled bookshelf. He held an old book and leafed through it with a corpse-like hand. The desk light beside him glimmered and buzzed, casting his looming shadow across the walls again and again.

He hummed to himself in that awful voice. He hummed a vaguely familiar song. I was almost too afraid to speak, but my confusion nagged at my vocal cords.

"Are you going to hurt me?" I asked.

The monster ignored me.

"What are you looking for?" I pressed.

No response.

I stared at him for half a minute, waiting for a word, a movement, another violent episode.

"Where is my mother?"

Nothing.

"I don't recall Frankenstein teaching his abomination how to read," I said. I don't know what possessed me to say that, of all things.

The Gorleth emitted a wet chuckle and tore his eyes from

the page to glare at me.

"No," he said, "the monster had to teach himself. He was abandoned by the only one he had."

He slammed the book shut and hurled it across the room. It exploded into a hundred thousand mixed up words that fluttered to the ground. The creature gingerly picked up another book and began to flip through its old pages.

"If you came all the way out here to read Epicurus—"

He silenced me with a hand.

"Defiant 'till the bitter end," he said, without looking up. "Tell me, Professor, what exactly are you qualified to teach? You know nothing about these books."

"Tell me what you want!" I shouted. "I know you've been following me. Why don't you just kill me already? I'm right here!"

The Gorleth slowly rose from the edge of the bed, still facing the bookcase in quiet contemplation. I held my breath, expecting to be beaten – or chewed – to death. He eventually turned to face me, unblinking, and lurched toward me like a bear.

He stopped a foot away from me. My back was to the wall.

"Do it, then," I said, gazing into his dead fish eyes.

The creature held still, looking down at me. He examined my chest and neck with a horrible hand. He dropped his face down into mine, pressed his cold nose against my ear, and growled in an impossibly deep voice,

"Soon."

Then he ambled away and continued his search. A few moments passed as he leafed through my mother's books. I slipped my feet into my shoes.

"Sit down, Professor. Try to rest while you can. I promise it'll be over soon. And I'm sorry to say, as I recall you're rather squeamish," he turned his head and looked at me, "…there will be blood." The Gorleth chuckled, and then began to hum that song to himself. That vaguely familiar song.

I knew I was going to die. But a worse realization dawned on me: he planned to torture me first. That was his game.

A hot feeling washed up from my stomach and into my

throat. I ran to the toilet and fell to my knees. This time, I dry-heaved. Sweat dripped down my cheeks and off my lips into the bowl. My skin went cold. My head felt a thousand pounds.

A shadow fell on me as I crouched by the toilet. The monster towered over me, blocking the entire door frame, eclipsing the light from the bedroom. He cleared a clot of phlegm from his throat and said:

> *"I found myself in a dark wood-*
> *-so dark that the way was lost.*
> *Ah, how difficult it is to convey*
> *The savage nature of that forest;*
> *Savage, dense, and unforgiving.*
> *The very thought of it rekindles my terror."*

I recognized his words. The creature must have found my mother's old copy of Dante's *Comedia*. I wiped my mouth on my sleeve.

"So, you can read," I said. "It still wouldn't earn Victor's love." I turned around to further defy him. "You'll get scholarships with that kind of—"

But then I saw that the Gorleth wasn't holding a book. His eyes narrowed at me, and a razor grin parted his lips. He continued:

> *"Through me the way into the suffering city.*
> *Through me the way to eternal pain.*
> *Abandon hope, all ye who enter here."*

We exchanged gazes for a moment, his blank and unwavering, mine surprised and perhaps a little impressed. Aside from my wife, nobody I knew could recite medieval poetry from memory. She would speak it to me, and I would attempt to return the gesture with quotes from my favorite literature.

The monster dragged a horrible claw down the door frame and tapped it twice, as if to signal something to me. Then he coughed and sputtered. His hands balled into giant fists. His strange fits returned.

"*Rak!..Rak!...Rugh!...*"

He turned around and disappeared into the bedroom.

I was alone again.

I turned back to the toilet and tried to spit out the horrible flavor in my mouth, then gazed out the window. The dark forest beyond the glass had always terrified me as a child, but now I thought of it as a sanctuary. My jacket was in the living room, and I knew it would be cold outside, but I'd rather freeze to death out there than die by the putrid hands of the Gorleth.

And my mom. Maybe she got out.

The creature continued to spasm in the other room, shouting and whispering to himself like a madman. As quietly as I could, I closed the lid of the toilet, climbed atop it, and grabbed at the window. It moaned in defiance as it scraped against its warped frame, but my terror inspired in me an unknown strength. I threw it open with the might of a gladiator.

"Get it all out?" the monster called from the other room. I could hear him opening drawers, looking for something.

I didn't respond. To cover the sound of my escape, I flushed the toilet with a foot, and then heaved myself through that window. I toppled to the ground outside with a painful thud.

CHAPTER 3

For a moment I lay there in silence, staring out at the distant tree line. The front of my mother's little house overlooked the ocean from a hundred feet up. If you were to walk out the front door on any given evening, you'd be greeted with a brilliant sunset that cast a thousand colors across the water's surface. Dozens of behemoth stones jutted painfully out of the sea, waiting to gut passing ships. The woods stretched from the sand for a dozen miles eastward and wrapped in a crescent shape around the backside of the house, where I now sat. Between the tree line and the window I'd just fallen from, there was a big meadow, which we considered our backyard. As a child I played here, but was forbidden to enter the forest. So I spent much of my boyhood surveying the woods from the edge of the meadow.

My mother would often scold me when she found me there. She was an avid hiker when my father was alive, but after he died, she persistently feared that I would enter the woods alone. She often made me promise never to go there without her, and I never broke that promise. At a very young age I had once been lost in a forest, and so I understood her concern.

The cry of distant wolves snapped me back to the present moment. I hesitated.

A rustling came from somewhere within the house.

I'll take my chances with the wolves, I thought.

I scrambled to my feet and sprinted headlong for the trees. No cool night breeze kissed my skin as I moved. The air was thick and musty, and unseasonably warm. The damp ground muffled my footsteps. As I glanced up, the clouds hung low and trapped the orange moonlight. In a few places the sky was clear, and tiny red stars peered down at me. They didn't twinkle at all.

They just stared.

I had no idea where I was going. I knew I had to find my mother, and to escape the wretched creature, but we didn't have a neighbor for miles. The town of Waldport was at least an hour away on foot. And it was dark. God help me, it was dark.

I reached the tree line and paused for just a moment, looking back at the house. Across the field, the Gorleth stared at me from the bathroom window, expressionless and unblinking. Half of his horrible face was covered in shadow, but in my chest I felt the grip of his silent rage. He was watching me. Daring me. Reveling in my fear. His gaze pierced into my soul, promising me that I would not escape so easily. He wanted me to know that my mother's house was now my prison, and that he was my executioner. I darted into the woods, disappearing from his sight. I prayed he wouldn't find me.

The wolves were silent now, as was the rest of the forest. No crickets chirped. No owls hooted. The place was unusually still, as it had been when I'd first arrived home.

I remembered that the highway ran through these woods, perhaps six or seven miles east. I could follow it into town and get help. It would be a long trek, especially in the dark, but my fear of the monster vastly outweighed all other concerns. All I could think of were those yellow eyes...those lifeless, yellow eyes.

As I waded deeper into the sea of pines, I finally heard sounds of life. A bullfrog croaked now and again, but in a sickly, sedated way. Once in a while, distant animal calls resounded from far off. At one point I even thought I heard voices, otherworldly whispers that echoed so faintly I could not distinguish them from my own imaginings.

The woods around me felt haunted. As I walked, I could feel my childhood phobia of being lost creeping over me. My fear took the form of writhing shadows, looming over me, watching my movements. The trees were rotted and decayed. Some of them were bent and drooping as if they'd melted; their claw-like branches reached out in every direction, desperately clawing the night. Whatever nightmarish presence that had taken root in my mother's home had somehow spread all the way out here.

If I can get far enough away, I'll be alright, I thought. *He can't follow me forever.*

No amount of reasoning assuaged me. I was trapped inside the Gorleth's world, and I had no idea if there even was a way out.

Something moved behind me.

Instinctively, I whirled around, squinting through the murk. The billowy fog that crept along the ground now wafted upward and all around me. In the distance I made out the ghostly form of a woman meandering between the trees.

I ran toward her.

"Mom!" I called out. "Mom? Is that you?"

No reply. The wraithlike figure drifted in and out of view. The fog rolled around and lapped at the trees like ocean waves.

"Is someone there?" I called again.

"Where…are you?" a soft voice returned.

"Mom?" I asked, "is that you?"

I edged toward the voice, but could no longer see anyone.

A branch cracked on the ground a few yards to my left. I spun toward it.

"Where the hell are you?" I whispered. "Stay still!"

Her form again came into view, but she was too tall to be my mother. From where I stood, her hair looked dark brown or black. I held still, watching as the woman slowly wandered in a half-circle around me. She didn't seem to notice me, and always looked downward as she weaved between the large tree trunks.

She cleared her throat.

"Who are you?" I asked.

She didn't respond.

"What are you doing out here?" I pressed. "Are you lost?"

She turned her back to me, and although I could hardly see her, she appeared to be wearing some kind of white dress. Her hair was nearly black, and draped across her back in thick locks. Her skin was fair and glowed in the foggy moonlight.

She looked like my wife.

"Emily?" I said.

An ungodly sound erupted from behind me.

"*Rak…rak…*"

It was *him*.

I gasped and whirled around, searching for the Gorleth, but found only a wall of fog.

"He's coming," I whispered. "Run!"

I dashed toward the woman. She ran ahead of me, moving effortlessly through the woods. I struggled to keep up. The creature began to hum that same song in the distance.

"I can't see," I whispered as loud as I dared. The strange woman pulled farther and farther ahead.

Heavy footsteps smashed twigs and leaves behind me. The Gorleth gave chase.

"Wait up!" I called a bit louder.

Tree trunks blew past me as I sprinted. I hit branches and tripped over roots. The woman was scarcely visible now. The fog and darkness embraced her figure, almost swallowing her up. She disappeared from my sight and made no further sounds, even when I stopped to listen for her. This left only the horrible sounds of my tormentor, searching for me just a short distance behind.

"Professor!" the beast called out, his voice like a saw. The words echoed forever. His yell antagonized the distant wolves, who responded in kind with eerie howls. "I can smell you," he growled. "You can't hide."

Not waiting to find out how keen his sense of smell really was, I dashed through the woods in the direction the woman had gone. Eventually, I heard no more of the monster, but I kept running anyway.

I ran for what felt like fifteen minutes.

Just when I'd begun to feel safe, a huge form appeared before me. The fog was so thick that I didn't see it until it was ten feet away. I yipped in fright and tried to stop, but it was too late.

I slammed face-first into a huge man in a trench coat. His burly form knocked the wind out of me, and my force sent us both into the ground with a tremendous thud. His reflexes were much quicker than mine. The man grabbed me by the shirt, and with some kind of karate move, he flipped me over and pinned me. He sat on me, too heavy for me to fight back. He raised his big fist into the air and held me by the throat with the other hand.

"Wait! Wait!" I cried.

"Who are you?" he shouted. I was so intimidated by the power of his voice that I froze up.

"Who are you?!" he shouted again, louder. This idiot was going to lead the monster right to us.

"Shh!" I whispered. "Keep your damn voice down! And get off me, you ogre!"

I looked around frantically, listening for my pursuer. The man paused for a moment, then relented, and allowed me to sit up.

"What the hell are you runnin' into me for?" he demanded. He was big, like a lumberjack, but not nearly as big as the creature. He looked about as disoriented as I did, and his five-o'clock shadow indicated to me that he'd likely been out here for days.

"There's something after me," I whispered.

"Oh yeah?" he responded in an unsympathetic voice. "Sounds rough. I got *three* somethin's after me, guy."

My words caught in my throat. Could it be possible that there was more than one monster? What could he be running from?

I studied his face.

"You...you look familiar," I said. "Where are you from?"

"Here," he replied, looking around with an uncertain expression. "I think."

"I'm from Waldport," I replied, "but I don't know where I am now." I wondered if he knew where the road was.

"That makes two of us."

The man sat down next to me and searched his trench coat for something, perhaps a cigarette. "Waldport," he repeated. "Never heard of it. That in Shropshire?"

I laughed at his bad guess. "It's...in the States."

For a few moments, he didn't respond.

"You know where you're headed?" he finally asked.

"No," I said. "Away. Anywhere. I just don't wanna be found." As I spoke, I glanced around, checking for signs of the monster. I heard nothing.

"Yeah me neither, on both accounts," he said. "Well, let's wander together, then. No use in being alone. Say, you haven't seen a kid out here, have you?"

I paused at the odd question. I thought of the ghostly woman but decided not to mention her.

"I haven't seen anyone out here but you," I replied. "And I'm happy to see you, believe it or not." I wanted to hug this stranger. For the first time in hours, I wasn't so afraid.

We stood up and brushed ourselves off, then wandered through the woods together. I warned him about the Gorleth, but he scoffed at my concern. As he laughed, he seemed immediately familiar.

He laughed like my father.

It was pretty dark, and perhaps my eyes were playing tricks on me, but he also looked a bit like my father – only decades younger. As we moved through the woods, I studied him carefully, and shared my ridiculous thought with him. He scoffed at me again.

"What did you say your name was?" I finally asked.

He stopped and looked at me squarely.

"I didn't. Listen pal, do you have eyes? You look older than me! And I never been to *Waldport* in my entire life."

Somewhat put off, I accepted his rebuke and walked on ahead of him.

"You gonna be okay there?" he asked.

I didn't reply.

After what felt like five or ten minutes, we resumed conversation, but he mostly babbled about how everything that was happening was part of some puzzle. Like this whole place was a projection of his own imagination. I barely listened.

Through some gaps in the canopy, I could see the moon. It glowed a sickly orange-yellow, and the fog carried the light to the forest floor. The beams lit up the nearby trees and reminded me of little light posts dotting the landscape, guiding me to some unknown destination. The only sound perforating the stillness was the crunch of leaves beneath our shoes.

The man abruptly halted and sank down to the ground. He stuck a meaty arm out beside him, silently ordering me to be quiet. Thoughts of the Gorleth flooded my mind, and I glanced around, terrified, squinting for any sign of him.

"What is it?" I whispered over his shoulder. He didn't respond.

Then, I heard it: rustling, directly ahead of us. Something big moved through the trees about a hundred paces away. It struggled and caused a commotion. In my mind, I saw the monster stomping his way through the woods, growling and thrashing about.

"No...it's him…oh God, he's f-found me again," I stammered. I took a step back and considered bolting in the opposite direction. My new friend grabbed my wrist with a stony grip. He pulled me along with him as he slinked forward, craning his neck to hear the sounds up ahead.

Then, I heard voices.

"Shut up!" a man yelled. "Come 'ere, stupid whore!"

The fragile voice of a young woman rang out, clear as a bell in the stillness.

"Don't!" she cried out. "Please! Please let me go!"

At first, I thought of the woman I'd seen in the fog. I thought of Emily. But this voice did not belong to my wife; the woman shouting now had a thick accent.

The big guy dashed off furiously in her direction, but not with the noble intent of a stranger coming to another's assistance. He moved with singular purpose, like a man rescuing his wife. His speed and ferocity surprised me, and I tried to keep up. We ran for only a few dozen paces before he caught his foot on a fallen branch and went careening to the ground. I came up behind him and helped him to his feet.

We had arrived in a clearing, and at its center stood a large barn. The building seemed out of place in the middle of the woods. There was no house or farm nearby. It sat in disrepair, obviously decades old and deserted for nearly as long. On the side from which we approached, there were no windows or doors.

"Let me go, you bastard!" the poor woman screamed. "Get your hands off me!"

The stranger broke away from me again, encircling the barn and screaming *"Adam!"* over and over. I could tell by the murder in his eyes that he knew both people inside.

Loud thuds emitted from the barn. As I followed his path around it, I could hear my new friend slamming his big body against a door and shouting.

"You monster!" the woman screamed. "They'll feed you to the wolves for this!"

It was her last scream, and it was forced through a waterfall of sobs. My heart fell still in my chest. I caught sight of my friend a second before he shattered the door and went flying into the barn, both feet off the ground.

I ran toward the door as fast as I could, ready to help the woman. Ready to tear this *Adam* guy apart.

CHAPTER 4

More fog rolled in to confront the moonlight, and the sky darkened. I could barely make out the innards of the barn. Hay covered most of the ground and was heaped in a few places. Bent and warped tools clung uselessly to the wooden walls, and hundreds of splinters covered the entryway where the door had shattered. My friend was nowhere to be found.

"Hello?" I called into the dark. There was no answer. A wolf howled somewhere in the distance.

"Anybody in here?" I asked. "Ma'am?"

Nothing.

I shuffled inside, careful not to trip on the debris that littered the ground. I made my way toward the back of the room, half-expecting to be ambushed.

"Hello?" I called again. "Hey man, where the hell are you? Did you find her?"

As I crept through the room, I perceived two figures cloaked in shadow. One lay on the ground, and the other stood motionless in the corner. The darkness obscured their features, but I was certain there were two people in this barn with me.

No movement. No sound. I inched closer, straining my sight, and desperately trying not to look scared.

"I can see you," I warned.

No response.

I took one more step forward, hands shaking, and then I realized what I was looking at. The standing figure was a man – a skinny man, like me, but probably in his mid-twenties. He was in fact not standing, but hanging by his neck from a short rope. His shoes barely scraped the ground. I worked up the courage to put my face closer to his.

I didn't recognize him. Dirt caked his face, and bloody scratches crisscrossed his neck and cheeks. I backed away, not peeling my eyes from him. I nearly fell over the body on the ground.

It was a young woman, but certainly not the one I'd met in the fog. Unlike the ghostly woman from earlier, this one had lighter hair, maybe dirty blonde. Blood streaked her face, making it difficult to identify her, but she looked young. Her red dress was ripped at the collar. The fabric was pushed up around her thighs.

Approaching the brink of a panic attack, I staggered away from the scene like a drunk.

"Hey…um…Somebody help," I said, barely squeaking the words out. "God, I…is anybody out there? Where are you, buddy? This woman… there's… someone's been killed."

My head spun. I struggled to think and speak, and my whole body trembled like a leaf in the wind. It took me more than a few moments to find the exit, and by the time I reached it, I was in tears. I felt an overwhelming pain in my heart, as if I'd just found my own family in that state.

Who was she? I wondered.

I stepped outside and gulped the night air for relief. It was stale, and offered me no solace from the horror I'd witnessed. The moonlight cast an orange silhouette across the misty sky. What light it offered barely reached this clearing, but was enough to reveal the edge of the woods, which formed a circle around the barn. I collected myself, chose a direction at random, and made my way to the trees. My friend was gone.

A choir of howls erupted from the woods ahead of me. The unseen wolves yipped and growled with excitement, no doubt excited by the arrival of their wandering dinner guest. I halted in my tracks, attempting to make out the size and number of my rabid enemies. They scampered and darted between the trees, careful to never fully reveal themselves in the moonlight. The only real shapes I could make out were their pale glowing eyes; a dozen pairs watched me from the edge of the woods.

I backed up a couple of steps, not sure whether it was

Felix Blackwell

smarter to make a mad dash in the opposite direction, or to move calmly.

Make a bunch of noise.

Or is that mountain lions?

Shit.

Suddenly, the shadowy things ceased their overture. The world around me fell deathly still.

I glanced over my shoulder to assess my exit strategy. The wolves guarded a half circle of the woods in front of me, and behind me to my right, the barn blocked my retreat.

I glanced over my other shoulder.

At that edge of the meadow stood a gigantic figure wreathed in darkness. The shadows he lurked in betrayed him – it was unmistakably the Gorleth. The monster peered into me, just like he'd done earlier from the bathroom window, and held perfectly still. Despite the distance, I knew that running would be a futile effort. I knew how fast he was.

I returned his gaze unflinching. We stood there, a hundred yards apart, staring at one another. With each labored breath, I felt terror's knives caress my ribs. The monster awaited my next move and glanced at the wolves.

He knew I had to make a choice.

"Do you remember the tale of Scylla and Charybdis, Professor?" he asked. His voice drifted lazily through the fog, like the sounds of a burbling stomach.

"Fuck you," I grunted.

He spoke of a Greek myth. Sailors feared a region of the sea, where two hazards lay waiting in the water, ready to devour passing ships. One was a giant sea monster, the other a deadly whirlpool. In order to avoid one, a ship would pass too close to the other and be destroyed.

"Let's go home, Professor," the Gorleth said, the patience in his voice thinning.

"You really believe I'd do that?" I called across the meadow, trying to spare myself time to think.

"I can't protect you from these woods," he replied. "This place is more dangerous than you think. You imperil yourself with every step you take! And there are far worse fates awaiting you there, in the dark, than the one I offer you." He pointed to the wolves.

"What is this place?" I asked.

"You tell me," he replied.

I hesitated at his words. What the hell was that supposed to mean? I shot a glance at the barn, then back to the monster.

"Those people in there…who are they?"

The creature didn't look. He never took his eyes off me.

"People? No people," he smiled. "Only you and me."

The Gorleth chuckled, and simultaneously, the wolves resumed their horrid baying.

"Now, Professor! Come with me!" he shouted. "You don't have much time!"

I was too afraid to move a muscle. I had no idea what to do. I was certain he meant to kill me, and by the look of his teeth, it wouldn't feel much different from being eaten alive by wolves.

"Come, or I'll rip out your eyes!" He screamed. Drool sloshed from his rotting lips. It caught the moonlight as it dribbled off his face. "*Rak!...rak!..Nuhh!*" The creature was seized yet again by a fit. Rage coursed through his huge form, and although he was some distance away, I could see his muscles flexing wildly from beneath his tattered clothes.

Why won't he just come get me? I wondered. The monster didn't seem to want to move any closer.

"If I have to come…over…there…" he struggled to speak through violent tics, "…I will *break* your bones."

The wolves wailed in glee.

I considered the idea that he was bluffing. I decided to test him. If I was wrong, I could run right into the wolves. Maybe they'd eat him too.

"Here I am." I opened my arms and held my ground.

The monster didn't budge. He just stood there, panting and shaking with rage.

"You can't come out here!" I laughed triumphantly. "What is it? The moon? What are you afraid of?" I asked.

Silence was his reply. I took a taunting step toward him,

and immediately in response, the wolves fell silent. I took a few steps back toward them, and again they howled.

The wolves and the monster refused to come near each other. Neither could take me so long as the other was nearby.

What the hell is this about? I wondered.

I turned back to the monster and eyed him.

"What *are* you, Gorleth? Where do you come from?" I demanded.

He bared his ugly teeth at me. With a voice that shook the forest for a hundred miles around, he screamed, "*That is not my name!*"

I nearly collapsed in fright. I'd never heard a scream so loud. The shock of it ensnared me and locked up my muscles. No part of my body registered my brain's command to flee.

Just then, a familiar sound echoed from the woods near the barn: the rhythmic crunching of leaves. I thought of my new friend, the man who looked like my father, but these footsteps were too light and quick to be his.

A tiny child, probably no older than six, burst from the tree line at full speed and raced across the meadow. He passed right by me, his shirtless torso lacerated and bloodied as though he'd crawled through a barbed wire fence. More likely his wounds were caused by the sea of jagged branches that protruded from the trees. This must have been the kid my new friend was looking for.

Speechless, I watched as the child bolted headlong toward the other end of the meadow, directly between the wolves and the Gorleth. I never saw his face.

"Wait, no!" I screamed, fearing he'd be attacked.

Although I had no children of my own, a parental urge overthrew my senses and washed away my recent predicament. I took off after him, arms outstretched, shouting for the boy to stop. The wolves moved to flank us.

The monster saw his opportunity and stormed into the meadow. The rage in his face morphed to a wicked glee, and I found myself shrieking with fear. But I didn't retreat. I kept running after the kid.

The monster intercepted me. His gigantic frame barreled into me like a truck, knocking me off of my feet and sending me to the grass. The boy disappeared into the woods, and the wolves receded into the darkness. Just before the black washed over me, I peered into the sky. The moon had not moved in hours…it remained fixed in its place.

The Gorleth stood over me and smiled a terrible smile.

Felix Blackwell

CHAPTER 5

The feeling of soft linen returned me to my senses. Fiery pain shot down my arm and back as I tried to move. For a blessed moment I didn't know who or where I was. Then I opened my eyes.

I was back inside my mother's house. It was dreadfully deformed, like a macabre funhouse. The bed I lay in was uneven and slanted. The bulging ceiling reminded me of snowy hills. The light in its center flickered. It took me a few moments to realize that I'd been gingerly tucked in.

Mom.

I mustered the strength to lift my head, which pounded angrily in protest. I saw that I was not wearing a shirt. I peered down the dark hallway toward what little bit of the living room I could see from here. Orange moonlight drifted in through the kitchen window and faintly illuminated the area, but no one was there. Outside, the crickets sang their dreary songs.

"Mom?" I called out, my voice frail and shaky.

The crickets stopped.

"Mom?" I called again.

"July 1st, 1975," a ghoulish voice erupted.

I whipped my head toward the sound, only to find the massive creature leaning against the wall next to the bathroom. In his gruesome hands he held a brown leather book.

"She's gotten worse," he spoke. "Emily confessed to me that the dream in which she commits suicide has returned. It has recurred every night for the past week, each time sending her from her sleep. Thus far she has rejected my advice to see a doctor. Instead she has withdrawn from me and spends most of her time painting or sleeping. Her boss called me, saying he was considering suspending her. I feel—"

"Where did you get that?" I demanded. I sat straight up in bed, ignoring the pain that flooded my body.

The monster dropped his arms to his sides, closed the book on a meaty finger, and gave me a disappointed stare. I fell silent. Several seconds passed, but his dead eyes remained fixed on me. He cleared his throat and lifted the journal again:

"I feel helpless. I've never heard of a dream like this one. Although I don't necessarily consider Emily to be suicidal, I fear she could become a danger to herself if her condition worsens."

The monster again dropped the book to his side, and glanced around the room, as if deep in thought.

"Professor, what do you think of dreams?"

"Why do you keep calling me that?" I asked.

"What?" his eyes met mine.

"'Professor.' Why do you call me that? I'm not at the university anymore. Nobody calls me that anymore."

"Ah, but I can think of one person who does," he said, smiling.

Only my wife used that name now, in the same way that someone might use 'dear' or 'sweetie.' But how could he possibly know that?

"What do you know about my wife?" I asked. "Do you know Emily?"

The Gorleth ignored me. His gaze drifted to the bookcases.

"What do you think of dreams, Professor?"

"That question makes no sense," I snapped, growing tired of his whimsy.

"Do you think they're meaningful?" he went on. "Omens, perhaps? Or are they just…random pictures and sounds?"

I had no idea how to answer him.

"I…I don't know. I think some of them are like, metaphors," I said, ending my thought abruptly.

"Well go on then," he pressed.

"When I was younger, I had a lot of nightmares about monsters—"

Felix Blackwell

"Terrible things, they are," he interrupted.

I glared into his hideous eyes.

"Indeed," I said. "And the worst ones, I realized, were just my mind's way of dealing with bad things that were happening in my life."

"These boyhood nightmares are news to me," the monster stated. He spoke in a concerned tone, but it was impossible to tell whether he was sincere. I had come to notice that this creature had a very *special* sense of humor.

"Of course they are, you idiot," I said. "You know nothing about me."

At that statement, the creature lunged at me, grabbing me by the throat and lifting me off the bed with one hand. He brought my face close to his. It looked wet and smelled like burnt steak.

"*You* are the idiot," he said. "And a failure." His lips trembled with rage.

The monster raised his other arm and, for the first time since his arrival, struck me – with an open hand. The blow was massive and sent me tumbling back onto the bed, jarring my vision and knocking me senseless. I lay still in shock, acknowledging that a closed fist probably would have killed me, and reminded myself to be much more careful in how I spoke to him. The Gorleth was becoming increasingly erratic. There was no doubt he'd finish me off soon. I shuddered at his earlier threat: "there will be blood."

"Ah! And this one is from just earlier this month!" he said with excitement. "September 18th, 1975. Emily has yet again threatened suicide. I don't know if it's her new medication or that she's beginning to lose touch with reality. She seems unable to decipher real memories from dreams and fantasies, and has again accused me of having brought a female student over while she was away. I swear on my soul I've never brought a student to our home, nor have I ever been unfaithful to my wife.

"She is otherwise coherent, and because of this I sometimes forget that she's suffering from an illness. Thus, I engage in unnecessary arguments with her, which have on a few occasions become violent. Two weeks ago, she threw a plate at me. It shattered against the china hutch, a piece that belonged to my grandfather. In a rage, I shouted that she was insane, and that I should have her committed.

"On the next occasion, only two days ago, she slapped me several times as I tried to restrain her from breaking a framed photo. She had never before struck me, and I felt compelled to hit her back, but I contained myself.

"I must admit that in my darkest moments, I've considered divorce. I don't know what else to do. I fear the medicine isn't working, and that Emily is too destructive to mend our relationship. I fear she's a danger to herself, and I'm the catalyst."

As the monster finished the journal entry, I buried my face in my hands and began to cry. Dreadful thoughts of my marital struggles swarmed over my mind, and the troubles I had tried for weeks to suppress came flooding back to me. The haze dissipated from my memory, and I finally remembered why I had come to visit my mother.

My recollections were dim and fragmented. I recalled moments of hatred. Not the empowering hatred for a nemesis, but rather the tormenting hatred for a friend. A hatred that clogs my veins like poison, corroding my resolve to love. A hatred that weighed impossibly on my conscience. It was sacrilege to me to despise someone I cared about so deeply. How could I forgive myself?

I recalled words – cruel, unforgettable words, spoken for no other purpose but to cut and carve and scar. Words dreamed up by the demons that dwell inside each of us, the ones who feed on our anger and starve with our forgiveness. They had fooled me and Emily into using those words against each other. It wasn't like me to do that; I'm convinced of the power of words to bring a person to ruin. I try to hold my tongue.

I recalled guilt – for crimes I've committed against my relationship, and guilt undeserved, which was assigned to me by false accusation. Guilt for permitting our marriage to come to ruin, and for permitting our love to become this farce. Guilt for

Felix Blackwell

wanting to leave. For not knowing the *right* thing to do.

"Don't be too hard on yourself, Professor." The Gorleth's raspy voice invaded my reflections, yanking me out of one nightmare and back into another.

I didn't respond.

He lurched toward me and placed a rough hand on my back. The feeling was enough to make me want to puke again, and I recoiled from him in disgust. He walked to the chair beside one of the bookcases. My shirt had been neatly folded and placed on the seat. The monster reached into the chest pocket and retrieved my father's pocket watch. He looked at it carefully.

"What have you done with my mother?" I asked.

"Ah, the saint!" he said without looking at me. "I've not seen her in *ages*! How's her health?"

Sighing, I lay back down and shut my eyes. I wished he would just kill me.

"It's almost time, Professor. But not quite yet." The creature tossed the pocket watch and the journal onto the bed, then lumbered down the hall into the dark.

My heart leaped into my throat. I reached out to retrieve the items. The watch wasn't ticking, and its hands were bent and warped. I picked up the journal.

My writing smeared across the pages, as though the ink had melted. Not a word of it was legible. How could the monster have read this?

I contemplated my next move. Did I dare try for another escape? What would the creature do if he caught me again? What would he do if I stayed? I knew that I was likely going to die either way, but there was a chance that my mother was somewhere outside, and I held on to the hope that I would see her again. On the other hand, there were wolves, and they hunted me with nearly the same zeal as the Gorleth.

For what felt like an hour, I considered my options. I felt helpless and indecisive, and I never made up my mind. Instead, I drifted into a dreamless sleep. With any luck, my heart would surrender and join the stillness that filled the room, and I would cease to be.

Felix Blackwell

CHAPTER 6

I was awakened by whispers. It took me a panicked moment to regain my senses, and the whispering ceased when I opened my eyes. The monster was sitting in the chair opposite the bed, facing me directly. His lidless eyes studied me.

"Were you watching me sleep?" I asked, revolted.

He didn't respond.

"What were you saying?" I demanded.

"Nothing you don't already know," he replied.

I felt rage building up inside of me. Nothing he said ever made any sense. I felt like I was going insane. I forced the anger out of my mind, and it was replaced with a kind of vacancy.

"If you insist on babbling, then tell me a story," I said, expecting no reply.

"What kind of story?"

"Tell me about you."

He stared into me without expression. When he spoke, his voice rose and fell in pitch, as if reciting a Shakespearean sonnet.

"There is so little I could tell you… that you don't already know."

"The only thing I know for sure," I said, "is that this is just a game. And I can see how much pleasure you take in it."

He snorted.

"And that you're ugly," I added, risking another beating.

He dismissed me with a snort.

"So fucking ugly," I said. "You make me *sick*."

The monster smiled, baring his jagged teeth at me.

"Not sick enough, apparently," he replied. "After all, you're still here."

"I've tried to leave! You follow!" I yelled.

He took his eyes off me and looked up at the bathroom window.

"Running away can't help you," he replied. "You're nothing without me…and I'm nothing without you. Why would I ever let you go?"

I shifted in the bed.

"If you need me so badly, then why are you going to kill me?" I asked.

The creature stood up, and with heavy footsteps, walked to the bed. He dropped down on it right beside me, sticking his face close to mine.

"What makes you think I'm going to kill *you*?" he asked.

I was taken aback by this question. Why the hell else would he be here? Then, my mother drifted into my mind.

"Wha…what do you…" I stammered. "Are you here for my mom?"

"I thought up a story!" he interrupted.

I sat in silence, unable to follow a train of thought.

"Why don't I tell you the story of a teacher I once knew?" he asked. "The story of a bright young professor, whose poor wife slipped into a deep depression. And in an act of baffling selfishness, he abandoned her. Walked out on her in her darkest hour. Left her for dead."

I knew his words were empty, but they singed me like fire.

"That's *not* what happened!" I yelled in defiance.

"Threw her to the wolves!" he shouted back, his voice blasting my ears.

That was the final straw. With an uncharacteristic burst of courage, I lunged toward the creature, grabbed onto his trunk-like neck, and choked him as hard as I could. His gruesome skin felt cold and stiff, and he did not react to my attack. He simply smiled. I realized that the Gorleth probably was not breathing in the first place. Undaunted, I began pummeling his face with my fist while screaming at the top of my lungs. He easily halted my assault and snatched me up in his giant hands. He stood up and dangled me in the air.

"You need to rest, Professor," he said, then dropped me

down onto the bed. I was shocked that he didn't break my neck.

After a while, I caught my breath. Tears streamed freely down my face, but I remained silent. The monster turned toward the bookcase. After selecting a book, he sank into the chair once again.

"*Cursed be the day,*" I said, trying to recall a quote from my favorite novel.

"What?" the Gorleth said with annoyance.

"*Cursed be the day, abhorrent devil, in which you first saw light.*"

He looked at me with surprise, and smiled as I continued:

"*You have made me wretched beyond expression. Begone. Relieve me from the sight of your detested form.*" I pointed toward the front door, which still lay in pieces in the hall.

"Impressive!" he said, lazily clapping his hands. "One of my favorites." Then, the monster cleared his throat, and spoke with the effortless passion of a theater actor:

"*I have love in me the likes of which you can scarcely imagine, and rage the likes of which you would not believe. If I cannot satisfy the one, I will indulge the other.*" He smiled a wide, fanged smile, and closed his eyes: "*Have a care; I will work at your destruction, nor finish until I desolate your heart, so that you shall curse the hour of your birth.*"

The monster opened his eyes and awaited my response, and seeing that I had none, he chuckled and resumed his reading. All the while, he softly hummed that familiar song. It drove me insane that I couldn't remember where I'd heard it before.

And so we sat in the room in this manner for hours. Eventually he grew tired of the book, and something out the nearby window caught his attention. Judging by the reflection in his putrid eyes, I guessed it was the moon. I remembered the way Emily used to spend hours on our balcony watching it, until I would retire from my writing and join her. I watched the monster gaze out the window for several minutes. It deeply disturbed me that he never blinked. I couldn't even begin to guess what he was, but I was curious about him nonetheless. I preoccupied myself with thoughts of Hell and demons, of ghosts and zombies, and of evil entities from the Jewish and Arabian mythologies I'd studied years ago. I could think of no creature quite like him.

A long time passed, and still the monster hadn't moved an inch. He stared, as if hypnotized, out the window.

"What the hell's so interesting?" I finally asked.

He didn't react.

Minutes later, he grumbled.

"What?" I asked.

"Don't know…what your…obsession is…" he said in fragments, "with that rotten forest." He never tore his gaze from the window.

"Obsession?"

Another long pause.

"Always so…curious…" he murmured so softly I couldn't be sure he was even talking to me. "So adventurous."

"What are you on about?" I pressed. He didn't acknowledge me.

I picked up the journal and tossed it at him. It smacked him on the shoulder and toppled to the floor.

"Anybody home?" I asked.

I watched him for a few more moments. He seemed entirely withdrawn and unaware of his surroundings. It was now or never.

I clambered to my feet. Sharp pains surged through my limbs, and I held back a gasp as I bent down to pick up my shirt.

"I have to take a piss," I said, staring directly at the monster.

As I walked to the bathroom, I glanced around, looking for my shoes. He must have taken them. I buttoned up my shirt.

The window above the toilet had been crudely nailed shut. The bathroom mirror lay in pieces all over the floor.

Cursing under my breath, I turned back toward the bed, and then had another idea.

"Looks like I'll have to piss outside then," I said, passing the monster and heading toward the broken front door.

"The… unknown," he said with great strain, "out there."

His hands clenched into tight fists, but he never looked away from the window. I took another step, but I was afraid to tear my eyes away from him. I was ready to run like hell.

"If you go…" he whispered through his teeth, "they'll find you…"

"I'm just gonna take a piss on the grass, I'll be—"

"Safe with me," he interrupted. "They'll… eat you… alive."

The monster never took his eyes off the moon. He just sat there, frozen beneath its glow. I calmly walked down the porch steps and then dashed off into the night. I didn't care about my shoes anymore.

CHAPTER 7

The motionless moon and the perpetual twilight threw my senses into disarray, making it impossible to judge the passage of time. I simply had no idea how long I'd been outside, or how long it had been since I had awoken in this disturbing world. The woods were difficult enough to navigate, and my lack of shoes slowed me considerably. I felt every twig and needle against my toes. The lonely crunch of my footsteps rang out in the silence.

I stopped and leaned against a strange tree, which groaned at my touch. No wind ran through the forest, and yet the trees moaned and shuddered all around me. My feet ached, so I rubbed them while I gazed up at the moon. I thought of the monster staring up at it at this very same moment. Something sickened me about his infatuation with it.

I never paid much attention to the moon since Emily and I started fighting all those months ago. When I was a boy, I enjoyed watching it. In fact, while I was working on my doctorate, my housemate was doing his Ph.D. in Astronomy. I spent long hours of our friendship asking him all the questions about the universe that I'd thought up as a child. When Emily and I met, I impressed her with my acquired knowledge of the stars, and we would often sit together under a blanket, gazing up at them. Like me, she loved the moon, and often included it in her paintings.

But when things changed, and Emily was either raging, withdrawn, or doped to Neverland on her medication, the moon played a different role in our relationship. It was no longer a source of wonder and inspiration, but a sad reminder of what once was. Sometimes I'd find her on the balcony, barely dressed, sitting in her chair and looking up at the night sky. She was so

Felix Blackwell

heavily medicated that she looked asleep with her eyes open. I remember how blue her lips were when I'd find her. I'd always get upset and either try to carry her inside, or wrap her up in a heavy blanket and sit with her. But it didn't matter what I said or did. Emily would simply sit there, unblinking.

Hypnotized…like the Gorleth.

A new awareness bolted through me. He reminded me of her. He looked just like her, sitting there in my mother's house, gazing out the window.

"Jesus Christ," I said, shuddering at the thought. "What the hell does that mean?"

I pushed myself off the tree and kept moving, unsure of whether I was going in the same direction as before. I needed to find the highway. It was my only way out.

I wandered, lost in a maze of trees, adrift in a sea of thought. I tried my hardest to remember where I'd come from before arriving at my mother's house.

There was a loud crash in the distance. It sounded like glass breaking. I stopped in my tracks and listened. After a short while, the noise repeated. I carefully approached the source of the noise, and after a few minutes, I heard a voice.

"Piece of shit," someone muttered. It was a woman. "You think it's that easy? Is that what you think?"

A familiar voice responded, but I couldn't make out what he was saying. He whispered, seemingly trying to calm the woman down.

"Don't touch me!" she shouted. "You don't get to touch me." She sounded a bit like Emily.

More glass exploded nearby. Those sounds were just as familiar as the woman's angry voice. I rushed toward the people. It made no sense that Emily would be out here in the woods, but then again, nothing here made sense.

"Emily!" I called out.

I searched all around the woods where I'd heard the sounds. I found no trace of anyone. I searched the ground for broken glass.

"Hello?" I called out.

Silence fell over the area.

Rage welled and erupted from me.

"God damn this place!" I shouted. "Where the fuck am I?!"

Not satisfied with my childish outburst, I looked around for a fallen branch. When I found one, I hoisted it up and smashed it against a tree trunk over and over.

"Let me out!" I yelled. "Wake up!"

Finally, I sank down against a tree and collected myself. I buried my face in my hands and tried to calm down. I tried to reassure myself that if I kept going, I'd eventually find help. I tried to focus on remembering something. Anything.

"Okay," I whispered to myself, panting. "Okay. Where was I?"

The sound of glass breaking ran through my mind, and I replayed the noise again and again. I tried to conjure up the woman's voice in the same way.

A memory flashed through my head:

She's standing in the kitchen, clutching a plate. I'm standing in the living room. I have something in my hand.

A suitcase.

I say something to her.

She laughs hatefully. Her eyes widen. I can see them smoldering from across the room. She says something to me.

"Is that right? You think you can just go?" I struggle to make out all the words.

She hurls the plate across the room. It shatters against the window sill next to me. I jump.

A terrible fear grips me. Not just a fear of her anger, but also a fear of leaving, and what it could mean. I say something else to her, in a calm voice.

"I don't know what to do," I say. Maybe that's what I say. Maybe it's actually "I don't know how to deal with you." But I'm angry. I feel hate boiling up inside. Maybe it's really "Fuck you."

She stares daggers at me, daring me to reach for the knob. Her teeth gnash audibly.

Felix Blackwell

Another plate flies at me. It hits the door as I open it.

Haze rolled over my mind, and the scene faded away. But at least I remembered something.

It was another fight that made me leave. I must have packed a bag and flown to my mother's house. I wondered if my mom knew I was coming. I wondered if Emily knew where I'd gone.

I knew for certain she wouldn't follow me here. My mother had advised me for months to leave Emily after hearing about her violent behavior. My unwillingness worried her. When Emily caught wind of all this, she began to despise my mother. The two would not speak to each other, and the strain on our marriage compounded. Emily would often mock me, telling me to "go cry to Mommy." She was needlessly cruel to both me and my mother. Deep down, though, Emily loved my mom, and I could tell that it hurt her to know my mom disapproved of her behavior. Sometimes, on her good days, Emily expressed great shame for how she acted, but refused my gentle prodding to apologize to my mom. She was embarrassed. She was proud. She would never come all the way out here.

So who was the woman in the woods? I thought.

I got up and kept moving.

I heard no signs of the monster, and no more voices. It was just me and the occasional howl of some ghastly animal in the distance, or the sad groaning of a tree. I worried the Gorleth would be out for my blood when he snapped out of his trance.

Get to the highway. That's the only important thing now.

My thoughts were fixed on Emily and my mother. My heart was heavy with guilt. I began to recall vividly my frustration with the entire situation. What my mother could never understand was that Emily *needed* me. I couldn't just abandon her; I was willing to put up with the abuse because I knew she was sick. For many months I forced myself to believe that this hateful person was not really my wife. I wanted to believe that Emily's true self was trapped beneath the dark surface, and that I could pull her out. My mother, on the other hand, believed that Emily was lost forever, and that only this malevolent shadow of her former self remained.

I feared what might happen to my wife if I divorced her. Since the onset of her depression, she was unable to work, so I was putting food on the table. She lost all interest in her friends and hobbies and withdrew from the world. She never went outside anymore. She quit painting. I was uncertain whether Emily believed that I would eventually come home, but a part of me intended to, even now. I feared for her life, and knew that I was likely the sole reason she had not yet killed herself. She was waiting for me.

My walk turned into a jog.

And yet, just when I felt compelled to race home and rescue Emily, my reason overthrew my compassion. I subjected myself to abuse in order to prevent Emily from hurting herself. And I did it with the hope that eventually she'd change. But was I actually doing what was right for her? Why should one of us suffer in order for the other to be happy? Maybe instead of trying to put out fires all the time, I should instead let everything burn to ash. I yearned for the thrill of new romance, and I knew I would not find again it with Emily. But could someone ever love me the way my wife did? My doubts were always in the back of my mind, whispering to me. Whispering like the Gorleth did as I slept.

A wolf howled in the distance. The hair on my neck pricked up. Something gave under my foot.

"Oh Christ," I said, knowing what had happened before even looking down. I had walked right into a pool of mud.

"That's...that's just great," I mumbled. I backed up a few steps, but my feet found only thick mud. I sprang off to one side, hoping to leap out of the puddle, but I sank even deeper when I landed. Mud swallowed my bare feet up to the shins.

For some reason, my first thought was, *thankfully the monster took my shoes...*

With each labored step the mud produced a slurping, sloshing sound that rang out in the night.

Another wolf howled, closer than the last. I shot a frightened glance over my shoulder.

"Shit!" I whispered, lurching another few steps forward. It was up to my knees now, and whenever I could pull a foot out, it made a sucking sound that was loud enough for any animal to hear. They'd find me.

Wolves began to wail behind me, maybe a hundred yards back. I twisted around to catch sight of them, throwing myself off balance. I fell to my knees and began to sink faster than before.

This is it, I thought. *I'm gonna drown.*

Even in my panic, a part of me was amused at the irony. I'd evaded a tireless demon only to find myself doomed to die in an ordinary mixture of dirt and water.

Howls rose somewhere in front of me. I was surrounded. In a desperate move, I reached into the mud to try to hoist myself back to my feet. It was no use; I immediately became stuck on all fours. My thoughts turned to my mother and Emily. A montage of all my past mistakes flashed through my mind, and a sad desire to apologize for them nagged at my heart.

"Emily!" I screamed. I wasn't sure why I called out to her. I wasn't sure if she was in the forest with me.

"Mom!" I yelled. No voice echoed back to me but my own.

Pale eyes gleamed in the moonlight, set into the heads of shadowy forms. I could barely make out their shapes in the gloom, but I knew they were preparing for the kill. I closed my eyes, helpless. They began to howl again, solemnly and in unison, announcing the finale of a long hunt.

I should have just left her altogether, I thought. *Maybe then I wouldn't be here.*

The wolves ceased their elegy.

I clenched my eyes shut, trying not to imagine what those phalanxes of teeth would feel like on my biceps, my calves, my neck. I sunk another few inches into the mud.

I held my breath. I lamented making Emily wait while I considered leaving her. I took too long to decide.

I hyperventilated. Fear's cold fingers walked across my

neck.

Death did not come. I dared to open my eyes, and glanced around anxiously. Tears glazed my vision, smearing the shadowy forms that surrounded me into one amorphous blur. The wolves simply stared back.

"Do it."

They just stared. Not one of them moved or made a sound.

I pitched my arm outward, slinging mud at a few of the beasts directly in front of me. They evaded my attack.

I looked at my hand and watched the mud ooze down my forearm. I lifted my other hand from below the surface. The little effort with which I retrieved it shocked and innervated me. I looked again at the wolves. They glared at me from the shadows, never inching forward, never moving close enough for me to make them out. I shouted as I hoisted myself to my feet, trying to frighten them off. I took a step forward. The wolves retreated a bit further into the woods.

I took another step, then another. With each footfall the mud became shallower. I shouted again. If I was going to die, I wanted to take a few of these pricks with me. I'd spent my entire life being afraid. For the last minute of my life, I wanted to be fearless.

"Come on!" I screamed.

The nearest wolf snarled defiantly. He bared his teeth, prompting the others to do the same, and only then could I make out the sizes of their mouths. Fear nipped at me, but I refused to acknowledge it. I pressed forward.

"Come and get it."

I'm not exactly sure what I did, or what they were thinking, but the wolves simply turned and trotted into the darkness, growling as they went. After a few moments, I couldn't hear their movements at all. I was alone again, and back on solid ground. The mud behind me was gone.

I vowed to try to understand this event later, but for now, I had business to take care of. I dashed onward, searching for the highway. Mud sloughed off my body as I moved.

Felix Blackwell

CHAPTER 8

My bare feet ached as they smacked the ground, and my heart thumped in unison with them. My mind vacillated between competing emotions. The strong pull of my guilt nagged me again to race home to Emily as fast as I could. Half of me wanted to run shrieking down that highway until I found someone, then drive directly to the airport. I wanted to hold my wife, to be strong for her, and to apologize for leaving. The other half of me wanted never to see her again.

A man's voice arose from up ahead.

"Damn it all," he grumbled. There came a sound of metal clinking against metal. I squinted through the fog and trees but couldn't see him.

"Come on, you miserable…" Fragments of his words were lost in the stillness. Then I heard a noise that was unmistakable: the sound of an engine, straining to start up.

A car! I thought. *That means a road!*

I hurried toward the racket. The car sounded broken, but I didn't care. There was another person. That was good enough for me.

I climbed up a steep hill. At the top, I beheld a joyous sight: a two-lane highway, freshly painted, cutting fearlessly through this wretched forest. And a hundred feet up, pulled to the shoulder, was a yellow car with a little man standing next to it. He disappeared behind the popped hood, then rifled through the engine while muttering to himself. I ran toward him, barely able to contain my excitement.

As I got closer, the fog cleared, and I read the bold lettering on the side of the car: TAXI. Could this be the same cab that had brought me to my mother's house?

"Hello?" I called out.

The man jumped, uttering a quick "Guh!" in response. He backed away from the engine and peeked around carefully.

"Who are you?" he asked. He adjusted a pair of thick glasses as he examined me. The man looked like a friendly old grandfather. His eyes were strikingly blue.

"Uh, I think…" I looked at the car again, "…I think I was your last fare." He was a foot shorter than me and had scraggly gray hair. As I spoke, he immediately beamed a cherubic smile, and opened his arms as if to welcome me.

"Yes, yes! Of course, I remember now," he said cheerfully. "What the devil are you doing out here? Your house must be ten miles from here."

Not knowing how to explain myself, I simply responded, "I'm…lost." I stuck my hands into my pockets and followed the cabby to the front of the car.

"Well, I'd tell you to hop in," he said, "but this heap isn't going anywhere." He gently kicked the bumper in defeat, then turned around and leaned against it. I can't really explain why, but I felt extreme relief in this man's presence. He was much friendlier than the man in the trench coat I'd met near the barn.

"Nothing works right in this place," he sighed. His gaze fell miles down the winding road, and he seemed to disappear into his own thoughts.

I turned around and looked down the road with him, adjusting my filthy shirt. It clung uncomfortably to my sweaty body.

"How long is the walk?" I asked.

"To where?"

"Into town."

The man scratched his eyebrows with his middle finger and thumb.

"Maybe fifteen miles," he replied.

"Well," I said, "I've come this far."

"You'd be doing it alone," he said, and turned to face me. "These old knees are hand-me-downs." He smiled.

"What is this place?" I asked, running my hand through

the hair on the back of my head. I picked bits of dried mud out of it like a chimp.

The cabby laughed a smoker's laugh and raised his bushy eyebrows. He looked up at the moon and pursed his lips.

"I don't really know," he said hesitantly. His eyes darted to me for just a split second, then back at the moon. He stood still and rigid.

Did he just lie to me?

"…but I've been here before," he added as a concession.

I looked at him with suspicion.

"Where is *here*?" I asked, taking a step closer to him.

He shrugged. Whatever explanation he wanted to give me, he knew it wouldn't be good enough.

"Feels like I'm in the devil's dreams," I offered, breaking the awkward silence.

"Who's Emily?" he finally spoke.

I fixed my gaze on him sharply.

"How do you know that name?" I demanded.

"M…my cab," he stuttered, "when I drove you here. You, uh, you were talking in your sleep."

"What did I say?"

"You just kept repeating her name. You seemed upset. You said 'no' a lot. 'Please' too." He backed up a step.

"I'm sorry," I said, "I didn't mean to—"

"Not at all," he interrupted, flashing his disarming smile again. "Come on. Let's give this old girl another try." He shuffled over to the driver's side and plopped down into the seat, feet still outside the car. I heard his voice from behind the glass.

"What are you doing out here anyway? I mean, really."

Before I could respond, the ignition sputtered, and the engine kicked on after a few seconds.

"A-*ha*!" the cabby laughed, clapping his hands. As he looked up at me, his smile was so big that his eyes turned into little blue slits.

"Come on, my boy!" he shouted, drawing his feet into the car and slamming the door shut. I grabbed the handle of the passenger-side door, but it was locked, so I hopped into the back seat. I nodded at him, and realized there was a little smile on my face too.

We sped off down the road. The car stank like old shag carpet and fake leather, but nonetheless I was overjoyed to smell it. I stretched my tired arms to the sides, leaned my head back, and closed my eyes. I heard the cabby flip the radio on, and out poured a calming mix of soft piano and violin, accented with intermittent static pops. My exhaustion caught up with me, and I felt a wave of lethargy slide over me like a warm blanket.

"She's my wife," I said without opening my eyes. The cabby responded with an affirmative "Mm."

"We had a fight," I continued. I wasn't really sure why I kept at it.

"You…wanna talk about it?" he asked. "Cab drivers are kind of like psychologists, you know." We both laughed.

I cracked open my eyes a bit and looked out my window. Dying trees rushed by me in scores. Through the windshield I could only see more of them, wrapped in fog, racing toward us as we passed. The empty road sprawled before us, slithering through the woods like a black snake.

I rubbed my eyes.

"I don't know what to say. In fact I've never known what to say. That's why I'm here. Emily isn't the same person she was when I married her. She's so angry now."

The cabby laughed, but not in a mocking way.

"My wife was a real battle axe too," he said, and kept laughing, as if remembering a time when she'd really let him have it.

"This is different," I interrupted. "They got her all doped up because of it, but that's changed her too. I gotta tell you, there are nights when I come home, and I'm scared of her. I mean, legitimately scared. Like I'm gonna walk in the door and she's gonna come at me with a knife or something."

I looked into the rear-view mirror and saw the cabby's expression turn grim.

"Wow," he murmured.

"The past few months have been one giant conflict," I

said, leaning my head against the window. It felt pleasantly cool. "I mean not just between us…an inner conflict too, you know? I have no idea what to do. *No idea.*"

The cabby let out a long, contemplative sigh. His little blue eyes darted around in thought, and he adjusted his grip on the steering wheel.

"What about a trial separation?" he said. "Maybe just a few months to…to let things cool off?"

Tears welled up in my eyes, and a lump caught in my throat. It was difficult to even speak the fears I'd been keeping inside.

"She'll hurt herself if I go. She's made that clear."

The cabby looked into my eyes through the mirror. He did not respond for several moments.

"This is grave," he said at last, "very grave."

"I'm afraid," I replied. "I'm afraid of her rage when I'm with her, and afraid of what she'll do when I'm gone. I feel like I'm being held hostage. I'm helpless…I'm not a man anymore. She took that from me."

The car hit a pothole and startled us both. He blinked and straightened his glasses. I sat up a bit and rolled my head around to stretch my neck. I felt the car lurch as he stepped on the gas a little.

"I'm tired of being afraid," I said, more to myself than to him.

"So you ran," he said. I couldn't tell if it was a question.

"We had a fight," I replied. "I left. I stayed at someone's house…and I remember being at the airport. I'm terrified of flying, so I usually take some anxiety meds."

"Anxiety?"

"Yeah, you know. Just to settle the nerves. I bet I took some, because frankly, I can't remember shit today." We shared another laugh.

"You know," he said, "I'll say this much. You smelled a bit sauced when I picked you up."

"Did I?" Our eyes met again briefly in the mirror.

"Don't be ashamed, my boy," he said, "it wouldn't be the

first time I picked up someone who was a bit…indisposed. That's why cabbies exist, right?" He smiled at me through the mirror again.

"I'm no lush," I said. "I haven't had a drink in years. In fact I was never a drinker at all."

"Well, sounds like you picked a good time to start!" he joked.

While the pills and booze explained my amnesia, the fact that I'd chosen to drink unsettled me. It's not like I was a recovering alcoholic; I'd been a teetotaler my whole life. What would make me do something so out of character?

"Did I say anything else?" I asked.

"Hm?"

"In my sleep."

"Oh, uh…a lot of mumbling…nothing I could make out. I wasn't trying to listen though. I usually keep the radio on, yanno?"

"Right."

"You were definitely dreaming," he added.

"A nightmare, sounds like."

"You remember it?"

"No," I replied. "But it seems like I woke up inside of another one."

I looked out the window again. The gnarled trees flew by. Hundreds of them. Thousands. And even though I grew up here, they didn't look like the trees I remembered from my childhood. None of it made any sense. Sick to death of trees, I began looking around the car instead. There were little signs on the back of the driver's seat, explaining fares and rules. A small placard next to it read, **DRIVER NAME: Magnus**.

"Magnus," I said, with a bit of power in my voice, "what a name!"

The cabby laughed.

"Magnus Farmer," he said. "Doesn't quite fit together, does it?"

"Still, a strong name," I replied.

"Makes you wonder why they'd give it to such a runt," he

chuckled.

"You know it means 'great'," I said. "Many small men have done great things."

"You read Latin?" he asked.

"I teach English. Well, I mean, I taught. I had to read a lot of old stuff in grad school. Original texts and such, you know?"

He laughed.

"One of those ivory-tower types had me readin' Chaucer," he said, "and not the modern version either. I mean, this stuff was like...Old English!"

"Middle English," I corrected. "And yeah, it's all Greek to me too."

We both laughed.

"You know, my friends call me Michael," the cabby said, after a deep sigh. "I prefer it."

"Michael," I repeated. "Who is like God?"

"What?"

"Who is like God? That's what it means," I said.

"Oh...I think I've heard that somewhere before," he replied. "I think it's the name of some angel." He glanced at me through the mirror.

"Yup," I said. "Well, Michael, you're my guardian angel for today. I didn't really feel like walking back to town. Funny coincidence that you should break down in the middle of the woods, just in time to give me a lift."

"Michael Farmer the Great, guardian angel and driver of the golden chariot, at your service!" he yelled, voice booming. He proudly bashed his hand against the horn, blasting the woods around us with its obnoxious sound. We laughed hard.

"It's good to meet you, really," I said. "By the way, I don't know if I mentioned it, but I'm—"

"I know who you are, my boy," he interrupted.

I went silent for a moment. The smile fell off my face.

"You know me?"

"Yes," he said, lowering his voice. "We've met before. Many years ago."

I tried to remember, but I couldn't place his face.

"When?"

"How much do you remember about your childhood?" he asked. "Before you were adopted."

I pulled the collar of my shirt away from my neck. A fresh layer of sweat crept over my skin. I shifted around in my seat, suddenly feeling like the air was too stale to breathe.

"Uh...bits and pieces," I responded. "It was a pretty tough time for me. They think I blocked some of it out."

"I know," he said.

I shook my head in disbelief and peered through the windshield, deep in thought. Michael kept his eyes on me.

"But how exactly do you—"

Something moved up ahead on the road. I saw it before Michael did.

"—*look out!*" I screamed.

The cabby jumped at my warning and the car swerved.

A huge form walked out of the forest and onto the asphalt, stopping in the middle of the lane and squaring off with the cab. I knew it was *him* before the headlights lit up his putrid face.

Michael slammed on the brakes. The car screeched in agony as it slid toward the monster. We were going too fast. He jerked the wheel in a desperate attempt to avoid the creature, and we fishtailed hard to the left.

I saw the monster flash past the right side of the car as it skidded by, and for just a split second, our eyes met. The cab veered into the oncoming lane. We flew off of the edge of the road, rolled down the dirt ravine, and smashed headlong into a big tree.

The engine died. Darkness washed over me. I fought to stay conscious, but my ears rang and my vision faded in and out. One of the headlights was broken; the other flooded the forest behind the tree for a dozen yards. Smoke leaked into the car, choking me. I felt something warm trickling out of my nose and down my lips and chin.

I tried to reach for my seatbelt, but my arms were completely numb. My eyes drooped shut and a tingly feeling wrapped around my head from the back, creeping forward to my temples. Soothing cold crept up my fingertips and over my body, inviting me into a gentle blackness.

CHAPTER 9

Emily climbs into bed with me and rests her head on my chest. Before I can open my eyes, I feel her hands touching my skin, and she begins to hum that old song. It was the one her mother sang to her when she was a girl. I wrap my arms around her waist and pull her on top of me. My hands find her face; I brush her hair aside and put my lips on hers. She's so warm.

"I love you," *I whisper.*

Michael's groans brought me back to my wits. I forced my eyes open and saw his blurry figure hunched over the steering wheel. There was blood all over him.

"Michael?"

I wiped my face, smearing blood everywhere. My nose felt broken. Strangely, I didn't feel much pain. I was just numb. I frantically unhooked my seatbelt and reached over, shaking Michael. He slowly lifted his head.

"Thank God," I said, squeezing his shoulder. "You okay? Can you hear me?"

He looked around, obviously dazed, and turned toward me. His right eyebrow was cut open. It looked bad.

"What happened?" he asked.

Before I could respond, the window next to me shattered to pieces, and a giant arm reached into the car. I shrieked as the hand grabbed hold of my neck and pulled me straight through the broken window. Michael watched in terror. He reached a shaking hand out for me to grab onto, but it was too late. The monster pulled me out of the wreck and threw me onto the soft ground beside the car.

"It's time, professor," he said.

I ignored him and flipped over onto my belly, trying to

crawl toward the road. My body was weak, but the sheer terror of death compelled me. I clawed at the soil, kicking my legs out behind me. Feeling was returning to my limbs.

"You can't avoid this!" the monster bellowed. "This is your punishment. I've waited long enough."

"Fuck you!" I spat. I felt the thudding of his feet against the earth as he bounded toward me. He caught up to me easily and dropped to one knee, poised for the kill.

"Get away from him!"

Both the monster and I looked back just in time to see Michael, blood smeared across his face like war paint, leap heroically onto the creature's back. He grabbed at the Gorleth's eyes and face, putting him in a headlock and blinding him.

The monster shrieked; his scream pierced my ears and paralyzed me for a moment.

"Wretched lamb!" he snarled. He reached back and grabbed Michael's neck, squeezing with inhuman strength.

Michael strained to look into my eyes. His face contorted in pain.

"Run!" he forced out through gasps and chokes. "Get outta here! Now!"

I scrambled to my feet and paused for a moment, tethered by my desire to help Michael. But when I looked in his eyes, I knew he didn't want to be helped. He had chosen to trade his life for mine.

"Go!" he commanded once more. He never let go of the monster, even as it beat and choked him. Michael kept his forearm firmly over the creature's hideous eyes, so that he could not see which way I ran.

I took one last look and fled. Behind me, I heard the monster flailing about, hurling himself against the taxi repeatedly to dislodge his assailant. I heard Michael's screams of agony. I tried not to imagine what the demon would do to the little old man. Blood ran freely down my lips, and tears streamed down my face.

In the distance, a wolf howled.

CHAPTER 10

Hopelessness weighed down on me as I moved. I had not yet abandoned my plan to make it to the town, but I knew that no matter where I ran, the monster would find me. And what was it "time" for? I imagined him snapping Michael's neck, and then my own.

I kept to the road, but stayed a few dozen feet into the forest. The monster was smart enough to know I'd follow the only landmark I'd found, and smart enough to be waiting for me wherever I went. But my hope was that I'd get there before he did.

My feet ached with every step, but I never slowed my jog. I wasn't tired anymore. Rage seared in my veins like fire. Vengeful fantasies of killing the monster clouded my mind; I imagined impaling him with a broken branch, or crushing his horrid skull with a rock. This state of mind persisted for at least a half hour, and I reveled in it.

"Oh shit," I muttered, stopping in my tracks.

I looked to my left, and then took a few steps in that direction.

Where was the road?

I clenched my eyes shut, furious and disappointed with myself. I'd gotten distracted. I must have veered off course.

I gave up after searching for a few minutes. I threw my hands in the air in defeat, then continued in the direction I'd been going. Whatever direction that was.

There's something I'm not getting here, I thought. *Something I need to see.*

I began to think carefully about the monster: his movements, his smell, the way he spoke. He was so vaguely familiar. He was like a bad impression of someone I knew. Then a memory flashed in my mind.

I hold Emily by the waist as she sits on top of me in bed. I move her hair back and the morning light illuminates her face. I feel the silk of her nightgown graze my thighs as she moves. She hums, and I smile.

I realized I must have gotten knocked out in the car wreck. I'd dreamed of her, and of that damned song. *That's* where I knew it from. It was *Emily's* song. The monster had been humming it all this time, but his voice was so ugly and off-key I never fully recognized it.

"Jesus Christ."

I began to shiver. My heart raced. It felt like a balloon was inflating inside my chest.

"Oh God, what did he do…" I said aloud. When I wiped tears off of my cheeks, I grazed my nose, and lightning bolts of pain shot across my face.

The Gorleth was impersonating Emily: every violent tic, every whimsical change of subject, every vacant stare, every Shakespearean recitation. He was mocking her descent into madness.

He *knew* her. The monster knew my wife.

My brain didn't know how to process this revelation. The balloon in my chest popped, and up rushed a hot wave of vomit. I fell to my knees and leaned against a big tree, spewing all over the ground beside it, again and again.

He knew my wife.

A million scenarios flooded my mind. My vision condensed to a tiny point of light. All I could see was the monster, standing in the same room with Emily.

How long did he watch her?

I tried to stand, but my legs were thousand-pound stones. Instead I dropped to my side and lay next to the bubbling mess of puke.

Did he kill her? Is that what he wants me to figure out? Has she been dead all this time?

It was too much to bear. I suddenly found the strength to stand, and new energy seethed through me. I took off running once again. I had to get to the town, get on a plane, and get back home. I had to know if Emily was alright.

Felix Blackwell

CHAPTER 11

There were no lights. No buildings. No landmarks. For miles and miles, there were only the moon and trees. It never ended. I could keep running in this direction, or arbitrarily choose another. It didn't matter. I'd never get anywhere. Everything looked the same. I felt no hunger or thirst, and was convinced I'd either be killed by the Gorleth, or wander the woods for eternity like a ghost. Which was worse, I couldn't begin to guess.

I found a huge fallen log and sat down against it. I rubbed my face carefully, avoiding my nose, and thought of my mother. I'd have given anything to see her in that moment. Anything.

Soft footsteps echoed from directly ahead of me.

I squinted against the fog, to no avail. But I could hear clearly. It was someone small, definitely not the monster. Maybe it was that little kid. Or my mom.

"Is someone there?" I called out. "Mom? Is that you?"

To my surprise, somebody actually responded.

"Hey, I'm here! Where are you?"

It was a girl's voice. Her words filtered through a thick accent. A young girl emerged from the mist before me, dressed in a school uniform that was caked with dirt and grime. She must have been out here for a while, just like the big fellow in the trench coat.

"Oh, thank God!" I cried out. "I lost the road. Do you know a way out?"

"I'm sorry," she said, "but I'm also lost. How'd you get here?"

As she came closer, I was surprised by the remarkable beauty of her face. Her voice was soft and calming. She looked young, probably seventeen or eighteen.

"I...I'm not sure," I replied. I tried to explain how I'd woken up here, but as I spoke, each word sounded more ridiculous than the last. Eventually I just shut up. The girl seated herself next to me and examined a deep cut on my arm. I hadn't noticed it yet. It must have been from the crash.

"Do you know how long you've been here?" she asked.

"I don't know," I replied. "It feels like days. But there's no sunrise, only dark. I haven't had to eat. I don't feel sleepy. It's like...time has just stopped."

She gazed up into my eyes as if to corroborate my experience. Both of us were lost souls, it seemed.

"I imagine this is what being dead feels like," she offered.

"You're so young," I said, adjusting my back against the log. "What are you doing out here all alone?"

"The last thing I remember was falling," she said. The girl looked up at the drab sky and pushed a lock of golden hair from her face. I was mesmerized by her composure.

"Falling?"

"Yeah," she said. Her accent made the words sound like poetry. "I was looking up at the sky, and I fell away. Or maybe it fell away from me." She took a sharp breath. "But when I got back up, everything was so different. I tried to run, and I screamed for help, but the only people I met were...like things from a dream."

My attention was peaked.

"People? Where?" I asked excitedly.

She looked around.

"I don't know where, because I don't know where I am now," she responded. "But they weren't people like you and me. Some of them were..." she paused, searching for the word, "...ghouls. With rotting skin. They wore strange uniforms."

Her words baffled me. Of course none of it made sense, but I supposed it was possible, given what I'd seen with my own eyes in this awful place.

While her gaze moved around the woods, I studied her face.

Felix Blackwell

As with the big guy from earlier, this girl seemed vaguely familiar.

"Have we met before?" I asked.

She looked into my eyes. Her brow furrowed.

"I don't recognize you."

Recalling how foolish I'd felt when I told the big guy he looked familiar, I dropped it. The girl and I had never met. I was probably just losing my mind out here.

A few quiet moments drifted by.

"What about the others?" I asked.

"Others?" The girl shifted against the log.

"You said *some* of them had rotting skin."

"Oh yes," she replied, her voice dropping to a whisper. She looked right at me, captivating me with her big eyes. "One was a horrible thing. A monster. Worse than the others. I couldn't see it clearly, only through the fog. It was too dark to see much. But it was tall. Taller than any person. And big, like a man. I ran away as fast as I could."

My stomach jumped into my throat. The revulsion I felt at the thought of *him* was uncontrollable.

"It hummed a song, didn't it?" I asked, despair clinging to my words.

The girl didn't respond right away. She just stared into my eyes. She could see the slew of dark emotions that overwhelmed me. Anger and fear mixed together into a black veil that shrouded my mind. My head ached, so I rested it against the log.

"Something's after you, isn't it?" the girl prodded.

"I tried facing him," I spoke. I raised my head back up to look into her eyes. "It was the first thing I tried. I've run from my demons before, when I was younger. I know you have to face them. But this…thing," I looked around nervously, "…He's different. He's hunting me, and no matter how far I run, he always finds me. It's why I'm out here in the first place."

Fear spread across her face, and she pulled her knees to her chin. I felt guilty for scaring her.

"What is he?" she asked, like a child listening to a bedtime story.

I looked away in thought, then back to her.

"The devil."

Of course I didn't really know what the monster was. But that was the first thing that came out of my mouth. The girl didn't blink.

"What does he want with you?"

I shrugged and picked at my fingers.

"He won't tell me," I replied. "Believe me, I've asked. He told me that he'd put me out of my misery soon. He says he can rescue me, but he needs more time."

The girl looked at me like she couldn't understand a word I'd said. Maybe it was the language barrier.

"I'm the mouse, you see. No fun if the cat kills me quick."

A smile spread across her pretty face.

"I escaped it!" she said excitedly. "There is hope."

I admired her optimism, but couldn't help shaking my head at her naivety.

"It's not after you," I said. "It's like a bloodhound, trained to seek a target. If he wanted to, he could have snatched you up and killed you right there. I've seen him do it." I grabbed a handful of soil and lazily tossed it back. "I can never escape."

The girl stared out into the fog, like she was thinking of something to say. I followed her eyes to the trees in front of us, and the ones behind them, wrapped in thick mist, and the ones behind those, barely visible at all. The monster could have been standing there, listening to us the whole time, and we'd never have seen him. He could be watching *right now.*

"What happened to your mother?" she asked, disrupting the stillness. I shot a glance at her.

"I heard you calling for her," she explained.

"Oh. I don't know," I responded. "That *thing* attacked her, and then she was gone. Just gone. Like she disappeared. Have you seen her?"

She took a deep breath.

"There's another person I haven't told you about," she whispered.

"There is?"

"Yes, I met a woman."

Goosebumps rippled up my arms.

"What did she look like?" I prodded. "Did she tell you her name? Was she looking for me? It might have been her!" I tried to calm myself and catch my breath.

"She was looking for you, yes—"

"Ah, then it's my mom!" I interrupted. "How did she look? Was she hurt? We should go find her now! Did she tell you where she was going? Where did you last see her?" I clambered to my feet in excitement, but the girl grabbed my shirt and tugged me right back to the ground.

"It wasn't your mother," she said. Her tone was grave. "It was someone else. *Something* else." She scooted closer to me.

I stared back at her, disturbed by my own thoughts as my imagination ran wild.

"She was scary," the girl spoke. "Very scary... She hummed, just like the monster I saw in the fog. And she was looking for someone."

I paused for a moment, contemplating this information.

"But how do you know she's after *me?*" I asked. The way the girl looked at me made my skin crawl. She was terrified for me.

"Whatever she was looking for... she said it was crying for its mother."

Her words churned my stomach. I could feel the blood draining from my face.

"Are you *sure* it was a woman?" I asked. Her description sounded so much like the Gorleth that I wanted to believe she was mistaken.

"I'm sure," the girl responded. Her voice lowered to a whisper again. "She didn't act normal, though. She walked...strange...and her voice was deep and..." she grabbed her throat and mimicked the sound.

"Raspy?" I said.

"Yes, that. It was like a monster, wearing a woman's skin. Her eyes looked dead. I've never seen anything like it."

Images of the Gorleth flashed in my mind; each of his

horrible mannerisms played out like a revolting film reel. The descriptions of this woman matched the monster's behavior quite well. I felt instantly perplexed and terrified at the same time.

Were there two monsters hunting me now? I wondered. There was no way anybody could mistake the creature's enormous size and features for a woman's.

"She also had shakes," the girl added, breaking my chain of thought. "She…she…shook, so angry. Like a sick person. You know? Like a crazy person." The girl struggled to find the word "convulse," but I understood her perfectly, and I knew exactly what she meant before she could finish her sentence. She was describing the monster. *My* monster.

"But how could the Gorleth appear as a woman?" I asked, more to myself than to the girl.

"The what?" she asked.

"The Gorleth," I repeated. "He takes his name from a story."

The girl ran her fingers through her hair a few times, combing little leaves and twigs out of it. She looked like she'd been on the ground. I wondered if anyone had attacked her.

"Has it ever changed its appearance in front of you? Does it always look the same?" she asked, grabbing my arm gently. "Think."

I thought for a few seconds, but the monster always looked the same. I'd stared into his horrible face enough to remember it for a lifetime.

"N…No," I finally replied. "He never—"

A twig snapped in the distance.

I jerked my head to the side, straining to hear where the sound came from. I poked my head up over the huge log just enough to see the nearby trees.

A voice seeped through the forest and barely reached my ears. I couldn't make it out. The same familiar song rang out in the night, far off at first, but approaching fast. My stomach knotted.

"He's coming," I said, without taking my eyes off of the source of the noise. The girl stuck her head up beside mine, squinting into the fog.

"Run while you still can," I said, grabbing her by the shoulders and turning her toward me. "He's not after you. You'll be safe if you leave right now!"

She looked into me with terrified eyes, but her expression protested my demand.

"No," she responded. Her eyes glazed with welling tears. Why she would risk her life for a stranger was beyond me.

I searched the fog again for the monster. The humming seemed to come from all around us now.

I looked back at the girl and shook my head. Her beauty defied the ugliness of these woods. She didn't belong here. I wanted to say something to comfort her, but the monster's humming grew louder and closer.

"He'll kill you if you get in his way," I whispered. "*Go.*"

Before she could react, the humming ceased abruptly, and we were alone again. The woods fell silent. We looked at each other with fright and then ducked back down behind the log.

A loud voice came from behind us.

"Professor!"

I shut my eyes.

Shit.

"Please! Please, come back to me! I'm sorry! I'm all alone and afraid!" he cried. Then a wet cackle echoed through the woods.

"It's him!" I whispered, pointing out in front of us.

A hulking form emerged from the gray, heading directly at us. He must have been able to see better in the fog than we could. He knew right where we were. Maybe he could smell us.

"Filthy rat," he snarled. "Hope has *forsaken* you!" The Gorleth stomped toward me, his dead gaze impaling me against that log like a sword.

The girl scrambled to her feet and positioned herself between the monster and me.

"Leave him alone," she demanded.

She cowered in fear as the monster approached her. I wanted to run up and shove her out of the way, but I simply couldn't move. My brain could not communicate with my legs.

The creature halted mere inches from the girl. He looked down on her, examining her carefully. His chest was soaked with Michael's blood.

"Don't hurt her!" I yelled in desperation. I finally regained control over my body and leaped to my feet.

The creature ignored the girl.

"Professor, come home! We must leave *now*. I can still save you from this place!" He held out a grotesque hand. The skin looked like grilled meat, and the fingernails were jagged and yellow. The girl looked back at me in confusion.

"Run!" I yelled at her. "Just get out of here!"

The monster looked down at her with a half-smile.

"Listen to the rat, child," he said, reaching down to her face and picking up a lock of her hair. "Flee, or I'll rip this pretty mane off your head."

"Don't touch her," I growled, surprised at the boldness in my voice.

"You owe me in blood," the creature replied. He shoved his way past the girl and bounded up to me, grabbing my shirt with both hands and yanking me toward him. Even though he'd grabbed me several times before, his strength always shocked me. He lifted me off the ground, brought my face to his, and sniffed me. The hairs on my neck became electrified with terror, and I shuddered as he moved his greasy nose across them.

"Fight her!" the girl screamed from behind the Gorleth. "Don't let her do this!"

Did she just say 'her'?

I held perfectly still as the monster examined me.

"Fight her!" she repeated.

What else could I do? Still in mid-air, I looked the monster square in the face and spat in it. I balled a fist and swung it like a club at the side of his head, roaring as I did. It smashed against his heavy skull with a wet smack. Pain reverberated up my arm to the elbow. I hit him *hard*, again and again, screaming with all the ferocity I could muster.

The Gorleth never changed expressions, never blinked,

and stood there still as death while I beat him until my hand couldn't take any more. He paused for a moment to see my reaction and then flashed his razor teeth. He loosed a gurgling laugh and lifted me over his head, then body-slammed me to the ground.

The impact was meteoric. If it had been asphalt I'd landed on, every bone in my body would have shattered. My vision went fuzzy and dark, and my strength abandoned me. My will flickered out like a candle.

The monster bent over me.

"Are you okay, little one?" he asked.

I turned my head and looked away, feeling like I was about to black out. From down here I could see the big trees and their gnarled branches reaching up to the dreary sky. The moon still clung to its hiding place, never moving, barely glimmering through the trees and mist.

Where am I? I wondered in my daze.

"Your friend is wise," he went on, stabbing an ugly finger toward the girl.

I had to tilt my head to see her. She cowered a few yards away from me and wept. Her softness broke my heart. Why was she here? What had happened to her?

"She sees things for what they are," the Gorleth said. He crouched down, dangling his face over me, and dug his hands into the soil on either side of my head. "Time's up."

"What have you done to Emily?" I demanded.

He wrapped his fingers around my throat, gently, and peered into my eyes.

"What have *you* done to her?" he retorted. His voice brimmed with sorrow, as though he were about to cry. I was surprised by his response; it was the first time he'd acknowledged a question about my wife.

The monster snatched up my ankle with his bear-trap hands, intent on dragging me to the slaughter. I was about to be "rescued." I didn't have the energy to fight back.

He turned to the girl.

"Do you want to watch?" he asked. He seemed genuinely

curious, and patiently awaited her response.

She didn't respond, except with a terrified and helpless gaze.

"Run!" I yelled from down on the ground. "For God's sake, run for your life!"

The creature yanked me around in a semi-circle and started toward the trees. I dragged behind him, screaming. When I looked back, the girl was gone.

CHAPTER 12

Trees slinked by. Wisps of fog fluttered around us as we moved. Bullfrogs choked out their warped calls.

The monster dragged me by the foot like a corpse to be buried. I slid painfully over twigs and pine needles and leaves. What was left of my shirt bunched up around my shoulder blades, and damp soil caked up underneath it, mashing against my skin. My back was scratched and bloodied to hell. I sobbed quietly in self-pity. What a miserable way to go.

"Quit your sniveling, Professor," the monster demanded. "Won't help you."

I tried to quiet myself and pondered what the girl had said.

"Don't let her do this."

Was that it?

"*Rak!..rak!..rugh*," the creature disrupted my thoughts with his disturbing tics.

"Why do you do that?" I asked. "What's wrong with you? I mean aside from that fuckin' face."

He shivered and grunted in response.

I couldn't understand. The girl had seen this creature with her own eyes. So why did she refer to him as 'her'?

"Where are we going?" I asked.

"Home."

"Why?"

"It's time."

"Why don't you just do it right here? Why does it make a difference where you do it?" I pressed.

He stopped and turned around to face me, but never let go of my leg.

"Suddenly you're interested?" he replied, anger seething

his voice. "Suddenly you care?"

My mouth hung open a bit. Nothing this demon said ever made sense, and no emotion or expression could be trusted. Everything he said was a lie, a trick, or an act.

"Of course I care that I'm about to be murdered," I said.

He laughed his disgusting laugh.

"It's all about you, isn't it?" he said. Then he turned and continued on, quickening his pace. He shuddered a few more times, swearing under his breath. I recalled Emily doing the same thing during her fits of rage. I wanted to ask the creature why he imitated my wife, but I knew I'd never get an answer. I guessed that it was just another tool in his special kit of psychological torture.

"I can walk, you know," I said. "It's not like there's any point in running away."

He snorted.

"Is Michael dead?" I asked.

No response.

"Is Emily dead?" I asked.

His head jerked a little.

"Would you really care?" he asked, not looking at me.

"I love her. She's my wife."

The Gorleth stopped in his tracks and threw the ankle he clutched to the ground. I shrieked in pain as it landed. Before I could even look up, he was upon me, grasping my throat with a monstrous hand. He squeezed so hard I could feel my eyes bulging out of my skull.

"No." he growled in an impossibly deep voice. "You *don't.*"

"What's that?" a voice called out from behind me. It was instantly familiar. A voice I hadn't heard in what felt like eons.

"What are you doing to my son?"

The monster jerked his head toward the sound and snarled with rage. His grip on me loosened. I lifted my head to see.

Mom.

She stood between two enormous trees about a dozen yards away.

A storm of emotions poured over me. I wanted to scream

out for her help, but I also wanted her to get away from the monster.

"Momma!" was all I could say. She was strong and unafraid, and looked immaculate for having just emerged from the woods.

Has she been out here all this time?

"The *saint*," the Gorleth spat. He bared his teeth as he spoke. "How nice to see you."

She ignored him and looked down at me instead.

"I love you, baby. Are you alright?" Her voice was calm and soft.

It was more than I could bear. I reached for her like a child. "Momma," I cried.

I rolled onto my belly and tried to crawl, but the monster dropped a huge foot down on my back and held me in place.

"It's *mine*," he said.

"Be gone," she replied, taking a step forward. The Gorleth wheezed as she approached.

"It dies if you come near," he said, moving his foot up to the back of my head. He stepped down firmly, letting me know that he could snap my neck if I tried anything. I could smell the old rubber of his massive boot.

"I know you won't do that," she replied, and took another step forward.

"Mom, please, get out of here," I said. "You can't help me."

He issued a long, low growl, watching her as she moved.

"Look what you've become," she said, gazing into my eyes. "You should be ashamed of yourself."

I couldn't tell if she was talking to me or the monster. Neither of us responded.

The creature looked down at me, into my eyes, with an expression I couldn't identify. He looked at me differently, as if with pity or remorse.

"I wish you were gone," my mom continued. "For good this time."

Upon hearing this, the Gorleth howled. He

hyperventilated and looked around in a panic, searching for something. His boot lifted from the back of my neck. He looked down at me.

"Come with me, Professor," he said.

"I'd rather die," I replied.

"Come!" he shouted. His voice was desperate.

"Leave my son alone, you *monster*," my mother commanded.

"*Rak! Rak!*" He twitched and thrashed his arms and head. He clutched himself tightly with both hands and turned away. We watched as the creature stormed off into the foggy darkness. We heard him screeching and muttering to himself for a few moments after he disappeared from sight.

My mom knelt down and cupped my face with her hands.

"My baby. Are you okay?"

"Momma," I repeated. She pulled my head toward her chest and held me.

"Where have you been, Mom? Where'd you go?"

"I feel like I'm losing you," she replied. "You're all I've got now, since Dad passed."

"What are you talking about?" I asked, looking up at her.

"She's pulling you away from me. I can never find you anymore."

"What are you talking about?"

"Why didn't you come back to me?" she asked, plucking a leaf from my hair.

"I've been lost," I explained. "But I looked for you this whole time!"

"Here I am," she said.

"I thought he killed you, mom. I thought you were dead."

We sat there for a moment in silence, just holding each other. For once, I wasn't worried about the Gorleth. Relief washed over me, and with it came the pull of sleep. Crickets began to chirp around us, a sound I'd not heard in a long time. I even felt a little breeze. The dead air of this world could move again.

"Why do you go on letting her treat you like this?" my

mother finally asked. "You've been miserable for so long."

I paused, not knowing whether she was talking about the monster or about Emily. I suppose her question was valid either way.

Suddenly, something clicked inside my head. I remembered the Gorleth's recitation of *Inferno*, back at the house:

"*I found myself in a dark wood—*
so dark that the way was lost."

I remembered his infatuation with my journal, and his relentless accusations that I didn't do enough for Emily. He twisted everything I said and used my guilt against me. He used my love for my wife against me. He used her condition against me. He used my fear of her death against me.

I remembered his mannerisms: the violent episodes, the tics and erratic speech, the vacancy and withdrawal. Every little bit of him was reminiscent of Emily in some way. Before, I thought he was imitating her behavior, as though he'd been watching us through the windows of our home, practicing his impressions. But he wasn't just a mockery of my wife. He was everything about her that I hated. The Gorleth was the monster inside her – the dark part of Emily that was slowly taking over.

With this realization, his most unsettling threat invaded my memory.

"What makes you think I'm going to kill *you?*"

Every muscle in my body seized up. I finally understood.

The monster was never going to kill me.

All this time, he intended to kill my wife. That was his ace in the hole. If I ever left her, Emily had it all planned out. It was revenge. She made the battle between her happiness and her depression contingent on my next move.

Emily was going to take her own life.

My mom squeezed me tighter.

"I always thought you'd be better off alone," she said.

"I know, Mom," I replied, sifting through the revelation. "I always knew I would be. I just thought that staying was the right thing to do."

She smiled.

"It *was* the right thing, sweetie. You fight for the one you love. We all do. You tried your best, but you must realize…you don't always win." She shook her head. "Sometimes things break, and they just can't be fixed."

"Yeah. I know that now," I replied. "I think I made things even worse by trying to fix them. I wonder if she'd have been better off if I'd ended things years ago, instead of dragging it out. I must have tortured her with her own fear of losing me."

"She did the same to you," my mom added. "Look what she put you through. Look what she's done."

"I'm sorry, momma," I said, sniffling. "I didn't wanna stay. I just didn't want Emily to hurt herself."

"You can't stop that," she said. "You never could."

My mom let go of me so that I could wipe my face. I lifted my filthy shirt and buried my eyes in it, patting dry the tears. When I looked up, she was gone.

"Mom?" I called out.

I looked all around, but saw only the dark woods, and the blank stare of the moon. I was alone again.

But I knew what I had to do.

The fog began to clear.

CHAPTER 13

As I walked, the temperature began to drop. A slight breeze kissed my skin, and for the first time since I came to this place, I felt like I could breathe. The fog thinned, and now I could see a bit better in the pale light. I headed in the same direction the Gorleth went, but this time, I was no longer afraid. I had a plan.

As I came over a small hill, something on the ground immediately caught my eye.

Is that snow?

I ran up to it and flicked some with my bare foot. It was cold and wet. Looking around, I saw little patches of it scattered everywhere. The breeze picked up a bit, and set the trees rustling and shivering all around me.

Wish I had my shoes, I thought.

As I continued on, the snow thickened and spread across the ground, covering almost everything. Some of the trees had fresh powder all over their branches. In ten minutes, I was walking through a regular winter wonderland. Snow fell all around me, gently, like the morning after a blizzard. It wet my hair and face, but I didn't mind at all. After being stuck in the stale, ungodly warm woods for who knows how long, I welcomed the cold. And it was *cold*.

Something else caught my eye: a black spot on the ground. It contrasted so plainly with the snowbound landscape that I could see it from fifty feet away. I ambled up to it, curious. As I got closer, I saw that it wasn't black. It was dark red in the gloom.

Blood.

A slew of grave possibilities raced through my mind.

Michael? Is he alive?

The girl? Did the Gorleth find her?
Mom?

From where I stood, I could see more spatters of it, leading in the direction the monster was headed. I jogged to the next patch. There were footprints — too small for a hideous creature.

My breath quickened as I followed them, and every few feet there was more blood. Someone was hurt. The footprints meandered aimlessly between trees, in random directions, and sometimes turned back. Whoever it was, they were lost.

"Hello?" I called out. "Is someone out there?"

I sprinted to and fro, following the trail of blood and prints, and barged right into an open meadow. It was about the same size as the meadow with the barn, but this one was covered in snow. In the center, I could see a lone tree stump.

Someone was sitting on it.

"Hey!" I called out from the edge of the forest.

The fog cleared a little more, revealing the jet-black hair of a woman facing away from me. She was wrapped in elegant white clothes.

The phantom woman. I'd seen her when I first escaped my mother's house.

"Are you okay?" I called out, starting toward her. "Are you hurt?"

She turned her head a bit, listening for me.

"Where…are you?" she asked.

As I saw her profile, I immediately recognized her, and my legs locked up.

Emily.

I tried to speak but couldn't. For just a moment, we both froze, and neither of us made a sound.

Finally, she spoke.

"You've come back."

Her voice was gentle and sorrowful, and shook me out of my stupor. I dashed toward her. My heart pounded.

My bare feet crunched through the snow as I raced to my wife. I never took my eyes off her, so I tromped patches of blood on the ground. Their warmth thawed the numbness in my feet.

My right foot fell on something sharp. A bolt of pain shot up through my body, and I toppled over.

"Ah, shit," I groaned, wincing as I moved my foot up to my lap. A shard of glass or porcelain jutted from my skin. As I yanked it free, blood collected at the wound and trickled down into the snow.

I looked at the object closely. It was a piece of a plate.

I forced myself up and limped on, throwing the shard into the snow behind me.

Emily never moved as I approached her from behind. I studied her form as I circled her. I recognized the cascades of jet-black hair, and the familiar shapes of her neck and back. Her white dress reminded me of the things she'd wear in the early days, when we'd spend our weekends on the town.

As I moved to her front, I saw more blood. It was sprinkled in places all over her chest and lap, and dried patches of it streaked her face, as though she'd wiped away tears with bloody hands. Her face was soft and sweet, the same one I'd fallen in love with all those years ago. It was the same sweet face that could turn to a monster's in a half-second.

This was definitely my wife.

This was Emily.

Her gaze fixed on her hands, which rested in her lap. She clutched a plate shard. Deep cuts crossed her arms. She'd slashed herself to ribbons.

"Oh my God," I said, falling to my knees and grabbing her wrists. They had bled out and gone cold. "Oh my God, baby, what did you do?"

"You came back," she said again. A weak smile spread across her face. She was pale. Her lips were blue.

I held her hands close to my face to inspect the cuts. They were bad, but they only oozed. She hadn't cut the arteries. Yet.

"Emily," I said, voice quivering. I closed my fingers gently over the wounds, trying to stop the bleeding. "*Why* baby, *why*." It wasn't even a question; I knew exactly why. I just didn't want to believe it.

She still clutched the plate shard tightly. It dug into her

fingers, and they bled a bit too.

"Are you coming home now?"

I didn't respond. I had no answer. I looked up into her eyes, but she didn't return my gaze. She just sniffled. Her expression was empty.

Emily's hand twitched, and I looked down at the shard again. She gripped it so tightly that her entire arm trembled. I feared she might stab me. I stood up and backed away a few steps.

"I've waited so long," she said, her voice withdrawn and distant. "Where are you?"

I forced myself to speak.

"Emily, sweetheart, look what you're doing to yourself. You don't really want this, do you?"

"Not me," she said. "You." She was gentle, but I could hear the accusation in her voice. She finally looked up at me. "How could you do this to me?"

A wave of nausea swept over me. The feeling was a mixture of rage and guilt. I didn't really know if her violence was my fault, or if she had just made me believe it through years of blame. I never knew who the real monster was.

"Emily," I said sternly, "you behaved like this before I ever left. How can you blame this on me? Please, I don't want to fight. I just want you to get better."

I took a careful step toward her with my hands out in front of me. I wanted to get the shard away from her. She moved it against her neck and held it there as a threat. I stopped moving.

"Sweetheart, please," I begged. "Look what you're doing. Please, please stop. Don't hurt yourself. Just put it down." I felt tears drip down my face.

"I love you," she said. Her face looked so soft and calm. It reminded me of how she looked on her medication. Her eyelids drooped, and her pupils bloomed wide open.

"I love you too, Em," I replied. "I just don't know how to help you. I've tried everything, baby. What more can I do?"

"All you have to do is come home."

"You know that won't change anything," I said. "I've left

before. I don't know how to fix this anymore. Leaving was the only thing I could think of that might help."

"If you love me, you'll come home," she responded. She never blinked. I wondered if she could hear me at all.

"My love," I said as gently as I could, "I've tried so hard. I've sacrificed so much. I've done everything I can for you." I clasped my hands against my heart. "I need you to do something for me now. I need you to see how much this affects me too. I want you to see how much your behavior hurts me. I love you, and I can't go on like this. I can't keep watching you hurt yourself. I can't keep letting you threaten me."

She looked over me carefully, considering my request.

"Please, Emily. Please put that thing down."

"Do you remember when we met?" she asked, gazing up at the moon. It peeked over the tree line, still fixed in place.

"Yes. Of course."

"I knew you were the one," she said.

"I felt the same way."

"I knew I could never live without you." She looked into my eyes.

Another threat.

"Trust me, Em. Being away from you is hard. I didn't want it to end up like this."

"But you left anyway," she said, and dug her toes into the snow. She wiggled them and watched the powder melt on her skin.

"Sweetheart, I had to go. You were violent. You attacked me. You accused me of things that never happened. I felt like I was gonna snap." I took another step toward her. Now I was within arm's reach. I thought about lunging for the shard.

"Please don't go," she said. Her eyes were big and wet. She finally looked like she could feel my words. "Please don't leave me."

She pulled the shard away from her neck and studied it, turning it over in her hands. She traced its edges with a delicate finger.

I felt a pang of guilt as I saw those eyes. My heart skipped a beat, and that primal male instinct took hold of me — the urge to be fiercely loyal to my wife, no matter what. I almost said, "Okay, Emily. I'll come home." The words were right at my lips.

A wolf howled nearby. I glanced over my shoulder and saw shadows darting behind the trees at the edge of the meadow.

"Things will get better," she said. "This time we'll make it work."

I didn't respond. I knew in my heart she was wrong.

"I know I can change," she added. "I know you can too."

The phrase was rehearsed. I'd heard it a thousand times before, and it always worked. It was the perfect excuse I needed to come back again. Just the right thing I needed to hear.

But not this time.

Wolves began to sing in unison all around us. Their dreadful howls were an appropriate score for the eerie scene before me: the dark forest, the ugly sky, my bloody wife. My bare feet protested the freezing snow. My skin crawled with each haunting bay.

"Emily, seeing you like this worries me, and hurts me," I said. "But it doesn't make me want to come back. It makes me believe things will only get worse. It makes me think you'll completely lose it because of me." I dropped my hands to my sides. She looked away.

"I can see how far you're willing to go," I added. "And I can't go there with you. I can't follow you to that place."

Her eyes narrowed and her expression fell to scorn.

"I told you," she said flatly, "I won't live without you."

"But you can't live with me, my love. You're always angry. You tell me I don't love you. That I don't do enough for you. I've given you everything. I have nothing left."

I took another step and placed a hand on her shoulder. She dropped her hands to her lap, gripping the shard gently. She wasn't going to hurt me.

"I think this has to end," I continued. "I believed for so long that I'd be responsible if you ever hurt yourself. But now I know that it's your decision, and you aren't going to hear a word I say. I can't blame myself for your actions anymore."

Emily stared into me. Her eyes lanced through me. Her voice became higher, more innocent.

"But I thought you loved me," she pleaded. "When I was in the hospital, you said you'd never go."

It was true. I vowed I'd never leave. God as my witness, I was convinced I could stick it out through anything. I was sure my love for Emily would be enough.

I thought about how to respond. How to justify going back on my vow. Guilt stung me as I spoke.

"What happened between us…what our relationship has become," I said, "is so far beyond the struggles I imagined we'd face. This has become something I simply can't handle, Emily. I won't live my life afraid that you're going to kill yourself to prove a point to me. I don't want to come home afraid, not knowing what you'll be like. I don't want to be afraid to fall asleep. Not anymore. I don't want to live this life."

"Well I don't want to live any life," she said. "Not without you."

Freezing tears dripped down my cheeks, but I maintained my composure. I rubbed her neck and shoulders to try to warm her up. She never blinked; she just stared into me, waiting for me to break. Waiting for me to be just weak enough to fall down that hole again.

The convincing hands of guilt slid across my back and nudged me toward Emily's empty promises. I wanted so badly to believe things would be okay, that we could work everything out.

The wolves howled enthusiastically. They sat still, encircling us under the trees at the rim of the meadow. I could just barely make out their dark forms. I thought I could see their sinister eyes. Emily didn't seem to notice them at all.

As I stood there in the snow, looking at my injured wife, surrounded by hungry wolves, I thought about everything I'd been through. It was a night of facing my doubts, my fears, my guilt. I thought about what my mom said. I thought about Michael Farmer. I'd gone through hell tonight, and I'll be damned if I didn't learn something from it. I reminded myself that I'd already considered my options and made up my mind hours ago. I knew what I had to do.

"Emily," I said, brushing the hair out of her face, "I love you. I'll always love you. But you can't manipulate me anymore. You can't hold this over my head. Whether I stay or go, I can't stop you from doing this to yourself."

She smirked and moved her tongue around behind her lips.

"You'll be all alone if you leave. You'll have nobody."

The wolves' howls reached a fever pitch.

"There are worse things than being alone. I can't stay just because I'm afraid of being on my own. You deserve better than that, don't you?"

The wolves fell silent.

I glanced over my shoulder, then all around me. They just stared, seemingly hanging on every word we exchanged. They were listening.

"Well, just remember," Emily said, drawing gently on her arms with the plate shard, "*You* killed me."

I shook my head and wiped my face. There was no place she wouldn't go. No words she wouldn't say. No line she wouldn't cross.

I blew out a frosty breath.

"I love you with all my heart, Emily. I love you more than anyone I've ever met. But I can't save you. And I can't stop you."

I touched her face one last time, cupping her cold cheek with a hand.

Then I let go.

"You killed me," she repeated. Her face was totally void of expression. Her eyes were dry. There was just nothing there.

Anger pushed its way to my lips. I swallowed it.

We stared into each other's eyes for what felt like an eternity. I was finally saying goodbye to my wife. I was finally ending our suffering, once and for all.

Then something changed.

She lit up a little. Not her expression, but her skin. The light was shifting across her face. I looked around in surprise. The shadows of the trees crept across the snowy meadow. My own shadow began to move.

Felix Blackwell

It was the moon. The thing finally moved! It was creeping up, up, over the trees, high into the sky. Its light was no longer a sickly orange, but now a pure, silvery glow. It looked normal again.

I turned my back to Emily and looked out to the tree line. The wolves stared back at me from the darkness, but as the moon crept up the sky, the gloom they hid in abated. Their menacing figures faded away as the light hit them, like shadows banished with a flashlight.

Without a sound, the wolves disappeared.

A feeling of triumph flickered inside me.

I whirled around to look at Emily, but only the tree stump remained. She was gone. The blood had disappeared too, leaving an immaculate snowy meadow. The last bit of fog withdrew deep into the woods, and I could see farther than before.

A light.

An inviting yellow light glimmered from beyond the trees. I started toward it.

CHAPTER 14

It wasn't long before I came upon a familiar scene: the back side of my mother's house. The light came from inside. It emanated from the bathroom window, where the monster had watched me escape. A heavy blanket of snow covered the field and draped over the roof, reminding me of the Christmas cards my mother always sent us.

For just a moment I paused, considering what was about to happen. I was no longer afraid that I'd be killed. In fact, I wasn't really afraid of anything, but I was certain the Gorleth would be waiting for me inside. My breath hung in the frigid air as I considered what to do.

I crossed the snowy field, glancing up at the moon. It shone down on me, bright and full. And the stars! They were no longer the unblinking red witnesses of my ordeal. Instead they twinkled in familiar yellows and whites.

I circled around the house and walked up the porch steps. To my surprise, the front door was intact. Inexplicably, it still stood, as if nothing had ever happened to it. It looked as new as it had on the day my father installed it decades earlier.

I pushed it open.

All the lights were on, and the warm air inside sent a flood of relief over my frigid skin. It felt like home again.

I stepped inside.

The house was immaculate. The shelves of books were in place. Nothing was strewn on the floor. No walls bulged, no doors bent. Nothing was warped. As I moved from the entryway to the bedroom, I heard a voice.

"In here, Professor."

I paused. It wasn't the monster's ugly voice that greeted

Felix Blackwell

me, but Emily's. It sounded labored and strained, but I was sure it was my wife's voice.

I cautiously moved to the source of the sound. The living room light was off. As I rounded the corner, I saw someone sitting on my mother's old couch.

"Emily?"

The figure didn't respond. It just sat there, still as death against the darkness.

I dragged my hand along the wall, feeling for the light switch. I didn't take my eyes off the shadowy form.

I found the switch and flipped it. The light flickered a few times, then popped on.

The sight revolted me.

It was the Gorleth who sat before me – I recognized his charred skin and yellow eyes – but now, his form was feminine. He looked like Emily, if she'd been burnt alive and returned from the dead.

"It's time," she said, grinding her jaw. The monster sounded just like Emily when she was raging. Her rotten lips twitched as she spoke, baring those razor-sharp teeth.

"Jesus *Christ*," I said, falling into the chair next to me. I couldn't even blink. I felt my stomach gurgle and go cold, like I'd swallowed a bag of ice.

"Off on your adventures?" she asked, glancing to the window. "Never was much for them myself. Too much of the unknown can kill you... But you already know that."

I said nothing. I was still too mortified by her appearance. *Keep it together*, I thought.

"So. Now you see," she said, examining my reaction with curiosity.

"…Yes," I replied, after a while. "I understand now."

"Do you?"

"It all makes better sense. I just didn't want to see before."

She laughed a sticky, wet laugh. Her black hair stuck to her patchwork skin and clung to her rotted cheeks. It disgusted me, but I didn't show it.

"I was lying to myself about you," I continued. "About

what you really are."

The monster stopped laughing.

"Is that so," she said, leaning forward. She dropped her hands to her knees. Her yellow eyes probed mine, searching for weakness. Not finding any, she rocked back and looked around the room, taking a quick breath.

"Like what you've done with the place," she said.

"Looks better this way," I replied.

"But how?" she asked. "As I recall, we left it quite a mess."

I glanced around, considering all the decorations: a picture of my father, an empty jewelry box, an old clay statue. It was just the way my mother had left it before I woke up in this nightmare.

"I escaped," I said. "But I chose to come back. This place isn't my prison anymore." I motioned to the woods beyond the window. "None of it is."

The Gorleth held her arms open, as if to welcome me.

"And yet I'm still your jailor," she said with a jagged smile.

I snorted, dismissing the comment. Her face twitched.

"You were never the warden," I said. "You and I are cellmates."

Her jaw clenched.

"Emily and I built this prison together," I said. "With every fight, every insult. Every excuse to carry on. Every time I told myself we could make it, I just dug the hole a little deeper. And now we're both trapped in here with *you*." I pointed an accusing finger at the monster.

She exhaled sharply, angered but intrigued.

"It took me this long to realize there are no doors. No locks, no keys. All either one of us ever had to do was walk away. And now, I'm choosing to do that."

"You are *nothing* without me," she snapped. But before she could further insult me, I cut her off.

"No," I said, speaking over her. "No, *you* are nothing without *me*. Emily and I created you together. You're the darkness that feeds on her misery. A mass of hate and fear and pain. You're a tumor, and you're not gonna stop 'til she's dead."

The monster snarled, jumping to her feet and pacing back

Felix Blackwell

and forth, never taking her eyes off me. I sat calmly, watching her. She pulled at her hair in anger.

"You know what I hate the most?" I asked.

She stopped in her tracks, glaring at me.

"You're not just the crazy inside Emily. You're my mistake too. You're everything I did wrong in this relationship. Every contribution I made to our downfall. Every failure. You are *my* goddamn fault."

The Gorleth shrieked with rage and grabbed a framed painting on the wall. She tried to yank it off, but it didn't budge.

I stood up.

"I love Emily," I said, "and that's why this marriage has to end. I'm casting you out. And one day she's gonna realize that she doesn't need you. She's gonna realize you have no power over her. You're nothing."

That was the last straw. The monster roared furiously and dashed at me, grabbing me by the neck with her leathery hands. I wrestled free and threw her to the ground with ease. She thudded to the floor with a screech. We both froze, each of us shocked by this turn of events. The Gorleth's terrifying strength had abandoned her.

She lay on the ground, staring up at me with hate in her eyes.

"You're an abomination," I said, shaking my head in disgust. "Using my guilt against me, while I'm trying to do the right thing for her."

"I'll take her from you," she growled.

"I love her enough to let her go," I replied.

"Suicide," she hissed, forcing a smile. Her pointy tongue flicked against those teeth.

"*Be that word our sign of parting,*" I said, pointing toward window and quoting a poem I figured the Gorleth recognize. "*Get thee back into the tempest.*"

She looked at my finger like a child banished to time-out.

I gazed out the window. I could see past the driveway and down to the cliff. Just beyond it was the sea.

"Fog's cleared," I said.

The moon was high and bathed everything in a soothing glow. The trees in the distance looked a bit less gnarled and warped. I felt like everything was shifting back to the waking world.

I turned back to the monster. She slowly picked herself up and faced me. She opened her mouth to say something, but I cut her off.

"You have nothing," I said. "Nothing left to take from me. Nothing left to threaten me with. No power. You are nothing."

She gnashed her teeth and snarled, shaking with unbounded rage.

"*Rak! Rak!*" she sputtered, unable to control herself. The monster dragged a claw-like hand across the couch beside her, but her rotted fingernails broke off as they scraped along.

"Begone," I said with finality in my voice.

The monster stopped twitching long enough to peer deeply into my eyes. Her lips trembled, and her throat bounced. Her chest heaved. She clutched her head with shaking hands and growled in pain.

With a final, defiant scream, the Gorleth shoved me aside and stomped down the hall. She threw the front door open with a loud crash, and without looking back at me, stormed down the porch steps and off into the night.

I turned and looked out the window. I watched her wade through the snow, toward the woods. The silvery moonlight illuminated her ghastly body as she went. She slipped between the trees at the edge of the field, thrashing about as she did, and disappeared into the darkness. That was the last I ever saw of the Gorleth.

I held my breath for a moment.

Then, I breathed. I felt like a newborn, taking in the air for the first time.

Something took me then, something I never thought I'd feel again – the warm and heavy weight of sleep. It wrapped its narcotic fingers around my body and dragged me to the floor, where I barely managed to crawl to the carpet before flopping belly-up. I lay there in the living room, flat on my back, just staring at the ceiling. My sight went blurry and my limbs turned to immovable stones. All my strength departed my body.

I surrendered to my lethargy and fell into a coma-like stupor. My eyes rolled back in my skull and my thoughts rolled around in my head. Faint memories of Emily flickered in my mind like distant lightning bolts. My eyelids slid shut. The last thing I saw was the moon, peeking in at me through the window.

I don't know how long I slept.

CHAPTER 15

Birds.

There were birds singing.

I didn't move for a few moments. I couldn't. I just listened.

I sucked in a huge breath, and felt water receding from my chest. The sensation startled me. My hand twitched as I raised my arm, and it made a splashing sound.

When I cracked open my eyes, I was instantly blinded by glorious white light. It dove in through the window and ignited the room in a fierce glow. My eyes adjusted after a few moments, and I saw little cream-colored tiles on the wall to my left. I reached up and touched them. They were damp.

I was in the tub. I barely remembered filling it.

How long ago was that? I thought.

I tried to speak, but a slew of gibberish poured out of my mouth. I felt like I'd been drugged. I could barely lift my head. I touched the water with my hands and splashed a little of it into my face.

It was lukewarm.

I must have been out for an hour, I thought.

I gathered my wits and stood up, leaning against the tile wall to ensure I wouldn't fall. I stumbled like a drunk out of the tub and onto the bath mat. The room tilted a bit as I regained my senses.

Through the window above the toilet, I could see the field. It was the brightest, most beautiful day I'd ever seen. The summer forest glowed a vibrant green, and hummingbirds and butterflies darted through the air. The breeze came through the woods and swayed the long grass. Not a single cloud dared hinder the sun's radiance.

Laughing with excitement, I turned around and picked up my clothes, which were still piled near the tub. I threw them on and walked into the bedroom, still dripping wet. There was something heavy in my pocket. I reached in. It was my father's pocket watch. I stopped and examined it.

The hands were straight, and corresponded to the clock on the wall above the bed. The watch pulsated gently in my hand as it ticked. It reminded me of a heartbeat. It reminded me that I was alive.

"Mom?" I called out.

I moved into the living room, and to my joyful surprise, I saw my mother. She had slept on the couch, as she often did while listening to the radio. She and my father used to stay up all night listening to it and talking. I think by continuing the tradition, she felt like he was still around, in some way.

I crept out of the living room and opened the front door.

The sunshine fell on my skin and washed away the remnants of my troubles. I stood there on the driveway, considering my dream as I stared out at the distant ocean. The water and sky were brilliant blue, smearing together at the edge of the world. The wind whispered through the trees, and the crisp air filled me with life.

I wanted this feeling every day – the feeling that I could be alone and happy. And that eventually, I could be loved by someone else. In that moment, as I stood in my mother's driveway listening to the symphony of a hundred cheery birds, I vowed to love myself. To me, this meant enforcing my boundaries and never living in fear.

I also vowed to love my wife.

I used to believe that love was measured in devotion. To me, the idea of staying with Emily was the most profound expression of love. But now I understood that love meant being loyal to her best interests. It meant letting go of her when I could contribute nothing more to her happiness. It meant giving her the opportunity for a new life.

Right now, I had to love Emily by letting her go.

PART II

How many nights I'm doomed to spend beseeching the divine,
that I'd happily trade my life to kiss your hands just one more time.

11 December, 1945

While many victims of abuse during the formative years are capable of recovering and go on to lead healthy lives, some are permanently debilitated. Ravaged by their pasts, they never overcome the trauma they endured, and often display complex psychological abnormalities. Many suffer the inability to cultivate or maintain personal relationships. Some victims even spend their lives emotionally disfigured, and isolate themselves from the world. Beyond those, there are a number of cases that I've only recently studied. These special few are most unfortunate: not only are they seemingly incapable of recovery, but in fact they degenerate into the very fiends that torment them — a prominent observation in the newly pioneered field of criminal psychology. In the very worst of these instances, the victim may become catatonic, as though the very processes of higher consciousness malfunction in an attempt to barricade the frail psyche from traumatic memories.

Recently I cared for a woman who suffered physical abuse throughout adolescence. A notably severe breakdown of her cognitive abilities was triggered by an encounter with a thug on the streets, who attacked her in an alley. Though she was spared serious injury, she has since been unable to return to a typical state of mind. While waking from her mental paralysis, which intermittently plagues her throughout our observations, she described to me (in a semi-conscious blur) a horrific dream world known to her and to other people she met within it as "the Nightmare."

According to the patient, this world is a strange and bewildering place where other victims of similar trauma congregate. She described it to me as a place where the minds of suffering people escape, yet even within this realm they are pursued by their emotional tormentors, who take archetype form of the victim's fears. It is seemingly inescapable, spare only the eventual recession of the patient's dissociative episode. Some of us, the patient says, are trapped there when we die. These people wander the Nightmare, unaware of anything but their own misery, as if "caught between here and somewhere else."

The imagination is well known to conjure vivid hallucinations in times of personal crisis, which are then misinterpreted as supernatural phenomena such as near-death experiences, ghost sightings, or demonic possession. All of these alleged miracles are more elegantly explained through psychology and neuroscience, without the need for spiritual interpretation. I resolve to study this patient further and help to end her cryptic, delusional episodes.

– César P. Arturo II, M.D.

CHAPTER 16

I still have nightmares. It's why I work so late. It's why I'm always exhausted, and why I smoke. A lot. It's why I go to bed after dawn. Something about the sunlight helps me sleep. If I wake up and it's still dark out, I sometimes have to fight off a panic attack. The darkness suffocates me. I never tell this kind of stuff to anyone. But after what I've been through, I'm not living another day without at least writing it down. Maybe I'll write a book someday.

"Sure. Right after you quit smoking," I catch myself saying. I'm hard on myself, but it passes the time. Being your own critic is like having an extra friend around. It keeps me company. Helps me forget that I'm alone.

So I stay up late, reading everything I can to help me explain it. To rationalize it. To make it not true. Maybe I'll find a study, or some similar anecdote somewhere, that will undo my belief that this is real.

It's the nightmares. They seem to be spilling into reality. I can't tell them apart and I can't be sure what is or isn't there. The latest heap of books I'd found in the town library revealed an article of interest: a little piece taken from the journal of a famous doctor a few years ago, just after I'd gotten out of the war.

Well, I didn't get out, really. It's the same story every soldier tells. My unit fell under heavy fire at Normandy. We were pretty green and were in a zone that wasn't expected to be entrenched with Krauts. I took a few good chunks of shrapnel to my right shoulder and leg, shoving a half-wit private to the ground. It was my arm or his neck, the way I saw it, and metal pieces aren't so easy to dig out of the jugular. The biggest of them barely missed my heart, which didn't surprise me – I'd made a vow in front of God that for all eternity, it'd belong to my fiancée back home.

I don't believe in God anymore.

It was during my two-month recuperation in a rickety French hospital that I got the second letter. I expected it might be orders from higher up, sending me back into the fray. But I was finished with that mess. I was out there shooting at people I didn't know and didn't want dead. I didn't want to kill anybody. I was just a kid. A smaller part of me hoped that I might be getting shipped back home, back to my fiancée.

It was such a harmless little envelope, pale yellow as I recall, but inside it was a bomb that incinerated my will to live. To this day, I never finished reading it.

I only got down to the part about how Anja had been murdered.

I met my fiancée in England in 1941. She was twenty, and I was about twenty-four. I was born in New York, but when the Depression hit, my dad moved us across the pond to a quaint little place called Pine Rest. He had money, and wasn't hit too hard, but his boyhood home in England was calling to him. With my mother having passed away only a few years prior, there wasn't any reason left to stay in the States. So off we went.

Anja and I lived near each other, and we went to the same church. She and her folks had emigrated from Germany to escape the coming war in '38, but it followed them here. Because of the constant bombings over London, we all tried to stay away from the major cities, and everyone in the community got to know each other pretty well. We were one big happy family there in Pine Rest, and Anja was the belle of the ball. Her hair was like spun gold, her eyes bright green, her smile enchanting. I can still remember her laugh, and the tingling feeling when she touched me. Electric fire. That's how you know that it's true love. I still remember her charming accent, which belied her fluency with the English language – she'd taught it to herself as a girl, as well as French.

"*Anne-juh?*" our fellow townsmen would say whenever they read her name.

"*On-yah,*" she'd respond, with that crazy smile.

Anja was brilliant, enigmatic, curious. She challenged me in every way. It only took me two years to figure out that I wanted to spend the rest of my life with her. So I proposed, she accepted, and we were to be wed.

That's when the first letter was delivered. It was 1943. To my horror, I'd been drafted, and was forced to leave Anja behind. I was so broken that I could hardly go about my life in the days before I left for training. Anja promised me that her heart would remain with me at all times, on the beaches and in the bunkers, and no matter what shape I returned in, she would love me forever.

She was my entire life. And now she was gone. Abruptly, violently, hatefully ripped from my arms. I'd been wrenched from a perfect dream.

In the coming months I learned her killer was a guy our age, one we both knew from the local church: Adam. He was a misunderstood little bean pole that never looked you in the eye. It seems he professed his longtime affections for Anja one day, and when she told him she was engaged, he fell into a jealous rage. That night, drowning in humiliation and booze, he kidnapped her and brought her to the barn in the woods behind his home.

There was no way anybody could have ever heard her screams. Adam hanged himself alongside her body, with a brief note of apology scrawled on a scrap of paper. I burned the note and pissed on his grave. If he wasn't already dead, I'd kill him twice.

To this day, I find myself paralyzed with hate. It poisons my blood. It's a festering tumor that grows bigger every time I think of him. And I think of him often. Every single day of my life.

I was already in bad shape because of my injuries, and from the shellshock. Every time I shut my eyes, all I could see was gore. The meaninglessness of war, the enthusiasm with which we turn each other into masses of red pulp, it all haunted every moment of sleep I could find. So when I learned of Anja's death, I spiraled into near-psychosis. While in that French hospital I began to experience bouts of catatonia, accompanied by hallucinations and something the doctors called "waking nightmares." The drugs they treated me with either did nothing, or made everything into one horrific blur, like I was living in a dream for days on end. I have no idea how I survived.

In October of '44 I was shipped home. I found myself back in Pine Rest at 28 years old with no life, no direction, and a broken heart. My father passed away within the year, but I continued living in his home because I had no place else to go. I thought about suicide, but that's not what Anja would have wanted. I had no idea how to pick up and move on, so I did what the army taught me: I survived.

I worked my ass off. I got a job as a small-town police officer, which was more rewarding than I expected it to be, so I found passion in it. As much passion as one could experience after such trauma, I suppose. And at the beginning of this year, 1946, I was promoted to Detective, which suited my personality better. I dedicated my life to my work, and found peace within it, but I still suffered from nightmares and panic attacks almost every night.

Everyone's had an especially bad dream, and until a few nights ago, mine was about Anja's death. But then a new one came. It was much more unsettling than the others, and took the color from my face for a few days. My hands never shook until that night, not even during the firefights from years ago, nor at the funeral. Since this dream, however, I can barely hold a cigarette to my lips. Which is probably a good thing, now that I think about it.

I opened my eyes and saw the ceiling. I lay on a stained and reeking mattress. The sheets had disappeared. The air felt icy, but the cold wasn't what woke me up. I'd heard a scream.

My room was different. The walls were made of rusty metal, and a little moonlight drifted in from a nearby window. As

I looked out, I saw dunes. It was an endless oceans of red sand that disappeared over the horizon. And coming toward me, crying, was my beloved Anja.

I don't know if she could see me. Her feet were bare, and she kept sinking into the ground. She struggled with every step. I hadn't seen her alive, even in my dreams, since the day I left for the war. To see her now, alive and breathing and coming toward me, was far more than I could bear. I felt tears explode from my eyes, and I bashed on the window as hard as I could. It would not break. She couldn't hear me.

I turned to look for a door to go find Anja, when suddenly I noticed a massive creature standing in the room with me. He stood over the mattress, examining it with his back to me. I'm a pretty big guy, and he was *much* taller than me. He wore no clothes, and his skin looked red in the gloom. On his shoulder was the same shrapnel scar I had.

I couldn't see his face, but I heard him say,

"Stay out."

I glanced back at the window but could no longer see Anja. Too afraid to move, I stood with my back and palms against the wall, trembling in fear. The thing had unusually lanky arms, and he scraped his long, brown fingernails over the mattress. He stunk of chemicals, and the odor scorched my throat. The creature turned toward me then, but thankfully there wasn't enough light to show his face. I felt my chest tighten as he reached out with a bony finger and poked my chest.

"Out."

The moment I felt his dagger-like nail on my skin, I leaped out of bed, paced around my room a bit, and threw up. I ripped my shirt off and kept wiping my chest with my hands, but I could still feel the monster's claw on me. I was still half-asleep, and began to wonder if I was having a heart attack. I walked toward my telephone, but suddenly the panic ceased. Quiet engulfed the room, and I read my watch: 1:10 AM.

That was a month ago. Tonight, the same nightmare jolted me awake. This time, my watch only read 11:41 PM.

"Tonight's gonna be a hell of a long night," I said to myself, lighting a cigarette. I would not sleep again until dawn. In fact, I refused to sleep again at all. Who needs sleep anyway? Just a waste of time.

CHAPTER 17

I spent the next day at work, trying to forget the thing I saw in my dreams. I dreaded the idea of going home, or getting sleepy, so I had plenty of coffee to keep me going. I went to the local library again on my lunch and sifted through more tattered books. It was rare that I found anything related to my situation, but today I got lucky.

The good doctor kept good notes, and he specialized in patients suffering from psychological trauma. Much of it was stuff I already knew about shellshock and the studies of men returning from war, but there were a few interesting entries about unusual dreams and sleep paralysis. The doctor talked about one dame who had it bad. Really bad. Her story reminded me of my stay in the hospital, suffering under the ten-thousand-ton reality that my future wife was gone. Taken.

I finished the entry and closed the book, taking a hard gulp of some coffee and realizing how warm it was in the station. It felt good, too good, and things got real cozy inside my jacket. It was an old brown trench coat my father had left behind. Around the department they started calling them "Trent coats" because I always wore one. The warmth relaxed me, and my eyes began to feel a little heavy. A wave of panic seethed up from within, and I stood up from my desk. I figured I'd get some fresh air and get the blood flowing to my legs. I walked through the office, which was now all but vacated, and caught sight of the wall clock as I walked by.

11:30 PM.

I wasn't excited about how early it was. I counted the hours until sunrise as I made for the front door.

"Headed home, Detective?" a voice called out behind me.

I looked back and saw pretty little Francesca poking her head out of the chief's room. She looked great. I pushed the thought out of my mind and looked away. She and my boss were the only others here this late, aside from the few patrolmen who passed through every couple of hours as the shifts changed.

"Just need a bit of air is all." I smiled, or tried to anyway, and opened the door.

Everyone at the department was aware that I'm a pretty tightly wound guy, but Francesca was one of the few who actually knew what was going on with me. She'd walked into my office a few months back and caught me in the midst of a nervous breakdown. The flood gate opened, but she didn't get scared off. I was surprised that she didn't. She'd always been there for me — during what little time we spent together, anyway. I'd never met up with her outside of the office. For my own reasons, I felt it was inappropriate.

Nonetheless, Francesca was a saint, and somehow always knew just the right things to say. She was a good friend. My only friend. I remembered this and smiled, this time sincerely, as I stepped outside.

A cascade of English rain poured from the dark sky. Every so often the winds would kick up and blow everything sideways, so I'd get hit in the face with the wet stuff even as I stood under the stone awning. I didn't mind. The blistering cold air felt good on my skin, waking me up a bit and lifting my spirits, and the raindrops washed away my concerns as they dribbled down my face. They pelted the ground so hard now that it reminded me of bullets slamming into the sides of French buildings. My heart fluttered instinctively and my breath snagged in my throat. It took me a moment to gather myself, but I soon dismissed the old fears, and blinked away the remnants of those visions, peering up now at the ugly sky. A sliver moon poked through the storm clouds every few minutes, but I wasn't happy to see it. Anja and I used to look at it together. I wished it'd go back to hiding.

The town seemed eerily quiet tonight. I peered up and down Church Avenue, and as far as I could see, all the store lights were out. No cars passed by. Nobody came and went. No people on the streets, no voices, no nothing. Just me and the empty whispers of the wind. A few street lights glowed soft yellow through the rain, but they didn't illuminate much of anything. One of them caught my eye as it began to flicker, then went out. The drone of pounding rain rose and dropped in volume, and my head started to spin.

After a few more deep breaths, my mind was quiet again, so I turned back to the door and headed inside. I walked by Francesca, who was back at her desk now, too busy to return my gaze. I glanced at the clock. 11:39 PM. I sighed and pulled my watch from my coat pocket. 11:38 PM. Tonight was gonna be a bitch.

I hated myself for living my life staring nervously at the time. I'd have struck up another conversation with Francesca, but hell, I was too tired, and I did have some legitimate work to be doing. I walked back into my office but left the door cracked open, just in case anybody wanted to stop by and chat. When I sat down, I looked out the blinds, just in case. What I'd give even to have my boss storm in and snoop around for a while, asking me about reports I'd filed days ago, or cases he knew I had nothing else to say about.

The minutes crawled by. I tried to busy myself with paperwork, but it failed to keep my attention. Eventually I became lost in Dr. Arturo's medical journal. He was a brilliant man. A man who thought differently. His observations were impeccable; his ability to evaluate the psyche's effects on the body was unparalleled. He even made a few hypotheses I'd never have come up with, and entries later, voila! His speculations are confirmed. And this all came from outside of his own field of expertise. Here I sat, wishing the good doctor had some counsel for me.

This discussion of dream states intrigued me. I flipped through the pages, wondering if any of it applied to my own experiences. I longed to end my nightmares and move on from Anja's death, but something deep inside of me refused to. As I considered the plight of my divided heart, I set the book down and shut my eyes, leaning back in my chair and stretching my arms. Memories of my fiancée invaded my mind: her kiss, her laugh, her smell. Then I saw her wandering through that desert again, and a myriad of emotions swirled in my mind like a hurricane.

It was more than I could bear. I rocked forward and stood up, desperately craving a cigarette. I reached into my coat pocket and retrieved one as I stepped out of my office again, then put it in my mouth as I strode to the door. I fished through my pockets for a lighter, when suddenly the entry doors of the police station swung open. When they crashed against the walls, the noise ricocheted throughout the building and knocked the cigarette right out of my mouth. The cacophony of splattering of rain came rushing in like ocean waves. Across the ceiling, lights flickered and went black.

A small, shadowy figure stood there at the door, holding itself with sickly arms. It lurched forward a step or two, coming right toward me. My hand instinctively dropped to my pistol. I couldn't make out the figure, but it stumbled toward me, gasping and dripping. The rain blasted the pavement outside and deafened me as I called out to it,

"Stop right there!"

Lightning crashed in the distance and momentarily flooded the building with brilliant white. I saw him then: a boy, maybe ten or eleven, clutching himself in pain. I raced over, sliding on my knees and just barely catching him as he collapsed. He looked up at me with vacant eyes. His lips trembled, but his words died in his throat. Then the boy's eyes rolled back, and he fell limp.

I looked around the station. Everything was dark.

"Chief!" I yelled. "Maddock!"

Francesca came rushing over to me.

"Maddock," I said, "call an ambulance! This boy's hurt."

A fatherly instinct surged through me, driving me to react. I hoped it wasn't too late to save the kid, but I could feel swelling on the back of his head, and one of his arms looked broken. I couldn't see his other injuries.

"Trent, the storm knocked out the power!" Francesca replied. "We've got to get him to the hospital."

I picked the boy up and raced outside, Francesca following behind. She opened my car door. I put the kid in the back seat, careful not to touch his mangled arm.

"Hurry, Trent," she said.

I grabbed my key and nodded at Francesca. I saw the concern in her eyes as I backed the car out and raced down Church.

"You'll be alright, kid," I said over my shoulder. I wasn't sure if he was conscious at all anymore. For all I knew, he might have already been dead.

CHAPTER 18

Through the city we tore, blazing past the local grocery. The rain's onslaught against the windshield made it almost impossible to see where I was going, but luckily, there wasn't another car on the road.

At last, a huge building glimmered from the darkness up ahead. It was the Pine Rest Memorial Hospital, nestled against a belt of towering woods at the edge of town. Only a few lights were on. Nobody went in or out as we pulled up. The car screeched as I stopped right in front.

I ripped the kid out of the back seat. He issued a moan of pain as I lifted him, but he didn't open his eyes. I kicked the hospital door open, startling a young receptionist inside.

"He wandered into the police station," I explained. "He's all beat up."

I couldn't even finish turning around before a gurney was shoved into my side. I set the boy down on it and watched as two men wheeled him away. I heard a doctor giving orders to two nurses as they drifted down the hall, but their voices faded to mere echoes. They turned a corner and disappeared.

When Anja and I first met, this building was owned by a paper manufacturer, and the largest employer in our town. Her father even worked there for a time until it went out of business. When the war came to England, the government turned it into a military hospital. The Nazis were bombing the shit out of London, so we hid our injured soldiers way out here.

I stood in the waiting room for what felt like hours. I thought about all the boys that came through here. I wondered how many never left this place. I wondered if I knew any of them.

Meeting this kid and seeing his injuries brought up a lot of memories I had tried to bury. My heart raced. I couldn't sit. My body tingled like there were a thousand ants marching under my skin. I read charts and magazines and pamphlets, but nothing could settle my nerves. I finally found my lighter, hidden deep inside one of my coat pockets, and decided to step out for a cigarette. The receptionist caught me halfway out the door.

"Excuse me, officer?"

It took me a second to realize she was speaking to me. Nobody called me officer anymore.

If I don't get a smoke soon I'm gonna break something.

"How's he doing?" I replied.

My hands started to shake.

"Sir, the doctor would like to speak with you," she said. She motioned for me to walk down the hall, where a nurse and a doctor were speaking to one another.

I made my way to him slowly, unsure whether I wanted to hear what he had to say.

"He didn't make it," I imagined him saying.

I couldn't take hearing that. Maybe I messed him up even worse by shoving him into the car like that. Or maybe one of those sharp turns I took knocked his lights out for good. I remembered the bump on his head, and examined the dried blood on my fingers. A frost crept through my veins, as though the nurse had injected me with ice water.

Before I could introduce myself, the man shot out his hand and said,

"Don't worry son, he's alright."

Relief washed over me, and I laughed nervously. I gratefully shook his hand and introduced myself.

"Trent Cadler, I work down at the P.R.P.D."

I looked the doctor up and down as I spoke, trying to memorize whatever I could about him. It was an old habit I'd learned from training. Or maybe it came before that. Maybe it was just the age-old paranoia. The doctor was older, old enough to be my father, and had a firm grip. His hair was grayish, and he wore a set of odd glasses. He must have been half my height.

His white coat read in elegant lettering, *M. FARMER, M.D.*

"Do you have an ID on the boy?" he asked.

"Uh, no sir," I replied. "I've never seen him before. I didn't get to speak with him. He just wandered into the department all messed up. He blacked out before I could ask him any questions. We had no power, so I brought him here."

Dr. Farmer turned to the nurse and said, "No name on him. Have Tracy prep the file." She disappeared around a corner.

A lot of people fear doctors, but I loved them. They'd saved my life. They had a confidence about them, the kind I wish I had. Hearing Dr. Farmer's voice settled my nerves like a morning cigarette.

"We had to go to the emergency generators," he said, pointing his pen at the ceiling. The lights flickered every now and then. "Storm came out of nowhere."

I nodded, waiting for the rundown.

"The boy's got some fractured ribs and a shattered radius, which the master surgeon may need to operate on when he's finished with his patients," he said. "We're a little backed up. Tonight the streets are quiet, but there's been an unusual amount of emergencies.

"The worst of his injuries, however, is a severe concussion. We've stabilized him and are monitoring it. But he may be here for quite some time, depending on whether his condition improves."

I rubbed my chin and was reminded that I needed a shave.

"Doctor, do you think somebody did this to him?" I asked.

He glanced away, and with a deep breath, said,

"It's hard to say. Anything could have happened. Fight with an older brother. Maybe the dad's a drunk. There are no bite marks; it wasn't a dog. No scratches, no cuts. It looks like he was whacked with a blunt object. But his arm makes me think he took a nasty fall, maybe down some stairs."

"I fell down a lot as a kid," I replied. "Never ended up under the knife. Maybe somebody pushed him."

The doctor took me up a rickety elevator to the fourth

floor of the building and walked me into the kid's room. He was just lying there, all wrapped up, not moving. Machines hummed and beeped all around him: an EKG, some sort of pneumatic contraption, a set of lights, and even a radio. A nurse jotted something on a clipboard in the corner. My heart swelled with pity as I approached the bed.

"He's stable, but unresponsive at this time," the doctor behind me. "We're unsure whether he'll come out of it or not, but he has shown signs of fleeting consciousness." He turned and walked out after having a brief conversation with the nurse. I didn't pay attention to anything they said.

I stood over the boy for several minutes, watching his face, wondering what had happened to him. I took the chair next to his bedside and sat down, trying to slow my racing heart. It felt like I hadn't slept in days (which was probably true). I was so tired from all the excitement that I actually wished I was home in bed.

I looked around the room. It was plain and clean, with a cheap painting here and there, a small window with white drapes, and ceiling lights that hung down a foot or so on cables.

"You got a nice setup here, kid," I said, not knowing if he could hear me. "They're gonna take good care of you…I don't really know what else I can do for you, but I promise, I'm gonna find out what happened, and if somebody did this to you, I'm gonna break the prick's neck."

I reached out and placed my hand on his, feeling the warmth of his little body, and felt a renewed twinge of pity. I never really had a soft spot for kids. I quit thinking about them after Anja died, so I was surprised that I was this upset over one I didn't know. After all, I'd almost perfected the art of removing myself from personal attachment.

I sat quietly for a while, playing the events of tonight over and over in my head. I figured I should give the station a call. Francesca was probably still there, waiting to hear from me, and the chief would have a thousand questions to fire off.

I figured now would be a good time to get up and finally have that smoke, but I needed to rest a minute. I sank in my chair, stretched out, and took a few deep breaths. I shut my eyes and tried to purge my thoughts of all the stress. It seemed to work, because I started to feel relaxed. And warm. The pitter-patter of nurses and doctors scurrying about the halls helped me feel like I wasn't so alone, and the gentle beeps and whirrs of the instruments surrounding the kid provided wonderfully comforting background noise.

I don't know how long I slept.

CHAPTER 19

I stretched again and rubbed the dreary webs from my eyes. It felt like I'd been out for a month. In fact, I felt like a million bucks. Who'd have thought I'd catch a few winks in a place like this? I chuckled, and reflexively straightened out my coat with my hands. As my sight returned, I saw the ceiling, and those lights dangling from it. They swayed, as if pushed by a gentle breeze, and creaked as they moved. Every now and then, they'd flicker.

Is it still storming out? I wondered.

The air felt hot and damp. I looked to the window across the room, but it was pitch-black, and I couldn't hear any rain against it. The door beside me was now closed. The hall outside sounded empty; the typical chatter and footsteps of hospital staff were strangely absent. As I looked around, I noticed that the pattern on the linoleum floor was uneven. A few of the black squares were crooked or too large – but I figured it was an optical illusion cast by the flickering lights, or by my tired brain.

A beeping noise, unlike the sounds from before, brought my attention to the boy's bed. At first I saw only the machines. Their chirps now distorted, as if I were hearing them underwater. The devices sputtered and reset over and over, and at times, sparks exploded from here and there. Some of the machines even looked burnt or melted.

"What…the…hell…"

I stood up and walked a few steps toward the bed. My pulse thumped in my neck. A lump of ice formed in my throat as I stared down at the empty mattress.

The boy was gone.

His sheets lay on the floor. It looked like he'd jumped out

of bed.

Or someone took him, I thought.

Only a few drops of blood remained on his pillow, no doubt from the wallop he'd taken to the head. The lights flickered and buzzed more rapidly now, as though my quickening heartbeat interfered with them. I ran to the other side of the room, careful not to trip on the spilled books and medical instruments.

Had there been an earthquake?

Memories of the bombings flooded my mind.

I calmed myself and pressed my hands against the nearby window, trying to get a view of what was happening outside – but saw only velvety black. An image of the hospital floating in empty space flashed across my mind. My skin went hot, and panic clamped down on my chest. I loosened my coat, and noticed that the lower ends of it were burnt.

I went for the door, ready to grab the first person I saw and shake the life out of him until I got some answers. But as I reached for the knob, the PA system crackled to life. An empty, robotic female voice seeped through it.

"Patient 606, please return to your room. Patient 606, please return to your room."

It took a few moments, but I finally got the door to budge. It almost ripped off the hinges as I shoved it open. Broken boards lay on the ground before me. Someone had nailed the door shut from outside.

I took a deep breath and stepped into the hallway.

It was an unsettling sight, to say the least. The once wide, bright hall was now a rancid mess. It looked narrower somehow, and the walls sagged and bulged. Stains covered the once-pristine floor, and my shoes stuck to the linoleum a bit as I walked. A gurney lay on its side a few yards ahead, and behind me, an abandoned wheelchair sat with a burnt blanket draped across it. Howls of wind broke the silence every so often, and water dripped somewhere off in the distance.

"Hello?" I called out. "Anyone here?"

My voice rushed down the hall and echoed back to me

distorted. I sifted through my pockets to find my watch, and when I retrieved it, it was caked with old dust. I brushed it off with my thumb and had to look twice at the time, because the second-hand was ticking much slower than usual, and it seemed to be going…backwards.

"What the shit is this?" I mumbled, knocking the watch against my palm.

A sudden noise jolted me back to my senses, and I spun around. A plastic sheet that hung from the ceiling of another room caught a draft and blew softly into the hall. I headed in the other direction, toward the elevator the doctor and I had taken. The hall lights flickered, illuminating the ugly mess. Most of them went dark, but the few that remained on were dim and scattered throughout the area. I paused for a moment to look into the other rooms for signs of the boy, but found only empty beds. Most were unmade, and some were torn up or overturned.

I reached the end of the strange hall and hit the call button for the elevator. A deep groan issued from below, probably the machinery trying to kick up, but nothing happened.

"Suppose I could use the exercise," I said. I followed the cob-webbed signs to the stairs and descended into the dark.

A dripping sound caused me to look up. A huge object dangled from the stairwell ceiling high above. It was wrapped in black tarp and hung from several thin cables. As I stood there trying to make out what it was, it flinched. I gasped and took off, leaping down the remaining steps by threes. Something had gone very, very wrong here.

I came to a door marked *3ʳᵈ Floor* and tried unsuccessfully to open it. Fortunately, the door to the second floor opened. I stepped into the hall, but forgot to close the door behind me, and it slammed shut. The sound ricocheted on for what felt like forever. I held my breath, pressing my back against the filthy wall, praying nothing had heard me. And just as some part of me expected, a score of horrific moans and screams echoed back to me through the corridors from far off. I held fast against the panic that rushed up inside me. The last thing I needed was to lose it here. I had to find the kid.

CHAPTER 20

The hall was almost pitch black. No drafts blew through here; someone had nailed all the windows shut, and the foul stench of decay filled the air. In the distance, a door slammed once or twice, and I heard coughing and sniffling from all around me.

As I passed by a room, I poked my head inside, and saw a man lying on a bed with all sorts of tubing and restraints covering him. In the dim light it was impossible to make out his features, and frankly, I didn't want to get a good look at him anyway. Something else caught my eye: a light coming from the window near his bed. I snuck toward it, careful not to trip on the wires that connected the man to his life support machines.

At first there was only darkness. Then, lightning illuminated my view, and I saw a big tree looming on the horizon. There was no city, no sky...only the tree. I waited for another lightning strike, but it never came. When I gave up and turned to leave, the man in the bed jolted violently against his restraints. His body contorted with unnatural force, and he whispered something I couldn't quite make out. Then he went limp. I yelped in surprise and stumbled out of the room.

As I stepped back into the hall, the nearby elevator kicked on. I stopped dead in my tracks and listened as it rumbled. It screeched to a halt on my floor. I ducked into an empty room nearby and poked my head out.

I needed to see who it was.

The doors didn't open for a long moment. My heart slammed against my chest. Then the elevator issued a soft *ding*. My heart stopped.

With a furious roar, the doors lurched open, and from the

darkness within came three massive beings. They looked like men, but taller, with broad shoulders and gray skin. Strange, decorative carvings aligned their chests and arms, and an oily black mucus seeped from them like blood from a wound. They had no faces, but instead featureless, flat stone slabs that narrowed at the chin. Gray, similarly unremarkable domes topped their heads, perhaps made of metal or stone.

As they exited the lift, their boots made terrible clunking sounds. The beings carried long metal objects that looked like ornate clubs, but I couldn't be sure in this darkness. As one of them passed by a well-lit room, I noticed that several thin strings of what appeared to be fishing line dangled from different parts of his body. At that moment I imagined giant, menacing puppets breaking free from their manipulators and scouring the earth in search of something to torment.

What the hell are those things?

The intercom crackled to life once again.

"Security code green. Missing patient alert."

I watched the creatures in awe as they separated and began searching each room. I knew they'd eventually find me, so I scurried down the hall, looking for somewhere to hide. I snuck through a door marked *Women's Lavatory.*

Inside, everything was stained and putrid, and a terrible green mold covered much of the tile and sinks. The whole place reeked of sickly-sweet perfume, something I imagined the corpses of old women wearing. Most of the mirrors had been shattered, spare the one at the far end of the room. As I passed by it in search of a hiding place, I caught a glimpse of my reflection.

I recognized my face, but the resemblance stopped there. My reflection donned the same white hospital gown I'd worn a few years ago in that French hospital, and bandages lined my right shoulder. I looked gaunt and pale, and my eyes peered back at me from sunken pits. As I reached up to touch my face, my reflection did as well.

A loud crash outside the bathroom shook me back to reality, and my gaze snapped toward the door. The puppet-men were drawing closer, and in only a matter of seconds they'd enter the bathroom I hid in. I abandoned my odd reflection and scrambled into one of the stalls. I closed the door and locked it, then jumped up onto the toilet so they wouldn't see my feet. Above me was a vent just wide enough for me to fit into, if I could make it through in time. I pried open the panel and hoisted myself in, straining to not cause a ruckus. I slid flat on my stomach, then crawled backwards over the hole and closed the panel – just in time to hear the lavatory door splinter open.

I held my breath as metal boots clattered across the wet tiles. The sound of heavy wheezing filled the room and echoed through the shaft I hid in, instilling me with dread. I drew a sharp, shallow breath, which almost gave me away; their movement and breathing abruptly stopped. For half a minute, the only noise I heard was the lonely drip of a faucet. I lay on my stomach, still as death, praying the creatures hadn't heard me. At last, a sound broke the stillness: the intercom crackled to life once more, and that empty voice poured through it:

"Medication time in five minutes. Please remain in your rooms and await your nurses."

The announcement was met with intense gasping and screaming from all corners of the hospital. I buried my face in my arms, trying to drown out the hellish cries. Every muscle in my body tensed, and freezing sweat beaded down my face and neck. The creatures left the bathroom, grunting as they did, and stormed off down another hall.

I waited until their echoes vanished, then I started to crawl through the vents.

I couldn't see much in the first room I passed over, but I did manage to catch a glimpse out the small window on the wall. A full moon glimmered in the empty sky behind the tree I'd seen earlier. This window puzzled me even more than the first. I distinctly remembered the moon being only a crescent at the police station. And the tree! When I saw it earlier through another window, it had leaves. Now, it was dead and gnarled. I wiped the dusty sweat from my face and shook my head in frustration.

You're having a psychotic break, I told myself. *None of this is real.*

I forced myself onward.

The second room I passed was full of people. Several patients, obscured by the dim and flickering lights, lay face-up in rows of beds. They shivered and jerked and mumbled strange things to themselves. Each one of them wore a blindfold. I watched through the vent for a few moments, too disturbed to pry my eyes away. One of the patients began to mutter louder and louder.

"N, nnn, n, n-nurse! Nurse! Nurse!" she screamed, then went back to murmuring softly.

"No! No no no!" the others cried out.

I continued forward, crawling on my forearms. Claustrophobia crept up my chest and clamped its burning fingers down on me. It was getting harder to breathe.

Patient 606, I remembered.

I drew a deep breath, forcing myself to remember why I was here in the first place.

"Hang on, kid," I said. "I'm coming."

CHAPTER 21

Crawling around a network of air ducts was a miserable endeavor. In ten minutes I'd only crawled about a hundred feet, and had found mostly dead ends. While conjuring a mental map of the paths I'd covered, I heard the sound of someone walking barefoot. I peered through a vent that overlooked a corridor.

It was the kid! He shambled around, confused, and maybe drugged. He no longer had any of the lacerations or welts I'd seen earlier.

"Hey! Kid!" I said, as loudly as I dared. "Up here."

The boy stopped and looked around. He said something in another language, then repeated it louder and louder. I shifted my body a bit in the duct, and my noise grabbed his attention. He kept yammering. He must not have known about the strange beings running around this place.

"Shhh!" I tried to hush him.

But it was too late. Someone heard him, and doors began to crash open from far off. The boy suddenly perked up out of his stupor and took off running in my direction. He passed me and ducked into a stairwell.

Soon after, the huge puppet men charged through the hall. They separated into nearby rooms, tossing beds and equipment. None of them figured to investigate the stairs. After a few moments they gathered, and then headed back the way they came.

What could they possibly want with him?

Eventually I crawled my way to the stairwell. I kicked a dusty vent open and leaped out. My shoes smacked into the linoleum floor with such force I was sure I'd given myself away, but there was no response from down the hall.

A window sat on the wall before me. Beyond it was not the abyssal blackness I'd seen before; a pale light seeped through it and illuminated the area where I stood. I walked up to it and peered out.

A thick fog shrouded much of what I could see, but I did make out a meadow of sorts, far down below, with a pond resting at its center. Sunlight shone faintly onto the grass, reminding me of how claustrophobic I was in this place. A young girl stood in the water with her back turned to me. She was naked. She was waded slowly through the pond, sometimes dipping beneath its surface. Against my better judgment, I bashed my fists against the glass and called out to her. Maybe she knew the way out. Maybe she could get help.

"Hey!" I screamed at her, pounding at the window. "Help me! Up here!" I knew I risked giving away my position, but for some reason, a powerful loneliness befuddled my senses when I looked at the girl.

"Up here!" I repeated. "Please, help!"

She seemed to have heard me, but couldn't figure out where I was. Instead she searched in the opposite direction, never looking behind her. I never saw her face.

Before I could yell again, a loud bang in the distance knocked the sense back into me, so I gave up and silenced myself. The fog rolled in thicker now, and after a few more seconds, I could see nothing at all out of the window.

Ashamed of my stupidity, I bolted down the stairs, halting at the *1ˢᵗ Floor* door and taking a deep breath.

As quietly as I could, I opened the door, and remembered not to slam it this time. My footsteps echoed differently now. The room sounded much bigger, but not a single blade of light cut through the darkness to confirm my guess. A row of windows glowed faintly along the far wall, but their light was too dim to illuminate anything inside.

I dug through my coat pockets with shaking hands, searching for my lighter, but instead I found some sort of paper. I yanked it out of my jacket, wondering what the hell it could be, and stuffed it under my arm to continue my search. When I found the lighter, it took several flicks to get going. It finally sparked to life, dispersing the darkness around me and revealing a small portion of the room. I inspected the paper and saw that it was an envelope.

A pale, yellow envelope.

I froze up, feeling my heartbeat slow to a frigid crawl. My breath snagged in my chest and wouldn't budge. A thousand terrible memories waded into my mind. Before I could decide to open the letter or throw it away, a woman's scream shattered my reveries and pulled me back to reality.

"You monster!" she yelled. "They'll feed you to the wolves for this!"

I stuffed the envelope back into my jacket, beholding with fright the words that emanated from the vents. Or maybe they came from inside my own head. I couldn't be sure of anything here. I listened for a while longer, but the woman never spoke again.

I made my way against the wall, feeling with my hands, until I found a light switch. Only two of the many hanging lights sparked to life, and even those flickered.

I was in a cafeteria. Tables stood in neat little rows, and a few trays of food still lay here and there. The sight reminded me of my hunger, and fresh pangs shot through my stomach. I stuffed the lighter back into my coat and approached a tray.

Upon it was a half-eaten cup of yogurt, an empty bottle of juice, and an apple. For the first time in what seemed like ages, I felt a little relief, and picked up the apple. It was bright red, even under the weak glow of my lighter, and looked fresh. I lifted it to my lips, closing my eyes as I did, and bit into it. The taste invigorated me, and my stomach gurgled in excitement. For whatever reason, an image of Francesca crossed my mind. I thought about where she was, and if she was worried about me.

Suddenly the taste went foul. I spat out both the bits of apple and the thought of Francesca. I scraped my tongue against my teeth and spat a few more times, and inspected the apple more closely. Its insides were brown and rotten. I tossed it to the floor, shrugging off the weird experience, and reached for the yogurt. A fly drifted whimsically out of the cup as I grabbed it. It too had gone bad.

I went to search the other tables for edible food, but the sound of cupboards opening and closing erupted from somewhere up ahead. I whipped around, searching for the source, and saw a husky man in a dirty uniform and toque, rummaging behind the buffet. He didn't see me, but impassively moved from one side to the other, picking up items and unscrewing lids. He didn't seem to be looking for food. In fact, he didn't seem to be doing much of anything except making a ruckus. He wiped his face with a meaty arm and sniffled. It almost sounded like he was crying. I sunk to the floor and hid myself in the dark. The man moaned in frustration and threw a canister of silverware at the wall.

I crept toward the door at the far end of the cafeteria, careful not to bump into anything. I tried not to take my eyes off of the man, but when I came to the windows, I had to look out.

An angry and opaque ocean lay hundreds of feet below, its waves crashing mercilessly against the lower regions of the hospital. The building reminded me of a ship sinking into a dark sea. The sound of the water rose steadily as I watched, eventually deafening me to any other noises that I might have otherwise perceived.

A few pieces of driftwood floated helplessly in the tumult, heaved and broken under the crush of water. The ocean stretched out to the horizon, where it met the churning sky. A few rays of brilliant sunlight penetrated the storm clouds and shone down on the water, but the world was mostly gray.

Each window I'd looked out so far had shown a different scene. I concluded that the windows could not be trusted. I tore my gaze away and backed out of the cafeteria through a door at the far end.

As I stepped out, I slipped in something wet and fell flat on my back.

CHAPTER 22

The door closed softly behind me. I scrambled to my knees, straining to see what had caused my fall. When I fished through my coat for my lighter, I noticed that the envelope I'd found moments ago was now missing. Confused, I located the lighter and held it near the ground, revealing that I'd slipped in a slimy, black fluid.

There were footprints: the bare feet of a child, leading down the hall and around the corner. With newfound hope, I touched a print to see how fresh it was. The liquid felt warm and thick, and as I touched it, I remembered that mucus shit running from the wounds of the puppet-men.

Then I remembered something. Anja's grandfather had been a dollmaker at one point in his life, and the family brought his favorite piece with them when they moved to Pine Rest. It was a terrifying thing, a clattering wooden puppet strung up on wires that dangled from a cruciform handle.

What did she call that thing? A marionette?

That's what those creatures reminded me of.

I wiped my hand on my lap and darted down the hall, following the prints. I patted my side to ensure my gun was still there. When the heavy metal pushed back against my fingers, a slight calmness seeped through me. A few more signs hung on the walls, the most exciting marked *EXIT*, with arrows pointing all in the same direction I was heading. Even better, the prints seemed to follow them.

Maybe he was a pretty smart kid, I thought. If he'd made it this far, he must have some brains. Finding his way around this place must be a nightmare, especially with those things stomping around looking for him.

Yeah, he's a clever one, I reassured myself.

I passed by more rooms, most filled with warped equipment, wilting like dying daisies. Why did nothing work right here?

"Damn hellhole," I muttered to myself.

The footprints began to change. Instead of the shape of feet, they soon became mere dribbles of the stuff, as though he'd just floated up into the air…

…or someone had picked him up, I realized. I halted right where the drops disappeared.

In front of me was a set of double doors marked *Reception*.

I shoved them open, ready to beat somebody to death with my bare hands. As I stormed into the reception area, I recognized the waiting room I'd sat in earlier.

A man stood there now, his back to me. He wore the unmistakable jacket of a doctor, and somehow it was pristine white – unlike everything else in this filthy hospital. He looked a bit like an angel.

I froze in place. He hadn't heard me; he simply stared out the little window near the front entrance. The doors were wrapped in chains, with a big padlock fastening them together.

We were locked in.

The doctor held a mop and rested his hands and chin atop the handle. He sighed and then began to clean the floor, humming a sad tune that reminded me of something Anja used to sing. I suddenly remembered how intensely hungry I was, but forced the thought out of my mind.

My hand hovered over my hip, ready to whip my pistol out and fill him with lead, but he made no sudden movements.

Oblivious, I thought, *just like the cook I'd seen in the cafeteria.*

I started toward the doctor, but as I neared the check-in desk, the sound of shuffling papers grabbed my attention. Two female receptionists in stained uniforms filed papers and typed on melted typewriters. Their mindless, repetitive actions made them seem almost inhuman. When one of the women turned to look at me, I noticed that her mouth had been crudely sewn shut.

I stood there in shock, unable to tear away my gaze. The

streaks of old tears smudged her makeup and painted purple streams down her cheeks. Her eyes were swollen and red, and she glanced up at me for a moment, but then looked away timidly and continued her dreary work.

"Uh...you seen a kid around here?" I asked her.

"Don't bother, they can't understand you," the doctor said behind me. "And even if they could, they don't have much to talk about, as you can see."

I turned around to face him. He continued mopping as he spoke.

"Those buffoons too dumb to catch you?" he asked. "I suspect they've turned up every bed and tray by now."

It took me a moment, but I recognized him. It was Dr. Farmer, but he looked different. He looked even older than before.

"They…" I examined every inch of the room to ensure I wasn't being distracted. Yet another old habit. "They're looking for me? Those things?"

The doctor chuckled and stopped his work.

"Oh no. Not you. Well not really."

"Who are you?" I asked.

"A friend." He replied so quickly he nearly cut me off, as if he'd read my mind.

"What the hell are those things?" I demanded. "What do they want?" I took a step toward him, and he recoiled in fear. As I moved closer, I noticed a few deep cuts on his hands.

"Slaves to a primitive ideology, I suppose," he said in a glum tone. "Mere puppets. You'd know more about it than I do, of course. Why, you were there. They want only to make everything just like them. To fix this world as they see fit."

I reached out and grabbed him by the lapels. I wanted answers, not riddles.

"The hell are you talkin' about?" I pressed. "What ideology? I want to know what you know about this...place. And if you don't tell me, I'll put a bullet right between your eyes."

I snatched my pistol from its holster and jammed it against the doctor's forehead, but it felt different in my hand. The doctor reacted with horror, but began to chuckle when he saw my confusion. The gun was all bent up, like it had melted and hardened, as with the rest of the instruments in this hospital. The barrel drooped down toward the floor, and the handle was so twisted I could barely grip it. Shocked, I released the man and inspected the weapon.

"Why does this happen?" I asked.

"Have you seen Patient 606, Detective?" he said, ignoring my question. "Do you know where he is?"

I got mad again, remembering my resolve to protect the boy.

"I don't know a damn thing," I replied. It was the truth, but I'd have lied even if I'd known.

The doctor leaned toward me and began to whisper.

"You *must* find him. They're looking for him, and when they catch him, they'll punish him for escaping. They'll change him."

A receptionist sniffled behind me.

"I've looked everywhere for him," I whispered back. "His footprints led me here. And even if I did find him, where the hell would we go?"

The doctor looked over his shoulder at the locked doors.

"The way out," he said. "The janitor can open it, I think. But they trust him. He won't give it to you."

"Give me *what*?" I asked, frustrated.

"The key, of course!" Dr. Farmer hissed.

We both looked around the room again to ensure no one had heard us.

"Where do I find the boy?" I asked, almost begging for the answer.

The doctor shrugged.

"He could be anywhere. You just have to find him first. Find him before they do."

I scratched the back of my neck.

"If they've already found him—" I tried to ask.

"Then it's too late," he said.

"But *if* they found him, where would they take him? Where

would I go?"

The old man ran his fingers through his hair and examined his hand. A tiny hint of red tinged his fingers.

"They'd take him to the basement," he sighed. "Down where the surgeons play God."

With that, Dr. Farmer withdrew from me and began to mop once more. I stood there like a statue, contemplating his words. When I looked up, he was gone.

CHAPTER 23

The thick hospital air and a nagging sense of guilt began to weigh down on me. Why hadn't I woken up when the kid got out of bed? And if he was taken, why didn't I hear any of it? I tried to remind myself that I wasn't really responsible for the kid, but goddammit, I couldn't make myself believe otherwise. And now it might be too late.

I left the reception area, following the signs as best I could in the dim light. A few unsettling noises echoed from the farthest reaches of the hospital as I moved: whispering, doors creaking open or slamming shut, and the malevolent cackling of an old woman.

I searched a few rooms, hoping to find a weapon, but discovered only useless tools that had been melted, bent, or warped. I accidentally backed into a tray of what looked like surgical instruments, and when they clattered to the floor, I noticed that they were featureless steel rods. At last I found a lone scalpel hiding in a drawer. Unlike everything else in this place, the knife appeared normal and could indeed be driven through somebody's skull.

I hated the idea of sticking anybody. I had to do it once in France, and the feeling never left me. The poor guy watched as his life poured out of him at the tip of a bayonet. He was some goddamn Kraut waiting to ambush the guys in my unit. The poor bastard was probably my age, but half my size. When he looked into my eyes, we both knew he wasn't going home. Maybe he had a fiancée just like I did. Maybe all he wanted to do was build a quiet little life with her, just like I did. I cried after that. He was the only man I'd killed in the war. I think. I hope.

At some point I found a large set of stairs that seemed to

go on forever, down, down, down, into the dark.

It took me a couple of minutes to reach the bottom. A single hanging light swayed gently at the end of the hall, flickering and crackling, and casting an array of dancing shadows on a set of double doors. A sign above them read *Surgery Ward*.

I sat down on those stairs and rubbed my eyes, recalling my incessant fear of blood: its warmth, the smell, how readily it splattered and spurted all over everything. I'd seen men bleed to death, slowly, crying for their mothers. Every soldier lived a different life, but they all died the same way – a bloody mess.

Suck it up.

I shoved the doors open and swallowed back my phobia. Another dark hallway lay before me, its floor and walls crooked and bulging, like all the rest in this endless maze. Three or four stained gurneys poked out of the many doorways or lay on their sides. The flickering ceiling lights illuminated a coat rack with dangling scrubs and operating gowns. I gripped the knife in my clammy hand. The metal still felt like ice.

Not knowing where to begin, I softly called out for the kid and poked my head into each room.

The third had me considering turning back and heading straight out of the ward. A graphic scene greeted me as I flicked on my lighter. It was another operating room, but this one had recently been...used. The far wall had been spattered with blood, and big, dried pools of it covered the table. Bent scalpels, jagged lancets and other surgical tools lay strewn across the floor, and a dripping faucet echoed through the silence. I walked to the faucet and tried to take a drink, but the water tasted like melted iron.

Gray static appeared in my vision, warning me that I was about to faint. I reminded myself that losing consciousness down here likely spelled certain death, or worse, a visit to one of these operating rooms.

As I turned to leave, I noticed a syringe with a long and cruel-looking needle glimmering from a nearby tray. I left the room and leaned against the door, trying to catch my breath. My fingers went numb and waves of nausea rushed up my chest into my mouth. I clenched my fists.

Where's your knife?

A vision of the scalpel flashed in my mind. I'd left the damned thing at the sink.

Even the thought of going after it made me want to puke, but I knew that if I was going to protect the kid, and myself, I'd need it. I pressed my forehead against the door as I stood, cursing under my breath.

"Goddamn hospitals," I grumbled. "Why'd it have to be a hospital..."

I turned the knob and the door creaked open.

The room was now immaculate. The blood had vanished. All the surgical tools sat neatly on their trays, and everything was dressed in white. It was as though no operation had ever taken place.

Breathe.

I walked briskly to the sink, retrieved my knife, and immediately left the place. The door locked as I pulled it shut. I didn't stop to wonder why.

CHAPTER 24

Move. Focus. Deep breaths. Someone needs you now.

I gnashed my teeth at the thought of Anja's death. The memory drifted into my head at least once a day, and each time it was like getting stabbed in the heart. It was ridiculous to blame myself for what happened, but some part of me interpreted my absence as a failure to protect her. Over time, that feeling evolved into irrational guilt. It was a monster that tormented me on a nightly basis. A demon I could never banish. But it gave me strength. It gave me motivation. It gave me the courage to succeed where I had once failed, and to be the man Anja once needed me to be. My only thoughts were of rescue. I needed to redeem myself, even if it cost me my life.

At the end of the long hall stood a tall wooden door. The elaborate carvings that adorned its surface befitted a church more than a hospital. Two smaller doors flanked it on either side. The left was labeled Basement, the right Morgue.

I contemplated them for a moment, then reached my hand toward the knob of the morgue door, hoping to get the worst of the three out of the way. A monstrous howl echoed from beyond it.

"Alright then," I said, feeling goosebumps ripple up my arm.

What's behind the fancy door?

I opened it and stepped inside.

This room was dark, but the echo of my footsteps revealed its cavernous size. I wondered if I'd found another cafeteria down here. I flicked on the lighter and strained to see just what this place was. Even in the dim light, I could tell the room was unlike any other in the hospital. Shackles and chains lay strewn about on the floor, and great pillars stretched from the polished stone floor up into the darkness. Rain pelted windows high up near the ceiling, but I couldn't see them. Several dozen candelabras lined the walls, and a set of black chains held up an ancient chandelier, which dangled over a long, decorative refectory table. A single chair sat at the far end of the table, bedecked with the same carvings as the door, and encrusted with glittering jewels. It looked like a throne.

I lit a few candles on the table and nearby candelabras, hoping to get a better view of the place. The tiny points of light failed to reveal the ceiling, but they illuminated a most welcome sight: a bounty of fresh fruit and roasted turkey, heaped in piles, fit to serve a dozen!

Who the hell is this for?

My hunger overwhelmed my curiosity and drove me to circle the table like a vulture. I ran my fingers over a steaming drumstick. My stomach churned. The smell overpowered me. I lifted a chalice of some red liquid to my lips – some sort of juice, or wine I suspected, and when it hit my tongue I swooned with joy. I pulled a bushel of grapes toward me. As I popped one into my mouth, I noticed the outline of a door across the room, concealed by a hanging tapestry.

The candelabra I'd lit stood right beside it. If not for the candlelight that danced across it in just the right way, I'd never have seen the door's outline. As I considered why the door had been concealed, and what might lay beyond it, the taste in my mouth turned vile. I spit out the grape bits and inspected the bushel more closely; it had putrefied there in my hand. I recalled my experience in the cafeteria and tossed the grapes away.

I picked up a banana. It looked ripe and yellow, even in the dim light. I broke it in half with my fingers. It seemed fine, but as I went to eat it, it softened to a stinking mush in my hands. The smell singed my nose, and I threw it to the floor as images of Francesca Maddock swirled through my head.

"What is this shit?" I whispered.

Everything I picked up rotted the second I placed it in my mouth. I grabbed handfuls of fruit and bit into them, but each attempt produced such rancid flavors that I might have preferred the taste of vomit.

By the time I came to the turkey I was covered in stinking juice, out of breath and clenching my fists so tight I could have snapped someone's neck. I ripped a hunk of meat from the bird and stuffed it into my mouth as quickly as I could, and for a few seconds, it tasted delightful. Soon after, like everything else, the meat spoiled and I couldn't force myself to swallow it. I backhanded a nearby chalice, spraying the sweet liquid all over the table. On the verge of frustrated tears, I sank down into the chair.

An explosion of lightning and thunder rocked the great room. The sound terrified me and dragged my attention up to the windows near the ceiling.

That must be ground level, I thought.

Another bolt flashed through the windows, momentarily flooding the room with searing light. It revealed a sight that wrung the breath from my lungs.

High above the hidden door was a tremendous, unmistakable portrait of my dead fiancée.

Anja.

She smiled down at me with those gentle green eyes I remembered from a lifetime ago. Her fair skin glowed like an angel's, and her straw-gold hair flowed around her face. One of her hands rested over her heart, and the other pointed downward, toward the hidden door beneath her.

My heart exploded in my ribcage. An ocean of sorrow bled from it, filling me up and drowning me. My hearing faded out, abandoning me with the intermittent flashes of lightning and the eerie painting.

"Anja?" I muttered through quivering lips. "Who...who put this here?"

I staggered to the portrait and fell to my knees. The floodgates finally opened, and I cried. I cried because I was afraid. Because I was alone. And because I could no longer remember why I didn't just kill myself when she died.

Then, I remembered the boy.

Eventually the lightning abated, and Anja's face disappeared into the darkness.

CHAPTER 25

After sitting in the darkness a while, I decided against entering the hidden door, and instead left the way I'd come in. I wanted nothing more to do with that room and its rotten bounty. And I never wanted to see that painting again.

As I stepped back into the hall, heavy footsteps pounded the staircase at the other end. Those marionette-things were making their way into the Surgical Ward.

Son of a bitch.

I tried to duck into one of the operating rooms. Every door was locked but one. Inside, I frantically searched around for a place to hide, but found none. I nearly slipped in a pool of the strange black liquid I kept finding, and it gave me an idea. I sat down, leaned against the wall behind the operating table, and yanked open my coat. I lifted my shirt and smeared globs of the slime on my stomach. Then I held the knife with a half-grasp and slumped over sideways, playing dead.

The marionettes kicked down doors and rifled through nearby rooms. Cold and hot flashes strobed up my limbs as the footsteps approached. From the floor I watched, eyes half-open and vacant, as the door to my room splintered into pieces.

Show's over.

A marionette sprinted over to me, backhanding an equipment stand across the room as it did. The damned thing must have weighed twice as much me, and sounded like it was made of solid metal. It stopped only a foot away and crouched down over my body, examining my "wound." The front of its head was a slab of faceless stone, a vacant display with no gaze or emotion. No eyes. No contempt. Nothing. Its emptiness terrified me, and I nearly lost my cool as the great being loomed over me. Its metallic head glimmered under the flickering ceiling light, and its scent invoked a memory of wet clay. With a huge, cold hand, it poked my stomach gently. I could hear the other two marionettes gathering at the door to see what was going on.

Just then, a scream broke the silence. I prayed they didn't see me flinch. It was a tiny scream, the innocent voice of a child.

The sound was muffled but close by. I remembered the morgue and basement doors, and wished I'd hidden in one of those. Maybe I'd have found the kid. The marionettes forgot about me and stormed off. A nearby door opened and shut, and I was alone again.

I jumped to my feet, trying to decide what to do. If I went racing after the kid, I'd surely run into those bastards, and who knows what they'd do to me. Then again, whatever terrible things they had planned, the kid seemed to be the target.

The morgue door had a dent in its center and a sticky handprint on the knob. I didn't hear anybody screaming, so I reasoned that the marionettes had picked the wrong room. I rolled the dice and chose the door marked *Basement.*

I found myself in a labyrinth of stone corridors. Stinking sludge trickled from every crack in the walls. There were little black footprints in here too. My heart soared; I knew I was getting closer.

I navigated the dark halls, following a network of dripping pipes that lined the ceiling. Even when I tried to walk quietly, my footsteps echoed on forever. I passed by electrical panels and a water main. After heading down a few short flights of stairs, I began to hear voices far off in the dark.

The halls opened up into large networks of chambers made for processing waste or purifying water...I wasn't sure which. Much of the machinery crackled and sparked or failed to operate. Eventually, the grinding of a big hydraulic pump masked my footsteps. With every turn I made, I grew more and more concerned that even if I found the boy, we'd never find our way back. The basement was a maze and seemed twice as big than the building above ground.

As I moved, I heard bits of classical music wafting through the stale air. It sounded like my father's prized record player. I followed the sound to a huge chamber with thin metal catwalks suspended over a pool of green water. Somewhere on the other side, far down a corridor, a man cackled. His voice was dry and wicked, and he screeched in another language.

He sounded like a Kraut.

Softer female voices mumbled in response to him, accompanied by the pings and clinks of little metal tools. Dr. Farmer's words resonated in my mind:

Down where the surgeons play God.

I prayed they didn't have the kid. At the thought, I felt like storming into the room and pistol-whipping the lot of them. I followed the metal catwalk, which took me high over the pool of green sludge. The noxious fumes radiating from it nearly pulled the puke right out of my mouth.

Something sloshed in the water beneath me.

At first, it looked like an animal swimming around. I knelt down on the catwalk, peering over the edge. The stench burned my eyes.

Something moved again, this time closer to the surface.

It was a naked woman.

I rubbed the fire out of my eyes and squinted through the gloom.

She was drowning. She couldn't get out. The woman writhed around, reaching up for help, but something kept pulling her down.

I nearly fell off the ledge in shock. I clambered onto the handrail and dangled myself over the pool, ready to dive in to save her.

A cloud of spun-gold hair floated up from the deep. I'd recognize it anywhere, even here.

Anja.

She floated underwater, struggling to move. Her head came up again, and our eyes met. She mouthed my name and reached out to me. Her fingers didn't penetrate the surface.

I seized up in horror and felt my entire body go numb. I

choked out her name, then remembered the sinister voices up ahead.

The drop was too far. They'd hear me. They'd get us.

I forced myself back onto the catwalk and backtracked, looking for a way down. A nearby ladder got me down into the slimy water.

It was only waist-deep, but the second it touched my skin, I nearly collapsed in agony from the brutal cold. The ripples created by my splashing shattered Anja's image, and I could no longer see her. Instead, a thousand tiny reflections of her drifted away from me, and eventually settled back into a featureless slick of green.

I sloshed around, searching for her with my hands, but found nothing. I waded over to a cement ridge and flopped onto it, shivering violently. My hands were pale blue.

I tried to hold it together this time. Memories of Anja danced through my head, carrying me into the past, then dropping me back onto that wet cement. Again and again. Something about this place unearthed the pain I'd worked so long to bury, and now my mind was casting the illusion of my fiancée. It placed her within my grasp, then ripped her away again, leaving me to watch as she dissolved like a ghost. I wanted to scream, to purge my despair, but I knew I'd give myself away to the beings that lurked down here.

I heard no voices now, only the sad music that came drifting from far off.

CHAPTER 26

I collected myself once more. I'd grown accustomed to it in this nightmare.

Don't trust the windows.

Don't trust the water.

Lesson learned.

I raced over the catwalk, this time without looking into the pool. All of this was some sort of hallucination, meant to impede me. But how did I get here? Had I completely lost it? At some point, I stopped trying to reason my way to an explanation.

A metal staircase took me down to yet another dimly lit chamber, this one with all sorts of machinery and tables. It was the kind of place a mad scientist would love. I could hear a strange man cackling again, babbling all sorts of nonsense. I stopped at the bottom of the stairs, hiding in the shadows. The only thing separating me from him was a waist-high wall.

I peeked around the corner. Across the room, I saw a wraithlike man and woman shackled to a wall. They'd been tortured, and now their weakness rendered them barely able to move, let alone struggle against their restraints. Closer to me, a tall, lanky doctor in a surgical apron and mask stood hunched over a table. Four blood-stained nurses surrounded him. They performed some kind of operation on an animal I couldn't identify. Their earlier discussion had ceased, and now the only noises to be heard were the pathetic groans of the two prisoners, and the eerie music that seeped from an ancient record player.

A few other operating tables lined the room, most of them freshly prepared for surgery. Large buckets of water near each table reminded me of the surgeries I'd read about in my dad's books on the American Civil War. I grimaced at the thought of being captured here. On the far side of the room, opposite the prisoners, a long hallway disappeared into the darkness.

A metal door directly across from me sat just beneath an old sign that read:

To Break Room, Reception, and Morgue.

I suddenly realized where I was. And I also knew exactly where those marionette bastards were.

Gentle footsteps pattered the stairs behind me. I spun around and almost cried out in joy.

The kid!

I reached out for him and pressed my finger to my lips.

"Shhh." I pointed around the corner.

The little boy definitely recognized me, and for a half-second I felt like hugging him. Blood caked his hands, as if he'd climbed over some barbed wire, or stuck them into a drawer without looking inside. A big bruise covered his cheek, and his hospital gown was torn here and there. The poor thing had no shoes, and his feet were covered in black muck.

"Jesus Christ kid, where the hell you been?" I whispered.

The boy couldn't understand me. He just stared into my eyes with a profound innocence. This place must have put him through the wringer just like it did me. But he seemed to be in decent shape. Hell, he'd made it this far on his own. I wondered then to myself: would I be the one to get him killed?

"Trent," he whispered in a strange accent, pointing at my chest.

I couldn't believe he remembered my name. A big smile spread across my face. He must have heard Francesca say it back at the department.

He then went on and on about something, but I couldn't understand any of it. His words vaguely reminded me of some of the Russians I'd met after the war. I shook my head at him. He stood up and nonchalantly descended a few more stairs, poking his head around the corner. He gasped.

At first I thought it was the blood that scared him. I got up to grab him. But before I could reach the kid, he stepped out into the open and started screaming things across the room. Terrified,

I ran over and caught him as he tried to dash over toward the prisoners.

"Mama! Tata!" he yelled.

For as small as he was, I was damn sure he'd rip my arms off trying to break free from my grip. It was like holding onto a rocket.

The surgeon's head whipped in our direction. He slammed a fist onto the table in frustration, spattering chunks of gore across his own face. The nurses gasped surprise. The kid didn't seem to notice the horrible surgery being performed; he only saw the poor folks shackled to the wall.

The prisoners perked up at the sound of his voice, and both screamed in unison,

"Dahveed! Dahveed!" They too had thick accents, and yelled other things in the boy's language.

The shock nearly buckled my knees, but I held him tight and watched as little David's parents struggled against their chains. They desperately reached for their son. The sight broke my heart, but I kept my eyes on the surgeon, who was now removing his mask, revealing a decayed face with teeth that looked like they belonged to a wolf. The nurses glared at me as well, their mouths sewn shut like the receptionists' upstairs, and their makeup streaking down their faces.

"This is a sterile environment!" the man spat, stabbing the air with a knife. "How *dare* you enter this facility without the master surgeon's permission!"

He had an accent too. A familiar one.

He was a Kraut.

He ripped his latex gloves off and threw them to the floor, cursing as he did.

"These are *my* patients! *Mine!*" he yelled.

"Time to go, kid," I said. I hoisted David up under my arm and took off running like a bat out of hell. He slapped at my arm, trying to escape me.

"Mama!" he yelled again.

I knew it was rough, but my primary concern was to get both of us out alive. His family would have to wait. In fact, I was certain we wouldn't be able to go back for them.

"Filthy whores!" The surgeon yelled at his nurses. "He's unclean! Seize them! Get them or I'll have you strung up by your entrails, you idiots!"

The nurses took off after us. They panted like dogs and moaned through the bloody twine that bound their lips. The horrific noises sent an electric shock of fear through my body, propelling me even faster through the dark.

I'd never let them take the kid.

The morgue door swung open right as we passed it and, lo and behold, the marionettes stepped into the fray. I sprinted down that hall, abject terror nearly lifting me off my feet. The kid saw them too and fell silent. His body went rigid. He'd seen them before.

We approached the end of the hall and I slammed shoulder-first into a wet, sticky wooden door. It budged, but not much, so I threw my heel into it over and over. The nurses and marionettes were closing in on us. I set the kid down behind me and turned around, looking for another door to try, and saw that our pursuers were only a few yards behind us. I pulled out my knife and shoved David behind me, prepared to defend him until my last breath.

CHAPTER 27

As the monsters drew near, the wooden door creaked open behind me. A withered hand emerged from the darkness and seized me by the coat, dragging me backwards into the next room. I fell flat on my ass. The door slammed shut and a man in a white coat secured the lock.

It was Dr. Farmer.

"How—" I tried to speak, but he cut me off.

"Quiet!" he whispered. "We have to leave! You have to get the boy out of here." The doctor grabbed me by the lapels and yanked me to my feet. His strength was astonishing. He and David exchanged a few words, but I couldn't understand any of it.

"Get the other end," he said, dragging a hospital bed toward the door. I assisted while David watched.

The doctor then pushed his way past us and ran to the end of the room.

"Let's move," he said.

It was some sort of post-op room, where patients were brought to recuperate after surgery. A score of beds lined each wall, many of them burnt. Some were occupied by mangled bodies. Dim lights flickered overhead, revealing the facility's rancid condition. As the room momentarily lit up, I could see that some of the bodies were in uniform.

This place reminded me of the French hospital I'd stayed in during the war. For a moment I forgot where I was, and time seemed to freeze as I looked around.

I approached one of the beds, recognizing the face of a man that lay in it. His jacket was decorated with medals, and he looked to have just barely survived some sort of head wound.

Bloody bandages obscured parts of his face, but I still recognized his features.

"Cadler?" he reached out to me with a weak hand.

"Roy?" I muttered. "What...what are you doing here?"

Roy Eberly took a sniper bullet to the brain not two minutes after we hit the beach at Normandy. He was my only friend in basic training. He had two little girls.

I reached out and grabbed his hand. It was cold.

"Trent," he whispered, "she's… she's here."

Something huge crashed against the door we'd blocked off. It would only hold for another minute at most. I looked over at Dr. Farmer and David, who were standing at another door on the far side of the room. They watched me in silence.

When I looked back at Roy, he was gone. The bed was empty. I felt a twinge of the old grief. This twisted place was eating away at my will to live.

I'm gonna die here.

As I turned to catch up with the doctor, another sight caught my eye: a window.

I knew it was a bad idea. But this one beckoned to me.

I approached slowly, afraid of what I might see. The ghoulish creatures outside the door banged even louder. Time was running out.

I peered into a velvety abyss.

There was nothing there.

I gazed into the emptiness a while, transfixed by it, when suddenly a figure stepped out from behind the glass. The emerald-green eyes of my beloved fiancée glimmered back at me. My guts knotted up inside me.

"Anja?"

Her delicate features glowed even in the darkness; her skin looked soft and youthful. The zest I'd fallen in love with was gone from her expression, replaced by a cold and distant stare. I felt every ounce of sorrow she carried as though it were my own, and a tidal wave of guilt and longing crushed my strength to dust.

Still, despite her obvious pain, Anja bore the gentle elegance I remembered. My heart thudded with the burden of a thousand emotions, each warring for my attention. Her mouth hung slightly open and her distinctive lips quivered with the words she whispered to me – words I could not hear, but my heart beheld them as an oath of undying love. Her golden hair whipped and fluttered across her face, some of it clinging to her tear-soaked cheeks. How I yearned to run my fingers through it one last time, to wipe the pain from her sparkling eyes, to feel her warmth on my fingers.

Anja pressed her hand against the window.

I lifted a shaking hand, placing it on the glass against hers, and could almost feel her touch. A delicate smile grew across her face, then faded away. I felt tears welling up, and when I tried to speak again, her eyes widened in horror, and she looked back behind her into the blackness. She stood on a narrow cement ledge dangling off the side of the hospital.

She turned back to me suddenly – and mouthed the words "let go." Then she fell. Her bright red dress flapped around her figure as she plummeted into the dark. It was the dress she'd worn when I had last seen her.

I howled her name over and over. I smashed my fists against the glass, but it would not break.

And then she was gone, and there was nothing more to see from the window.

I screamed until I was hoarse, long after the abyss swallowed her up.

A hand clamped down on my bicep. I whirled around expecting to find myself in the clutches of the marionettes, but instead, it was Dr. Farmer. He shook me hard.

"You fool, hurry!" he shouted, rattling me back to my senses. "They'll find a way around!"

The marionettes had stopped trying to break down the door. Everything was silent.

"Did you see her?" I asked, barely cognizant. "Did you see my fiancée?"

The doctor didn't respond; he simply yanked me toward the back door. I gave in and fled with him and the boy down another hall, arriving at a decrepit elevator.

We wasted no time getting into it. I half-expected the lift wouldn't move, and imagined the marionettes slaughtering us inside it.

Almost magically, the buttons flickered to life. The doctor pressed one of them and the doors slid shut. I put my arm on David's shoulder and looked down at his dirty face. He looked up at me with tears in his eyes.

Yes, losing someone you love. I know that feeling.

I rubbed his head and forced a smile, then turned back to Dr. Farmer.

"Why are you helping us?" I asked him. "Who are you?"

He didn't look at me.

"I...I just couldn't let it happen again," he said, pulling his sleeves down to cover the deep lacerations on his forearms.

"What happened to you, doctor? Are you alright?"

The elevator lurched to a halt. The doors groaned as they opened, revealing a little room with strange metal contraptions.

The doctor stepped out of the elevator without a word. Dozens of candles, ablaze with eerie light, lined the walls, illuminating a series of medieval torture devices. A few macabre paintings clung to the stone walls. A large, dusty mirror stood at the far corner of the room.

My breath calmed. My muscles relaxed. My eyelids drooped. This place felt warm and sickeningly comfortable.

In the middle of the room sat a large wooden table. A body lay face-up on top of it. High up on the wall, a painting of Anja hung, smiling down on the body. It was the same as the painting I'd seen in the great hall.

Dr. Farmer escorted David past the table, shielding the boy's eyes and guiding him to a small door across the room. As they left the room, the doctor briefly looked back at me.

I paused to look at the body on the table.

"Trent," the doctor called gently.

I ignored him, examining the body. It was a man, held in place with heavy chains attached to the wrists and ankles. He was dressed like a medieval court jester.

A black veil covered his face.

I reached out to remove it.

"Trent," the doctor said louder, "there's nothing here for you."

As my hand neared the veil, the body violently jerked and set me back on my heels.

"Jesus Christ!" I yelped, feeling my heart leap into my throat.

The man groaned softly. I grabbed his hand, asking if he was okay. As I touched him, he recoiled in fear; his hand balled into a fist that ripped from my grasp.

"No! Please!" he begged.

I tried loosening a shackle, but couldn't.

"It's okay, man. It's alright. You're safe now," I said. "How'd you get here?"

He fell silent. His head turned in my direction.

Did he recognize my voice?

"Who's got the key to these fuckin' things?" I asked.

The man didn't respond.

I slid the hood off. When I saw his face, I choked. Every muscle in my body went rigid. He'd been beaten to a pulp, but I recognized him.

I knew that face.

The face I see every time I shut my eyes. The man who killed my fiancée.

Adam.

We stared at each other for an eternity. The universe collapsed into the room, and nothing existed but us. Malice crept over my heart, freezing it solid. I saw fear in his eyes – a terror I hadn't known since the war.

Seconds crept by. My gaze pierced his tattered form. My hands trembled with rage. Adam cowered before me in a way that fulfilled my darkest desires. The feeling sickened me, and I felt the urge to puke, but I swallowed back my emotions and stepped toward him. He squeezed his eyes shut and begged for his life. The monster inside me breathed in his suffering and grew stronger for it.

Felix Blackwell

"Why are you here?" I demanded, grabbing his face and forcing him to look at me.

"Trent...Trent, I...please," he cried, "please God don't hurt me." His tears dripped onto my fingers, and suddenly I pitied him more than I hated him. I thought about bashing his skull against the stone table. I breathed out the murder inside me.

"I'm not gonna hurt you, son. Just answer me."

He coughed and sputtered bloody flecks.

Something moved inside me. Something that couldn't move for all these years. I finally saw him as a man, rather than the animal that took my fiancée.

"I'm so sorry for what I did, Trent," he sobbed. "I deserve this." His words were slow and slurred. Blood covered his yellow teeth.

I let go of him, examining my hands and looking around the room. My gaze fell onto the standing mirror in the corner. My reflection was accurate, except for a thin silver chain that hung around my neck. A small key dangled from it. I looked away from the mirror and down at my chest, but found nothing.

Dr. Farmer and the boy watched me in silence from just outside the door. They allowed me to plumb the depths of this event alone.

I'd always dreamed of exacting revenge upon Adam Howle. *Fantasized.* I wanted closure, not just for me, but for Anja. I wanted to look into the face of the bastard who did this to us – to see him alive and full of terror.

Adam muttered something as he lay dying on the table. It snapped me out of my trance, but I couldn't be sure if I'd heard him right:

"...the hands of retribution outstretched, taking pieces from me..."

He spoke vacantly, as though he were already gone.

"What did you say?" I turned back toward him.

"Trent..." he reached out to me. The shackle restrained him.

Rage filled me again. I wanted to pummel him until every bone was shattered. I wanted to smite him in Anja's name. But I knew she wouldn't want that.

It took every drop of my will not to reach down and wring the wretched breath from Adam's throat. I wanted so badly to end it for him, but even more than that, I wanted to honor Anja's wishes. Allowing Adam to turn me into a monster would disgrace her memory.

I crouched down beside him and examined the chains that restrained him.

"You're my prisoner here, aren't you?" I asked.

"No," he whispered. He pointed a shaking finger at the painting of Anja. "The lamb."

With that, Adam closed his eyes, and gently passed.

A memory arose inside of me then. It was a bit of advice given to me by our old pastor. I hadn't spoken to him since Anja's funeral. He implored me to one day find forgiveness, and let both my fiancée and her killer rest in peace.

I shrugged the feeling off, and shoved the hood back over Adam's head. I didn't want to look at his face anymore.

Felix Blackwell

CHAPTER 28

I followed David and Dr. Farmer through the little door, only to find a thick tapestry blocking my way. As I ducked under it, I almost collided with a candelabrum. I recognized this place immediately. The giant room with the refectory table sat before me, delicious-looking fruit still piled in heaps atop it. The shadowy painting of Anja leered down at me through the gloom. That secret door I'd noticed earlier turned out to be the way into the torture chamber.

My torture chamber.

I hurried past the feast and caught up with my companions. We headed straight out of the surgery ward. When we climbed up the last set of stairs and walked back into the reception area, I breathed a sigh of relief. Anywhere was better than down there.

As we approached the front desk, one of the poor receptionists saw us coming and leaped to her feet, knocking a stack of paperwork onto the tile floor. She trotted away down a hall, the clicking of her high heels echoing on forever. A door slammed in the distance and then she was gone.

The doctor seemed to be calculating our next move when the intercom crackled to life again. A dark and familiar voice seeped through it.

"Patient 606 has been spotted wandering the first-floor entry hall."

Dr. Farmer shot a frightened gaze at me. I held my breath, waiting for his decision.

There was silence. Even the remaining receptionist made no sound; she only looked at us with surprise. Then, the grave clatter of metal boots resounded from far behind us, down in the surgery ward. It was time to go.

"Run!" the doctor bellowed. He took off, rounding corners faster than we could keep up. He seemed to know where he was taking us. I prayed he had a plan to get us out of here.

We entered a stairwell and fled up to a door marked *3ʳᵈ Floor*. Dr. Farmer yanked a keyring from his jacket and opened it. The marionettes barreled up the stairs behind us. As we dashed through the hall, we had to dodge gurneys and boxes. The lights flickered wildly, casting our ghoulish shadows across the walls.

Our lumbering pursuers were never far off. We raced through several rooms and halls, sometimes passing by groaning patients as they lay in their beds. One man had fallen to the floor and was crawling toward us as we passed. I saw him out of the corner of my eye, and when he began to croak my name in the voice of my dead father, I didn't look at him. I only ran faster.

"Where the hell are we going?" I shouted at Dr. Farmer. He didn't respond.

The marionettes were closing in. The screeches of metal doors echoed throughout the hospital as the creatures tore through them. We were running out of places to hide. At the end of a long, bending corridor, we found a lone door. It sat slightly ajar, but wouldn't budge when I pressed my weight into it. It was barricaded from the other side. We squeezed into the room one by one. David babbled strings of words I couldn't understand. The only thing I could make out was "Mama".

"I know, kid," I snapped, forcing myself through the small space.

Dr. Farmer got in last, and just in time; the marionette-men had spotted us and were rumbling down the hall.

"It won't hold them!" the doctor shouted at me.

The room was like the one I'd woken up in, when David had first gone missing. The bed had been pulled against the door. I grabbed a table and stacked it atop the bed. Not a moment after, the first of the marionettes slammed against the door. His thunderous force rattled the windows. Dr. Farmer leaped onto the bed and held the door with his body. He gazed at me helplessly. He'd run out of ideas.

The room had no other doors, and the only vent was too small to squeeze through. Not even David could get inside of it.

There were, however, two windows. One of them was sealed shut with prison bars, and one was not.

I ran over to them, afraid of what I might see.

The left window displayed a typical Pine Rest forest. I gazed at it for a moment, and when David looked too, he began yelling in delight and pointing, then pulling hard on my coat.

"What is it, kid? You see somethin' out there?" I strained to see anything but the dimly lit trees.

David had gone wild by now, and was already banging his fists on the glass.

"Hold on a second there," I said to him, and pushed him gently away from it. I examined the bars of the other window; it looked out onto the same forest except from an inexplicably higher vantage point. My eyes fell on a small barn, partly shrouded by the darkness.

It was a rotting shack, ignored for decades and allowed to decay. I'd never seen it before, but it felt so familiar, as though I'd visited it in a dream. I stared at it unblinking, forgetting the sounds of David's yelling and the door splintering behind us.

A sense of doom washed over me, but not the same terror I'd felt in the crosshairs of the three beings just behind the door.

And then I saw him.

Adam.

He was down there, making his way toward the barn in a pair of dirty overalls. He dragged a woman along with him. She fought and scratched every step of the way. I recognized her immediately. Her voice rang across the woods and filled the room we stood in.

"Anja!" I screamed at the top of my lungs, frightening little David. My heart clenched in my chest.

The son of a bitch was going to kill her.

"Adam, stop!" I yelled, louder than I thought possible. I thrashed and beat the steel bars that blocked the window.

He ripped open the barn door and forced her inside, then

slammed it shut.

I exploded with rage, grabbing a nearby chair and slamming it against the bars. I put both feet on the wall and pulled on the metal frame with all of my strength, nearly tearing out my own spine in the process. But the bars just would not give.

The marionettes finally broke through, heaving Dr. Farmer to the floor. As I looked back I could see them shoving things out of the way to open their path. I turned and looked at the barn once more. It was gone. Only the empty forest remained.

"God damn it!" I screamed. I hurled the broken chair at one of the marionettes. It shattered uselessly against the creature's body. The being looked at me with that faceless metal plate, then flipped the bed across the room with its gigantic arms.

I ran over and picked David up with one hand. With the other, I smashed the unbarred window, ignoring the hot sting of shards piercing my skin. I shoved him through, letting him go when I was sure he could safely land on the ground a few feet below.

I turned back and took one last look at the barred window, then at the marionettes. I jammed a middle finger into the air at them.

"Not as long as I'm breathin', fellas."

CHAPTER 29

The marionette-men came straight for me, their hulking forms blocking out the dim light from the hall. I turned and flung myself through the window, crash-landing in the dirt below. The cool air hit me, and forced its way into my lungs like the first breath of a newborn.

I jumped to my feet, looking for David and preparing to engage our pursuers. But as I turned around, I could find neither the boy, nor the window I'd jumped through. The hospital was gone. I was alone in the foggy woods.

I ran a few steps in every direction, trying to find my bearings, but could not. A full moon pierced through the trees above me, casting pale-orange light across the earth.

I had to find the kid, and I had to stop Adam. Maybe if I stopped him here, it would change something. Maybe I'd get to see Anja again.

But where was the barn? And the hospital? Was it possible that I had dreamed it all up? Had I sleepwalked into the woods? Did the kid actually exist?

Don't trust the windows, I reminded myself. *Don't trust anything.*

I was so deep in thought I almost didn't hear the footsteps of an approaching person. By the time the noise was close enough to pull me from my musings, I was knocked over by a man running full-speed. He crashed into me and we both plummeted to the ground. My back seized up in pain as he landed on top of me. I reacted before I could even think. I grabbed him by the shirt and easily wrestled myself onto him, then pinned him. I raised my fist, ready to beat him to death.

"Wait! Wait!" he begged, turning his head away.

"Who are you?" I shouted.

He wriggled and squirmed and kept looking past me as though he was expecting someone else to come through the woods.

"*Who are you?!*" I yelled, pulling him closer to me.

"Keep your damn voice down!" he hissed. Black hair clung to his sweaty forehead and dangled in front of his eyes. "And get off me, you ogre!"

I looked him over for a minute and complied.

"What the hell are you runnin' into me for?" I whispered, eying him up and down.

"There's something after me," he said, glancing around nervously.

I've never seen anyone look such a wreck. At least not anyone besides me.

"Sounds rough. I got *three* somethin's after me, guy," I replied. I wished I could find my cigarettes.

The man didn't share my amusement, and hardly looked at me. But when he brushed his hair out of his eyes, he stared into me, amazed, as though he recognized me.

"You...you look familiar. Where are you from?" he asked.

"Here, I think," I replied. I looked around, remembering that I had no real idea of where 'here' was. For all I knew, we were wandering around on some plane of Hell.

He didn't take his eyes off me.

"I'm from Waldport," he said. "But I don't know where I am now."

"That makes two of us," I replied, sitting down and taking a moment to relax.

He sniffled.

"Waldport," I continued. "Never heard of it. That in Shropshire?"

The man laughed like I was an idiot.

"Uh," he said, "it's in the States."

I nodded and shrugged. It was quiet for a few moments.

"You know where you're headed?" I finally asked.

"No," he said, shivering. "Away. Anywhere. I just don't wanna be found." His eyes darted around again. It wasn't very cold to me, but then again I'd been locked in that stifling hospital for the past several hours. Or days. Who knew?

"Yeah me neither, on both accounts," I replied. "Well, let's wander together, then. No use in being alone. Say, you haven't seen a kid out here, have you?"

"I haven't seen anyone out here but you," he said. "And I'm happy to see you, believe it or not."

We picked up and began to walk, whispering every now and then, and occasionally pausing to listen to the stillness of the woods.

"If you hear anyone humming, run for your life," he warned.

I laughed, thinking he was joking. The sound of his footsteps died away, so I turned around to see what the holdup was.

"You laugh like my father," the man remarked.

"Yuh?" I replied. I had no idea what kind of response he was looking for.

"That's why you look so familiar..." The man walked closer, studying me.

"What did you say your name was?" he asked.

I suddenly wondered if this man was a patient from that hospital.

"I didn't. Listen pal, do you have eyes?" I said. "You look older than me! And I never been to *Waldport* in my entire life."

He accepted my rebuttal and walked on ahead of me, scratching his dirty hair. Poor bastard looked like he'd been tromping around out here for days.

"You gonna be okay there?" I asked. He didn't respond.

Several minutes passed, as well as hundreds of trees. I yawned and grew bored of the woods.

Better than where I just came from, I reminded myself.

"So what's your story?" he asked, dropping back and walking alongside me.

"I don't know," I said. "I just woke up like this I guess. Seen a lot of crazy shit."

He laughed, I didn't.

"I think I'm starting to make some sense of it all," I added. "But I'm still working on it...I don't think any of this is random. It's like someone's reading my mind. My past. My secrets. And coloring the world with them."

The man shrugged at me and said, "So I'm just a figment of your imagination, eh? There are a lot of new ideas in academia right now about reality as a subjective construct. It only exists because there's someone there to experience it."

"That doesn't make any sense," I replied with a snort.

"No, not really," the stranger replied. "But neither does this place, right? I've got a few books I could recommend to you – if we get out of here, I mean."

"Okay, professor," I said dismissively.

He shot me a suspicious look.

There was an eerie calm in these woods. The smell of the wet soil invaded my nose, and the air, however stale, was infinitely sweeter than what I breathed in that awful building. There was no breeze at all, and the only sounds we heard were the songs of the frogs and crickets. They seemed morose, however, sharing our despair as we trudged through the endless murk. Their music came to us as though it had traveled thousands of miles and had been warped and detuned in the process. I felt so distant from the world that I couldn't be sure I was even alive. I imagined myself as a ghost, unaware of my own demise and desperately seeking answers I'd never find. It frightened me, but the sound of my own beating heart anchored me to a place that allowed me to press on. I refused to die here.

I asked the man about whatever he'd been running from, but he didn't want to talk about it. Maybe he feared I might think he was crazy. Then again, I don't think he'd believe me if I told him about the marionettes, so all was fair.

Something moved up ahead.

I jolted to a stop and sank to one knee, raising my arm to signal him to halt. He held still.

"What is it?" he whispered.

I didn't reply.

Something was making an awful racket up ahead, past the trees. Something big.

"No..it's him...oh God, he's f-found me again," the man said. He started backing up. Twigs snapped beneath his feet. The idiot was going to give us away. I grabbed him by his pant leg and told him to shut up.

At first I heard only muffled sounds, but then I began to make out two distinct voices. I dragged the man forward with me and strained to make out what the voices were saying.

Finally I realized that one of them was a woman. And then I knew exactly what was happening.

"Don't! Please! Please let me go!" she cried.

Before I could even think, I was in full sprint, blinded with hatred, blazing toward the voices like a meteor. I cut through shrubs and flew over logs, nearly breaking my neck as I tumbled over a twisted branch. The stranger came up fast on my heels and helped me back to my feet.

"What the hell's this doing out here?" he asked.

I brushed myself off and looked up. My sight blurred.

The barn.

It stood right in front me: the dark place where my misery was born. The one part of the earth I swore I'd never go to. Its shadow loomed over me, weighing my heart against all of my fear and guilt. I couldn't bear it. My stomach churned and my head reeled. Confusion and nausea wrapped me in a sinister embrace. A terrible force emanated from it, pushing me away, compelling me to flee. But I heard her voice again – Anja's voice – and my strength was renewed.

"Let me go, you bastard!" she screamed. "Get your hands off me!" The harsh words sifted through her dainty accent.

I searched frantically for a way in. On the far side of the barn was a faded black door. I beat and kicked it, screaming my fiancée's name. I heaved my entire body against the rotting wood, sending great cracks splintering across it. I roared my bloodlust, but neither Adam nor Anja seemed to hear me. A great struggle ensued beyond the door; he must have been roughing her up pretty fierce. I couldn't see what was happening, but everything transpired with terrible clarity in my mind's eye.

Hatred became my strength. Revenge became my purpose. I wished now that I had brutalized Adam back there on the table, when he was the object of my cruel amusement. My slave.

With a final sob, Anja cried out, "They'll feed you to the wolves for this!"

And then all was silent.

My words failed, but that didn't stop me from channeling my rage into grizzly snarls. I wanted to kill Adam Howle with my bare hands. I wanted to watch his eyes roll back as I choked the worthless life from him. I took ten steps back and ran at the door as fast as I could. I shut my eyes and imagined shattering through it, crashing into Adam and crushing him beneath me.

The door exploded into a thousand rotten splinters. I sailed through the frame, two feet off the ground, and barreled into the side of a staircase, almost knocking myself unconscious. I tried to blink away the spots and prepare myself for the slaughter. After all these lonely years, after all this agonizing guilt, my chance for redemption was now.

Adam's time had come.

CHAPTER 30

I lay sprawled on a fine hardwood floor. Bright lights blinded me. An ornate chandelier came into focus. I managed to sit up.

I was in some elegant hallway. An expensive runner rug stretched across its length. At one end of the hall stood a door flanked by decorative glass windows and a coat rack. It looked like the front door of a house. I closed my eyes, trying to figure out if I'd knocked my brain around in my skull.

I looked at the wooden door that I'd broken through. It lay in a hundred pieces all around me, and I had the cuts to prove it was real. But there was no forest outside. No moon. And no frantic stranger. I had exploded from a tiny closet full of shoes and coats. I even smelled like old leather.

I looked down the hall in the other direction.

There was a kitchen. A middle-aged couple cowered in it, screaming gazes locked with mine. I recognized them, but couldn't recall from where, until little David rounded the corner.

"Trent!" he yelled.

He ducked between them and ran up to me, throwing his arms around me in a tight hug.

"Daveed!" the woman called out.

I remembered now.

They were the prisoners...his parents.

Barely able to think, I hugged the boy and then slowly rose to my feet. His mother took a step back, and his father eventually came to me and examined my wounds.

"It's alright," I said, keeping him at arm's length. "I'm fine."

The man seemed to understand me but replied in the same

unfamiliar language David spoke. I shrugged at him. David turned to his parents and held a brief conversation with them, probably regarding just how the hell he knew me.

How could he explain it? I just fell out of a goddamn closet, I thought.

"Nice setup you got here," I said, noting the opulence of the house.

Suddenly, the father hushed everyone. A noise came from outside – boots smacking on the wet cobblestone road. David's eyes widened with fear. We both knew what was coming. His parents, however, seemed to have no recollection of the creatures from the hospital. They exchanged confused looks.

David screamed something at them and then ran up the stairs, pausing at the top.

I rifled through the closet, trying to find something to use as a weapon. There was nothing, not even a lousy umbrella. My pistol was still badly deformed; it sat uncomfortably in its holster at my side. My knife was gone.

I ran to the front door, flicked off the light switch and peered outside.

We were in some European town. Quaint little houses pocked the wet hillside and nestled under the glow of street lights. It reminded me of Pine Rest before the war.

The picturesque ambiance was broken as dozens of marionettes stormed up the road, splashing through puddles as their boots collided with the stones. There must have been fifty of them. They broke off into groups and headed to each house.

I ran at the boy's mother and father, trying to coax them to hide. Before I could convince them to get out of the hall, the front door came crashing through. Glass shards slid down the hallway to the place where I'd woken up.

Four of the giant beings spilled into the house, knocking things over and stomping across the wood floors. Their heads were slick with rain, and their entire bodies shimmered like metal. Everywhere they set foot, they left sticky black residue.

I was the only thing standing between these sons of bitches and their prey – an innocent child. Why they wanted him I still could not understand, and what they would do to him I could only imagine.

If I die, I'm taking them with me.

No room for fear now. No escape. There was only one option. I roared furiously and barreled down the hallway toward them, leaping into the air and crashing into the group shoulder-first. Despite their gargantuan size, I was able to knock all of them back and took two to the ground with me. I heard the piercing screams of David's parents behind me as they scrambled to get away. I felt the fiery sting of metal clubs cracking down on my back and legs. But the pain didn't faze me.

Better me than the kid.

I wrestled with one of the marionettes and tried to kick the legs out from under another. The other two bludgeoned me with their clubs. I knew I couldn't keep it up forever. As David's mother and father ducked into the kitchen, one of the beings scrambled over me and raced after them. Another headed up the stairs after David. I tried to rope him in by grabbing one of the thin strands of wire that dangled from his body, but it slipped through my hands and tore my skin. Searing pain shot up my arms, meeting the ache of my back where I'd been clubbed.

Narrowly avoiding a bash to the head, I leaped to my feet and took my closest foe down atop the one still on the floor. They were big and heavy, but they sure didn't expect a fight. I only had a second to get away before they were both up again. I bolted up the stairs to catch the one heading for David. I jumped onto his back and wrapped my arms and legs around him, inhibiting his movement. We teetered sideways, breaking through the wooden handrail and careening to the floor below. I landed mostly on top of him, but my shoulder took a nasty hit from the fall, and the injuries all across my body began to take their toll. Things felt a little heavier now. The world slowed down.

Dying to protect a child. Not a bad way for a cop to go out.

I looked up through the fray and saw David poke his head around the corner, watching helplessly.

Three of the creatures faced off with me in the narrow hall, destroying bits of the walls and floor as they swung their clubs. I was quicker than them, however, and through some stroke of luck or old combat reflex, I disarmed one of the marionettes and used his weapon to protect myself. I thrashed my arms around and hit every one of them that I could, shoving them away from me or dodging their attacks so they'd strike each other.

At last I saw an opening and took advantage of it. With the last bit of my dwindling strength, I whipped the club in an upward arc. It connected squarely with the faceplate of my nearest foe, sending a hideous crunching noise throughout the house. He collapsed to his knees and clutched his head. Deep cracks ran across the faceplate.

For a moment, time seemed to stop.

David slowly inched his way down the stairs, unblinking, mesmerized by something I didn't see. Then I received a blow directly to the back of my head, and with that, I fell to the ground, defeated. It was up to David and his family to get away now.

Paralyzed, I watched as the boy stood on the stairs, looking down at the marionette I'd injured. The barren slab of its face had broken apart. The creature cradled the wound with its heavy hands. The fourth marionette had retrieved David's parents and returned with them, shoving them through the hall with its club. The mother was in tears. The father begged.

The two other creatures stepped indifferently over their fallen comrade and seized David, lifting him off the ground and dangling him in mid-air. I tried to move, but all I could do was watch. David's gaze never left the injured marionette.

And then, something began to happen. The being with the cracked skull began to pick and pry little bits of stone from his head. The pieces dropped to the floor with heavy thuds. He slowly rose from his knees to his full height and looked at David. For a long time, the two gazed upon one another, unmoving, their stillness more unsettling than the entire altercation beforehand. Nobody breathed.

David had no fear in his eyes. He didn't seem worried by the fact that he and his family were about to be taken. His face bore a contemplative expression that baffled me. The boy no longer looked up at his pursuers with horror, but rather down on them with a calmness I could not decode. The two beings that held David set him down.

With a deafening racket, the marionettes, who had shadowed David's every movement, who had inflicted unimaginable torment upon him, collapsed lifelessly to the wood floor and broke into thousands of pieces of rubble.

CHAPTER 31

The four of us stood in quiet shock as the dust settled. David's parents gripped one another with a relief that, on some level, stung me. The boy sat down on the bottom stair, not saying a word, lost in thought. He gazed down into the only part of the injured marionette that had not disintegrated – its head. I knelt down and scooped it up in my hands.

It was even heavier than it looked, and felt warm as I turned it in my hands. I wanted to look at the place I'd struck him with his own weapon.

The stone had broken away.

There was a face.

It was the face of a man, brimming with emotion, betraying the stoic countenance of the mask. It *was* a mask, after all.

His face was twisted with grief and disgust. Dirt-caked streaks of old tears meandered to his chin. Wrinkles creased his young forehead, and bags swelled under his eyes. It seemed he'd been full of anger and sorrow, and the mask existed to hide it. His blue eyes were fixed in a withdrawn gaze, witnesses to the terrible things he'd done. His lips were full and healthy, barely exposing pearl white teeth. He was just a kid. The same age I had been, back in the war.

I looked to David for answers. The expression his face told me he understood what had happened, but that he was lost in his own revelations. For now, my curiosity would have to wait.

David said something to his mother and father then; I could guess what. They returned the phrase. With tears in their eyes, they waved goodbye to him. Then, they were gone.

The boy walked toward me, stepping over the heaps of rocks, and grabbed my hand. The lights in the house began to dim and flicker as they had in the hospital. The sounds of a hundred boots outside faded away. He looked up at me and said something; it sounded like "Jeng-koo-ya". I smiled and pat him on the head.

"Sure, kid."

David pointed to the front door.

It lay broken on the ground, but its frame no longer encased a view of the neighborhood outside. Instead, there was a sea of red sand beneath a purple, dusky sky. It was the desert from my dream.

A heavy grief overtook me. I recalled the image of Anja wading through the sand, struggling with each step. But the notion that she could be out there right now silenced my mind. The familiar pain of her loss churned and roiled within me, becoming a fiery desperation. My heart thundered in my chest.

Could she be here?

I felt David let go of my hand. He knew what I had to do even before I did.

I gathered the courage to move, and walked to the door.

Sand spilled into the house with each gust of wind. Anja's unmistakable scent hung in the air. I breathed her in, just as I had done when she was in my arms all those years ago. The aroma was narcotic and devastating. I didn't look back at David. I knew he'd wait.

Broken bits of glass crunched under my shoes as I moved to the door. A warm breeze stung my eyes.

Into the desert I stepped.

It stretched on forever, vanishing into the star-littered heavens. The sand danced and swayed under the whipping winds. I walked across it with remarkable ease, as though I weighed nothing at all.

The dunes writhed around me like serpents, and when I came to the tallest of them, it collapsed and fell away, revealing my fiancée.

"Anja?" I said. My voice was lost in the wind.

She walked toward me from far off, a big smile glittering

on her face. Her liveliness defied all reason, and her movements were instantly familiar.

She's alive.

Her eyes met mine. I took off in full sprint toward her. What countless nights I'd spent awake, begging for one more chance to see my beloved Anja, dying a little more with each unanswered prayer.

She saw me running and dashed toward me, holding her flowing dress up with one hand while the other kept her hair out of her face. How gracefully she moved. How delicate she was. Every atom in my body ignited with primal desire. I *had* to feel her against me.

As I neared her, I began to feel heavier. I didn't move as fast, and I no longer felt like I could glide over the dunes. My shoes plunged a few inches into the sand. Every step I took sank me deeper into the desert.

Nothing can stop me. I've earned this.

I fought harder. I nearly ripped my calf muscles apart trying to yank my feet free. Anja suffered the same problem; the ground swallowed her up to the knees. We trudged toward each other, sinking to waist-deep, never breaking eye contact. Tears dribbled down our faces. Joy gave way to panic. I tried to call out to her, but my voice caught in my throat. The wind howled my frustration.

At last, we could move no further. Anja and I were both chest-deep, and with every flinch, I felt myself sink down. I reached helplessly for her. She wiped her face and returned a loving smile, the one that had snagged me like a lame fish when we'd first met. She was just the way I remembered her. Her smile beamed with love. Her eyes emanated the forgiveness I so frantically longed for.

And then, I understood.

Every dream, every painting, every vision of her in that hospital invaded my mind. And I finally got it.

Anja wasn't trapped here. She was free, and always had been; her face displayed it clearly. What remained of her in this nightmare was merely the ghost of our past that I jealously clung to. But my sorrow could never return her to me. My guilt could never revive her. My stubbornness could not save her. There was simply nothing I could ever do to have her back again, and I was wasting away in body and mind refusing to allow myself to move on.

For so long I had obsessed over her murder, and my torment, that I'd lost sight of something much more important. I'd forgotten to honor her. I'd forgotten to celebrate the gift of Anja's love and the remarkable story of her life.

Over the years I'd deformed Anja's memory into a symbol of life's unfairness. She was my best friend, my fire, my purpose. She was a wonderful daughter and a beloved member of our community. A noble soul. But instead of those things, I chose to focus only on the fact that she'd suffered. That she'd been taken from me. All this time, I should have reminded myself of what she'd taught me. Of what we'd cultivated together.

Adam was wrong. Anja wasn't really my prisoner here. I was the one wearing the shackles, condemned to walk alone in this nightmare with my empty memories. The phantoms of my fiancée that tormented me here were nothing more than reflections of my own desires. They were not my love. They were not my Anja.

My fiancée was long gone from this place.

It was time for me to leave too.

It was time to surrender my dark obsessions. Time to allow myself to be entirely conquered by Anja's absence, and then to let that absence go.

I stopped crying. I was at peace now, and my heart no longer bashed against my chest. I was no longer a hostage of my agony and guilt.

I knew what I had to do.

Anja looked at me with the loving gaze I always remembered, and placed her hand over her heart. She blew a kiss to me.

I tried to mouth the words "I love you", but she placed her finger over her lips and hushed me. Nothing needed to be said. She already knew.

I took one last look at her, taking in all of her beauty and softness. I breathed and felt and tasted her, and it was every bit as soothing as it had been all those years ago. This was my last goodbye, and I'd been putting it off for an eternity. The end had finally come.

With that, I turned around and walked away. David's house sat alone in the distance, drifting in the ocean of red sand. With each step I took toward it, I climbed out a little. I was soon on top of the dunes yet again, free to walk toward the front door. The boy waited patiently for me there. We exchanged no words. He held out his hand again. I took a deep breath, then placed my hand in his.

I never looked back.

David and I made our way down the hall and into the living room. There was a little couch and a cozy-looking armchair. Upon the couch sat a small frame with a photo of David and his parents. He walked over to it, picked it up, and laid himself down. I found a familiar yellow envelope resting on the chair. I picked it up, no longer afraid of the words it might contain, and plopped down into the seat.

I opened the letter. It was the first one Anja had written to me that contained the word "love". I held it against my chest. My eyes eventually closed.

The lights in the house flickered for a moment, then went out.

I don't know how long I slept.

When I awoke, I was still in the ugly chair right beside David's hospital bed. He was awake now, and looked to be feeling much better. The room was immaculate. Out the window I could see Pine Rest. The brilliant sun shone down upon it, and the birds sang in reverence of the new day. I checked my old watch and found that its hands were once again straight and functional. I turned my gaze to David. He smiled back at me and wiped the sleep from his eyes.

"Morning," I said. "You're lookin' alright, kid."

He turned and gazed out the window, probably as eager to leave this place as I was. I stood up, fixed my coat, and instinctively reached for my cigarettes. I pulled them out and looked at the package.

"You know David, I think it's time I quit smoking."

PART **III**

An angel's choir erupts in full when she sees fit to speak,
a sound as sweet would make the knees of sturdy Atlas weak.

CHAPTER 32

The noise of an argument disturbed my sleep, causing the sea in my dream to churn and roil. It was my mother and father. Lately, they'd been fighting more than ever, and now I was used to waking up like this. The folks in town had been acting strange too; there's always chatter of some impending doom nowadays. It felt like everyone I knew had gone mad.

I opened my eyes. Sunlight poured through the window near my bed and blinded me for a moment. It felt warm and comforting. The birds chirped merrily outside, and the wind had finally stopped whipping. I rubbed the sleep from my eyes and looked around the room – and my heart sank back into reality.

My baby brother's cradle sat in the lonely corner. Gabriel was only four months old now, and he'd fallen ill a week ago. His unrelenting fever now stoked the flames in my parents' confrontations. He'd already seen the town doctors, and none of the medicine they were giving him was helping. To make matters worse, we had used up nearly all our money trying to help him. The only good that came out of this predicament was that our parents, despite their constant bickering, seemed to have rediscovered the meaning of family, and showered both of us with constant attention. But I could see them getting desperate for money and a cure.

I spent the days of late spring walking everywhere: to school or the market, and back again to our little home tucked in the forest. It was good living so far out of town, and I didn't mind the walk. it gave me plenty of time to think or practice my singing, not to mention exercise. I was already getting a lot of attention from the boys, and secretly I took pride in knowing I was more adventurous than any of the other girls in my class. Whenever my friends and I ran into the boys from across town, I beat the snot out of them at climbing trees.

Lately, however, I'd been tending to my brother in every way I could. Despite my parents' support, they could do nothing to soothe Gabriel's pain. I wanted to save him as much as they did, but I didn't have any idea how to handle a situation as grave as this. He was so sick that he hardly even cried anymore. He would just lie still, whimpering pitifully. There were times when it hurt too much to even look at him. I cried myself to sleep to the sound of my mother doing the same in the next room.

One day I'd had enough, and I decided that doing something was better than doing nothing.

The kids at school talked about a hermit who lived deep in the forest. We joked about him at school and told scary stories about him when we hiked, but most of us had never seen him. In a small town, everybody knows everybody, so getting famous was as easy as being a little different. The hermit's identity was mysterious, so naturally, rumors swirled about him. Some called him a killer, and others said he was a vampire. I knew many stories about him, but I liked best the ones my father used to tell when I was little.

He called the man the "mushroom farmer." My dad described him as a grim hunchback who scoured the wilds, seeking exotic plants for crafting potions and poisons. The hermit's visage haunted my dreams for years.

As I grew older, I stopped believing in such fairy tales, and assumed the man was probably a simple outcast that liked to keep to himself. After all, my family lived a mile into that very forest, and none of us were crazy.

I'd been living in the same place all my life, and had explored much of the wilderness that surrounded it. But I'd never been to where the hermit supposedly lived. I was always warned to stay away from the southeast reaches of the woods, where the trees were so thick they blocked out the sun. It was dark and gloomy there, a perfect setting for all the town legends – mostly stories of werewolves and witches dragging children off into the night. Last year a boy had disappeared, and rumor had it at school that a water spirit had dragged him down the river that leads into the Southeast Woods. They never found him.

Desperation is a funny thing. It makes people do things they'd normally believe were crazy. A teenage girl wandering into the woods to find a hermit sounded pretty crazy to me, but I refused to spend another day look down at my brother and wishing I could save him. I figured if I wanted to find a creepy old recluse, I should go to where the legends were born.

CHAPTER 33

The next morning, my brother was in particularly bad shape and wouldn't eat. I laid him in his crib and sang to him, but he didn't move. He just stared up through the window. His eyes looked vacant, like he knew the end was near.

Gabriel's misery justified my decision. All night I'd plotted my journey to the Southeast Woods, and now I was ready. I slipped on my clothes and readied a small pack of food and water, then kissed Gabriel goodbye. I told my parents that I was going into town with friends, and that I'd bring Millie, our Golden Retriever, with me.

Looking back on my father's ridiculous stories, I now prayed there was some truth to them. Maybe this hermit knew something about medicine that Gabriel's doctors didn't. I had little expectation that I'd find him, and even if I did, I had no clue what I'd say.

"Gee mister, I heard you're a wizard and came to ask if you could use magic to save my little brother!" I'd sound like an idiot. Still, I was willing to take the risk for a chance to help Gabriel.

I walked outside and summoned the dog. We took the main road until I could no longer see our cottage. We climbed over a little stone wall and cut across a big green field. There was a lot of abandoned land out here; many of the farmers had died in the war around the time I was born, and their families had moved elsewhere. I loved to sit in those empty plots and watch the wind swirl the grasses around. Beyond the field we reached the south-flowing stream. This was my path, and I would stick with it for around two hours until I came to the Far Fork.

Over the years, I'd named a lot of places in the woods. The Far Fork was where the stream diverged into two smaller brooks.

One flowed southwest, the other southeast. I'd never explored beyond that point because the woods grew much thicker and darker there. The gloom seemed to radiate from it, warning travelers to turn back. Sometimes I'd stand at the fork and peer into that place, trying to catch sight of the monsters fabled to dwell within it. Today, I planned to go inside.

Our walk was peaceful. The last of the spring snow had melted away, and the forest was in full bloom. The trees grew full and green once again, and wildflowers exploded in dazzling purples and yellows. The birds competed with me as I hummed songs I knew from my father's record player, and the trickle of water and whispers of the breeze harmonized in vibrant symphony. An occasional lash of wind stirred the leaves all around me, and their dancing stirred my soul. I knew I wouldn't be back for several hours, so I drank my water sparingly and keep a steady pace.

After an hour of brisk walking, I stopped under a big tree to rest. Millie lapped from the stream and barked at a squirrel. Butterflies drifted between the yellow and purple wildflowers. I smiled and closed my eyes, leaning my head back and feeling the scattered sunlight move across my face.

"I never want to leave," I said to the dog. I could hear her pitter-pattering through the grass and nipping at the dragonflies near the water. The babbling stream looked irresistible, so I kicked off my shoes and waded into it. The water's icy kiss invigorated me. With renewed energy, I alerted Millie that it was time to press on.

As I approached her, she dropped her head low to the ground and growled. Her fur rose up on end and her eyes narrowed. She bared her teeth and circled me slowly, looking off in the distance. I spun around in the direction she stared.

"What is it?" I asked. "What do you hear?"

I felt it before I heard it. The ground rumbled. It was faint at first, but grew stronger with each passing moment. I could feel it in my body, and suddenly a thunderous roar erupted. It came from far away, and was gone in another few seconds. I darted down the stream with my shoes and pack in hand, trying to find a suitable tree to climb for a better view. By the time I'd found one, the world was quiet again. Whether it was an animal, an engine, or something else, I never knew, but I never wanted to hear that sound again.

I scratched Millie's head and tried to calm her down. Her frisky demeanor eventually returned. I dropped down on my butt and slid my socks and shoes back on, then checked my pack. We still had another hour of walking ahead of us, and the time was approaching noon. I worried that we wouldn't be home until dark, and my parents would be furious. At least I had plenty of time to dream up a good excuse.

Looking down the stream, I gulped back a sense of dread that tried to creep up my throat. There was no room for fear now. There was only hope, only courage. Only Gabriel.

CHAPTER 34

As I suspected, the remaining hour before reaching the Far Fork went by in what felt like minutes. I was afraid now, but refused to let it hinder my progress. We stood at the diverging streams for a long time, taking it all in.

"This place is dangerous," I whispered to Millie. "Stay with me, okay?"

She looked right at me, and somehow I felt she understood. We gazed into the Southeast Woods, and immediately I felt eyes upon me. With a deep sigh, I gathered myself and pushed off the bank, treading into the darkness as quickly as I could.

The Southeast Woods seemed frozen in perpetual twilight. Owls hooted and crickets twittered lazily. Here, nature didn't produce a cheerful song, but a dreary lament. While the rest of the forest bustled with life during the day, the Southeast Woods felt ghostly and still.

The air smelled stale here, and the ground felt damp beneath my shoes. Fog crept about, casting the old trees in a sickly pallor. A few rays of light stabbed through the canopy here, I imagined them as glowing swords plunging into the darkness of this place. Millie's tail whipped my leg gently as she trotted alongside. It reminded me that I wasn't alone.

"We have to stay near the stream," I whispered. "I don't want to get lost here. Use that nose of yours."

I moved quietly, fearful to disrupt the stillness. This place felt unwelcoming, as though the very trees around us leered menacingly at our presence. They seemed taller and older than the ones closer to home. Their long trunks cast a labyrinth of sinister shadows across the leafy floor, discouraging me from walking too slowly and allowing them to snatch me up in their branches.

Stop acting like a child, I thought to myself. *Don't be afraid of nonsense.*

My scolding did little to convince me, and I grew more and more wary as we continued on. Even Millie's demeanor changed. She no longer panted carelessly with her mouth open, but instead had an inquisitive expression on her face. She strained to see what awaited us beyond the great veil of fog and trees, and sniffed the ground much more often now. She seemed worried, and stayed closer to me.

After a few minutes, I could no longer see where the woods thinned behind us. The gloom pushed down on me, and the air became so thick and musty it took work to breathe. There were more hills here than back up north near my home, and as we continued south, the ground began to slope downward. Each time we came over a grassy knoll I half-expected to see a werewolf. Suddenly my mind raced with all of the terrible creatures I'd read about in my dad's books. Thankfully, after a half hour of walking, the worst these woods could muster was a flock of noisy crows feasting on a deer carcass.

At some point the canopy grew so dense the light rays no longer penetrated it. It felt so long ago that we'd last seen the sun, and I began to lose track of time. The dark was affecting my mind. I felt dazed, and for a moment, I could no longer recall why I had come here in the first place. I sat down beneath an impossibly large tree. Its roots poked in and out of the soil like snakes, and they fanned out over a wide area. Millie plopped down next to me. My canteen was half empty now. From so many years of hiking throughout the wilderness near my home, I had learned that the distance I could explore was limited by how much water I had with me. I always turned back when my canteen was half empty. I'd never broke this rule before, but I had to break it today.

I decided we'd explore for another hour and then return to the Far Fork. If I timed everything right, I'd get home about an hour before it started to get really dark. It seemed like the perfect plan.

CHAPTER 35

Ten minutes – or thirty – drifted past. I could no longer tell. My sense of time and distance failed miserably in these woods. As we wandered, Millie picked up an interesting scent and began sniffing furiously at the ground, trotting to and fro.

We crossed the stream heading west, then cut south again. The dog intermittently paused and looked around or sniff the air. This continued on for quite a while until she came to a complete stop and sat down.

"Well?" I questioned her.

She gazed back at me vacantly. I sighed looked up at the trees.

"That's the last time I trust you to do anything except drool—"

"Of all the peculiar things…" a voice behind me interjected. My skeleton nearly leaped out of my mouth.

I whirled around and beheld a man standing a few yards away. He was short and hunched a bit, craning his neck to get a better look at me. He wore a tattered woolen cloak and a scarf that bobbled with his squirrely movements. In his weathered hands he carried a bundle of twigs, and clutched it as though he feared I'd take it. Gray hair slithered across his greasy head and jutted in every direction, and his eyes glinted from his dirty face like little blue gems, studying me through a pair of spectacles. A crack forked across one of the lenses.

What was most remarkable about him was the fact that he'd walked straight up behind me without rustling any of the leaves that covered the forest floor. He moved so quietly that I'd sooner believe he'd dropped straight out of a tree, or appeared out of thin air like a ghost. Millie didn't seem startled at all, as though she'd expected this meeting, and hardly moved when he engaged us.

The man removed a handkerchief from his pocket and swabbed his glasses without taking his eyes off of me.

"Why are you here?" he asked. "Are you lost?" He spoke gently, trying not to cause me any further alarm.

"You scared me!" I yelled. "Who are you? How did you sneak up like that?" I took a step back. The man finally blinked and looked away, thinking of what to say.

"No one's asked my name in years... it's become special to me, and I'd like not to go handing it out to strangers," he said. "And as far as being quiet, well my dear, if you'd lived out here as long as I have, you'd have learned to surprise your prey as well!"

I took another step back. Millie crossed between us and growled at the man. I was ready to run as fast as I could in the opposite direction, but the man stuck his open hand out to signal me to wait.

"N-no no, I'm sorry, I didn't mean it that way. Why, these stubby little legs couldn't outmatch you! You're in no danger, I assure you," he said. "What I meant was, when you live out here, you have to learn to be sneaky, in order to surprise rabbits and birds and the like. Even then, they're quite a challenge...no, no, I prefer plants because they don't have to be chased!" He laughed nervously and relaxed his posture. After clearing his throat, he continued in a jovial voice, "Alright, let me start over. It's Magnus. And I approached you because I haven't seen anyone this far out in the woods in months. My apologies for scaring you...just wanted to ask if you were lost. I must look ghastly," he chuckled. "I don't own any mirrors, you see. Fragile things don't last long out here."

I eyed him sharply, but then remembered why I'd come here in the first place.

"I... I am somewhat lost, yes," I replied. "I've never been here before."

"Why on Earth are you here?" he asked. "And alone?"

"I'm looking for someone," I said, "a man who lives in the

woods. People in town say he makes medicine. And my name is also special to me, so please forgive me that I don't share it."

The man thought long and hard for a moment, scratching an ear. His face was clean-shaven, which struck me as unusual for a man living in the woods. He either had a house out here, or he was lying to me. The air felt a little colder, and I shivered.

"I know this man," he said, then paused. "But he's a terrible thing. It's true, all those stories you've heard. Well, most of them. I suspect he lives in the area, because I've seen his tracks here and there. It is peculiar…very peculiar…" he trailed off and craned his body, looking out into the dark.

"What's peculiar?" I asked impatiently.

"The tracks, you know," he continued, slowly returning his gaze to me. "They...change."

I cocked my head. "What do you mean?"

"Well you know. They're different, the farther along they go. Haven't you heard the stories about bear men? Screaming in pain, walking around with stretched bones."

I shook my head and offered a nervous laugh, then told him there were no such creatures in the world.

"Oh, but how do you know?" he pressed. "Have you been? Have you seen all the world? All the dark places? Why, you haven't even visited this place before!" His voice dropped to a dreary whisper, and he leaned toward me. "Why, they could be watching us…right...now…"

We both glanced around the forest in silence, then back at one another. He suddenly put his fingers to his mouth and hushed me, then cocked his head.

"You hear that?" he whispered.

I shivered more. Another ten seconds of silence went by, when suddenly the man yelled "boo!" and threw his kindling up into the air.

I screamed. He apologized through a fit of ill-concealed laughter.

"You're awful!" I shouted. "How can you scare people like that?" Millie was very entertained by all of this. She wagged her tail furiously and barked in delight. She trotted over to give

Magnus an approving barrage of licks. He patted her on the head.

"Oh dear, I'm so sorry. Hah! You see, I don't get to chat very much with others these days. I sometimes daydream about playing little tricks on people who come through these parts.

"I am that man you've heard of, yes" he continued. "But unfortunately, I can't cast spells or brew magic potions. I'm no wizard. I'm just a man, living out the end of his days in the quietest place I could find."

An awkward silence fell as I realized I'd wasted my time coming out here.

"Say, my shack is nearby," he added, sensing my disappointment. "It's quite cozy, if I do say so myself. I hunt small game once in a while, but my favorite foods grow in the dirt. And cooking is my specialty!" He paused, still smiling, awaiting my reaction.

I considered his words for a long moment, and then realized that I had very little choice but to trust him. He was strange, that was for sure, but by the look of him, there was no way he could catch me if I ran. He must have been pushing seventy years old, and walked with a slight gimp.

"Are you hungry?" he continued. "I can make you some hot stew."

Swallowing down my fears, I agreed, and called the dog to me. Millie trotted back to my side and nudged her cold nose against my leg.

"How far is your home?" I asked.

Magnus turned away from me and scanned the area, then pointed with a stubby finger.

"Ah, about a five minute walk this way. Let's be on then!"

He picked up his firewood and hobbled away. I followed a safe distance behind. Millie slobbered all over herself.

CHAPTER 36

As we walked, the woods began to darken even more, and I realized that dusk was upon us. I longed to race home, to be at Gabriel's side.

Magnus distracted me with his ramblings. By the time we reached his shack, I learned that he'd owned a small house in town, but when his wife passed away, he came here. They were avid hikers in their youth, like me, and they'd found the Southeast Woods to be particularly enchanting. To avoid the torment of her death, he left behind most of his things and lived a simple life in the forest, but still wandered into town for supplies now and then. The last time he'd made the journey was around two months ago. I also learned that his favorite food was a soup he himself had concocted, with roots and mushrooms and vegetables from his little garden.

We came upon a little shack. It looked surprisingly well-constructed. Little lights glowed from inside.

"Magnus," I said, "I've never met someone with your name. Or your accent. Where are you from?"

He hesitated for a moment at the door. Without looking at me, he responded,

"Far away. Ah, but it's such a long and boring story. You'd fall asleep where you stand!"

He obviously didn't want to talk about it, so I didn't press.

"Some folks call you the Mushroom Farmer," I said. "Did you know that?"

"Oh yes," he laughed, turning to face me. "Some boys spotted me picking moon caps north of here a few years ago. They ran off screaming, and I didn't even try to scare them! Made me feel a bit like an ogre, actually."

"Moon caps?" I repeated.

"The purple ones. Big as a dinner plate. Chop 'em up and fritter 'em with some onions and peppers! Wonderful!"

"Ah," I said.

Magnus dropped his bundle at the doorstep.

"I never hurt anyone, you know. Not a soul. But you don't have to do that to become a legend around here. Just be a little weird and you're set."

He opened the door to his tiny cottage and welcomed me inside.

"You're well on your way to fame too, my dear," he said, "walking around by yourself in the woods all day. They'll say we're in love!"

To my surprise, and Magnus's, I laughed. For the first time in hours, I felt a bit less afraid. I examined the outside of his home before stepping in. It was made from wood and stone and mud, but looked quite charming, like something from a fairy tale. A flimsy wooden fence encircled it, barely able to contain a strange garden that grew out of control.

"Why the fence?" I asked.

"What do you mean?" he replied, kicking off his shoes.

"Well," I said, kicking the mud from my shoes, "it's the sort of thing you'd see in town."

Magnus chuckled and shrugged.

"My wife would have liked it."

We headed inside, and I closed the door behind me, ensuring it was unlocked in case I had to flee.

There was a makeshift fireplace, and a wooden breakfast table with two hand-carved chairs beside it. A couch rested to the left of the fire beneath a window, and to the right, a comfortable armchair with hundreds of old papers stacked around it. A large animal fur sprawled across the wood floor, perhaps a bear's, and two more covered the windows in lieu of curtains. It was difficult to imagine Magnus taking down a bear, even with a gun. I realized I was very interested in learning more about the strange fellow.

The little man rushed around, getting a fire going and

picking up pots and rifling through cabinets.

"I've not had a visitor in months, maybe years," he said, "but I'm glad to have one now. Come and sit. I'll make you some stew."

As I sat, I picked up one of the many papers piled nearby. The handwriting looked professional, and the paper must have been fifty years old.

Tomato bisque à la Magnus Farmer, it read.

"So you were a chef, then?" I asked.

Magnus scurried to and from a bubbling pot, dumping in mushrooms, sliced tomatoes, garlic, onions, peppers, and a myriad of aromatic spices. It smelled like it had already been simmering for hours. While zipping around, he said, "Well, my father taught me nearly everything I know about food. That's how I got my wife to marry me, I think! Hah, I'd have been all alone if I didn't have a knack for cooking."

We talked for a while as the stew finished. My gaze moved around the room and fell on a piece of parchment on a nearby shelf. Dozens of little mushrooms were drying upon it.

"What are these?" I asked.

Magnus briefly glanced up from his work.

"Oh, those," he said, "they're, uh, for dreaming."

I looked closer.

"I've never seen ones like these. Do you cook with them?"

He stirred the pot and pulled some wooden bowls from the cupboard.

"Sometimes I make tea with them," he said reluctantly. "They're quite rare, so I'm careful about what I do with them."

"But they help you sleep?" I asked.

"They're Dream Callers," he said, hobbling up to the table with the pot of stew. "They help you see things you didn't know were there. But they're only for adults!"

I looked at him, then down at the mushrooms again, intrigued. Magnus chuckled and turned away to fetch some spoons. As he did, I snatched one of the mushrooms and hid it in my coat pocket.

CHAPTER 37

Magnus poured a good amount of his stew into a bowl and set it in front of me.

"It's quite hot," he said, "but I'll be surprised if it isn't the best you've ever eaten." He sat expectantly; a big smile spread across his round little face.

He was right. It was incredible, and I nodded in satisfaction. He clapped his hands in delight.

"So, my dear," he said. "What could have made you come out here all alone?" He began to eat his soup, and seemed more interested in it than in my story. Across the room, Millie grunted in her sleep. She lay passed out on the fur next to the crackling fire.

I didn't know nearly where to start; it all seemed crazy that I'd wander out into the wild to find some kind of shaman. I realized how embarrassed I was to tell Magnus the truth, but I'd already come this far.

"I...I hope you don't think I'm crazy," I began. He continued eating without looking up.

"It's my brother," I said. "He's only a baby, but he's already dying. We don't know why. His fever has worsened over the past few days, and I'm afraid it won't be long now. My parents have taken him into town to see the doctors, but—"

"Ah, so you don't live in town?" Magnus interrupted.

"N...No," I replied, unwilling to tell him the exact location of my house. "We live north of it."

"Ah, the farmlands!" he chirped. "Many beautiful views there. Oh, and the sky, I remember seeing the stars out there. Deep in the woods, all I can see are the damned branches, by the millions! They're like spiders."

I nodded and redirected the conversation.

"Yes…but the doctors don't understand what's making him sick. I love my brother so much. When I see him just lying there, when I see that the medicine has no effect, I feel my heart breaking. I hear my mother crying late at night.

"In school, I heard of a man who made potions that made an ugly girl beautiful, and ones that stopped soldiers from dying. I came here looking for that man. I know it sounds stupid, but I'll do anything to help Gabriel."

Magnus finally looked up and sat his spoon down on the table. His glittering eyes found mine.

"Fever, you say? Does he shake?"

I nodded.

"Young lady, as I said before, I'm no sorcerer," Magnus said in a glum tone. "I just make foods and drinks that are healthy. I can't make potions. I once found a boy who'd eaten the wrong berries in the woods, and a girl who had ugly rashes on her skin, but those conditions are easily treated. This is how rumors are spread about me. I can't cure your brother…" he trailed off, and looked over his shoulder toward the kitchen. My heart sank in my chest. "…But we may be able to give him a fighting chance, to allow the doctors more time."

His sudden change of demeanor sparked a flicker of hope in me. My eyes widened as Magnus scampered off to what looked like a spice rack. Jars of plants and powders lined its shelves, and as he rifled through them, they clinked and clanged together, causing Millie's ears to twitch in her sleep.

"You say he's got a fever, and that he shakes," he said, his voice full of conviction. "And does he sleep a lot?"

"No," I replied, "he hardly sleeps at all."

"I see," he whispered, more to himself than to me. He began to mix powders and crush herbs in a small bowl. After a few minutes, Magnus produced a jar of dark brown and green powder. He strained it through a sort of filter, which removed most of the leaf and stem bits, and then added in a few pinches of this and that. It was riveting to watch him work, and for a moment, I forgot all about my own stew. When I finally remembered it, I gulped it down before it got too cold.

Magnus brought the completed medicine to me and asked me to hold out my hand. As I did, he poured a small amount onto my palm, and said, "Mix this amount into his water or milk for three days. If on the third day he seems to be getting better, use the rest of the jar. If he doesn't feel any better, stop using it. You'd be treating an illness he doesn't have."

I was thankful for his efforts, and for his food. I offered my hand in friendship and he shook it with both of his. They felt dry and rough.

"Thank you, Magnus," I said, feeling a lump in my throat. "You're very kind. If it doesn't work, should I come back?" I asked.

He smiled at me, but his joy quickly faded.

"I'm afraid this is all I can do," he replied. "I'm only guessing here. There's only one plant that treats fever around here, and it doesn't work on everything. Either way, I'm sure Gabriel will appreciate your efforts."

I nodded and looked to the door.

"Must you leave now?" he asked. "It's late… the woods are dangerous this time of night, especially for a young lady."

"I know they are," I sighed. I was exhausted, and Millie was in a coma on the floor. I looked at her and then back up to Magnus.

"I have to," I said. "I know it's dark. But my family will be worried sick about me. I know the way. And I need to get this home as soon as I can." I shook the jar in my hand. "I don't know how long he has."

Magnus looked over to the small bag I'd left near the door.

"Could you use more water and food then?" he asked, and walked over to his pantry without waiting for a response.

"Yes," I replied, "I almost forgot how low on water I am. Can you spare any?"

He was already on the job, grabbing a large jug and pouring it carefully. He wrapped a pastry and what looked like beef jerky in a blue cloth, tied it, and stuffed it into my pack. He then grabbed a small lantern from the windowsill and lit it with a match he produced from his coat.

"Take this," he implored, "I have plenty more for myself, and it'll be pitch black by the time you get home." After, he paused and looked at me carefully. "I know how your brother is feeling, but how are you? You don't say much about yourself."

I took a deep breath and sank against the wall.

"Nobody's asked me that since Gabriel got sick," I admitted. "We've all been so worried about him that we've almost forgotten about ourselves. I'm not angry for it. I only wish things could go back to normal. I miss being a kid sometimes. I'm not even seventeen and I feel like an old woman."

Magnus responded only with a look of concern.

"I've been having nightmares," I added. "Probably from the stress. Awful things haunt my dreams. Thankfully they're so scary they wake me up, so it ends quick."

I sighed deeply and reached to open the door.

"Thank you again, for everything," I said, and called Millie over. Magnus smiled.

"It was my pleasure," he said. "So nice to make a friend. Be safe on your journey home, and should you ever find yourself in the Southeast Woods again, do drop by for more stew! Oh, and uh, please don't tell anyone about me...there are enough stories floating around out there. If I wanted to be a celebrity, I wouldn't live in a forest!"

We both shared a laugh and said goodbye. As I exited the cottage, Magnus called out to me.

"May it help you find your way, if ever you are lost," he said, pointing at my coat. My heart skipped.

Did he know I took one of his mushrooms?

I smiled and walked out the door.

CHAPTER 38

Darkness had fallen over the woods. Crickets sang their lullabies for miles in every direction. The croaks of frogs and toads echoed all around me, some deep and some shrill. The night's song was rich and vivid, like the backdrop of some dark fairy tale. A cool breeze kissed my face and sharpened my senses a bit. Millie and I strode up the path toward the northern woods. I was anxious to see my family.

I thought about everything Magnus had said to me. He was a wiser fellow than he'd let on. Polite as he was, I sensed a drearier undertone to his words, as though he had less hope for Gabriel than he wanted to admit. Either way, he was a wonderful host and a kind man. I felt bad for believing all of the stories I'd heard about him, and for joking with my friends about what a nut he must have been.

And what did he mean about finding my way? I inspected the little mushroom in one hand as I walked. Magnus knew I could find my way back home. He wouldn't have let me wander off so easily if he thought I might get lost. He also knew Millie could probably found our way back. I looked up and saw the dog trotting a few yards ahead of me, sniffing the ground on occasion and looking back to make sure I was close behind.

He must have meant something different. But what? If I wasn't lost in the woods, where would I be lost? Maybe he was talking about losing myself in a metaphorical sense. Lost in life's chaos, perhaps.

I suddenly realized that even though I knew the way home, I was more lost than I'd ever been. I was at a crossroads in my life, not only with my brother and parents, but with myself. School would be over soon, and then I'd be off to an academy, or to marry and have children. A storm of possibilities clouded my mind and drowned out my senses, hushing the world around me. I couldn't imagine what lay ahead. Right now, all I wanted to do with my life was explore the woods, play with my brother, and perhaps write a little poetry.

I stopped walking. Millie paused and studied me over her shoulder.

Magnus had me figured out better than I did. He saw my wanderlust for what it really was: escapism. Gabriel was dying. My parents were drifting apart. The whole world and its weight dangled from a thread, ready to crush me underneath. And I was out scraping my knees, going on adventures.

Millie whimpered at me. I walked up and hugged her. I always felt like she could understand what I was thinking.

"Look at me," I said. "I'm too old for this stuff."

I should have grown out of playing in the woods years ago. Better yet, I probably should have left exploring to the boys. But I was different. I wasn't interested in curtseying and cooking and meeting gentlemen. My father would be ashamed to know I was out getting dirty and cut up and looking for old hermits.

My God, what's the matter with me? I thought to myself. *I could have been kidnapped!*

I threw my arms into the air, cursing under my breath. I was disappointed with myself, and I knew my parents would be disappointed with the woman I'd grow up to be. I still acted like a kid, and now more than ever, they needed me to grow up.

I wondered if Magnus thought I was a fool, or a freak like him. I imagined myself growing into an old vagabond, sulking through the dark, collecting firewood and talking to myself. I even imagined myself with a dirty gray beard.

I looked down into my palm at the mushroom, and then up into the branch-shrouded sky.

"I am lost," I spoke into the night. "Show me the way then, Magnus."

I brought the mushroom to my lips, took a deep breath, and ate it.

CHAPTER 39

The taste was awful and bitter, like chewing on a horse saddle. I chewed it quickly and swallowed, then gulped down a few mouthfuls of water. It was surprisingly cool, and washed away the foul aftertaste. My stomach gurgled, and I stood still for a brief moment, wondering what I had just done to myself.

"Not for *young ladies*?" I asked Millie, and then continued on, laughing. We quickened our pace. I didn't want to be in the Southeast Woods late at night. I looked behind me out of some childish fear of being watched, and then brushed away the feeling as best as I could.

As we walked, I pulled the jar out of my pack and unscrewed the lid. It smelled like tea, but tasted terribly bitter. I wondered if it was even safe to eat. What if Magnus was a demented psychopath all along?

No, I reassured myself. There was no use in imagining all of the horrible things he could have put into the mixture. He'd used some of the same ingredients in our soup. He was a kind man, and just seemed lonely.

I caught myself deep in thought about a multitude of topics. My mind wandered and raced and danced, briefly touching on what felt like nearly everything one could possibly imagine. I was so entertained with letting it run freely that I felt my eyes growing heavy – not in a sleepy way, but as though I were being hypnotized. I suddenly realized how cold my hands felt, so I put the jar back into my pack and stuffed my fingers into my pockets. It was no use. I imagined a delicate frost creeping its way up my fingers and toes, to my forearms and legs, turning my skin blue as it moved. My heart fluttered at the thought of becoming too cold to even make it home, and I was forced to stop and catch my breath.

My awareness of the world around me became more intense and vivid. Objects appeared more distant, as if I'd withdrawn from every possible direction. Thoughts rushed toward and away from me like trains through a dark tunnel, and always left a new web of ideas to scour. My emotions vacillated from excitement to fear to serenity to contemplation, over and over. My limbs went tingly and numb, as though the imagined frost had entirely overtaken me. My body stiffened, and I started giggling and walking like I was underwater. Millie looked confused by my behavior and sniffed at me.

After several minutes of this, stomach pains awoke me from my trance, and my skin shifted from icy to warm and sweaty. My neck went hot, as if I'd soaked in a bath for too long. As all these new feelings washed over me, a sudden urge to lie down on the ground overwhelmed me. I wanted to feel the earth against my body.

"Something...strange...is happening," I said to Millie.

We came upon a small grove. In the distance I thought I could see the Far Fork, but the dark was playing tricks on my eyes. Millie had the same idea and plopped down onto the ground. I followed suit. The grass felt soft and fluffy as I fell into it, and I imagined I was floating on a bed of clouds. I gazed up between the branches and into the sky. Thousands of luminescent jewels flecked its breadth, and the thick, syrupy light of a full moon drenched the grove in silver. The crickets and toads serenaded me with their music, and every sight and sound and emotion melted into one sensational blur.

I let go, ready to experience whatever magic had overtaken me without trying to control or understand it. A tide of narcotic energy hummed through my body, pulling me deeper into the strange world I'd found. My last memory was of the stars dripping down the ethereal dome of the sky. Then, all went black.

I don't know how long I slept.

CHAPTER 40

A terrible roar jerked me from my sleep. It was the same noise I'd heard earlier in the day, before we'd reached the Far Fork. I struggled to sit up. The ground rumbled, and I imagined water rushing beneath its surface. The knoll squirmed beneath me like it was coming alive. Gravity pulled me in every direction, and the sensation of falling jarred my balance. I grabbed at handfuls of grass, trying to anchor myself to something before I flew off into the sky. My hands found the roots of a nearby tree, and for a brief moment I clung to them, but they too began to writhe and elude me like angry snakes. Sharp pain shot up from my stomach and into my chest. The wind shrieked through the forest, bending millions of branches and stripping the leaves from them. The trees groaned in pain.

I held myself in a ball and cried. The world morphed into a horrific creature that howled and fought against me. Every muscle in my body clenched. I held my breath and waited for the end to come.

Then, everything stopped. The ground ceased its convulsions, and the screaming wind calmed to ominous whispers. The monstrous noise abated, leaving trees groaning all around me.

Finally, I lifted my head and brushed the leaves out of my hair.

The sky looked different. The stars had vanished, leaving a vacant abyss that peered back at me. The moon hung overhead, but it had waned to a dim sliver. I gazed up in awe, my jaw dangling open. There was nothing. I saw a universe of absolutely nothing but the lonely moon.

I pried my gaze from the horror above me, only to find I'd

woken up in a very different place from the one I'd passed out in. Everything had warped. A thick fog, much thicker than before, flooded through the forest. Gnarled and dying trees surrounded me, reaching out in desperation with their wooden claws. They no longer stood straight and tall, but instead grew misshapen, some of them covered in what looked like throbbing tumors. Odd fungus clung to the trees and draped from their branches like melting spider webs.

The grass beneath me felt brittle, and the air tasted stale. The forest stunk of decay – a stark contrast to the drifting scents of herbs and flowers that hung within it earlier. Crows cawed harshly in the distance. The crickets had fallen silent, and the only other sounds I could hear were the deepest croaks of the bullfrogs. Whatever evil that had been lurking in the forest before had now conquered it.

I got up and staggered a few paces. I tried to call the dog, but her name caught in my throat. As I turned to her, my heart stopped.

There, sitting in the grass, was Millie. She stared down at my body, which was still sprawled out where I had been a moment ago. I froze, speechless, looking down at my own hands and back at the body on the ground.

I called out to her, and her ears perked up, but she didn't look at me. Her gaze fixated on my lifeless body, which I'd somehow left behind. Millie whimpered, nudging my side and licking my face, but I simply did not wake up. I stumbled over to my body and touched it. The skin felt cold. I checked the pulse. My heart beat faintly.

My mind reeled with confusion and terror. I wanted to scream out for help, but I was afraid of what attention I might attract. What happened? Where was I? I checked my own pulse, and checked the pulse of my body on the ground once again. Both beat in unison.

I reasoned that as long as I kept myself alive, my body wouldn't perish, and vice versa.

I reached out to touch Millie, but the closer my hand got, the more it felt like I was reaching into a fire. I pulled my hand back and examined it for burns. Nothing.

I considered running north in hopes of getting home, but it would take hours, and I didn't want to leave Millie in the Southeast Woods by herself. I decided to make my way back to Magnus.

A noise in the distance interrupted my panic: a far-off instrument chirping, or perhaps someone singing. The sound faded in and out, lost in the maze of trees.

It wasn't my imagination. Someone was playing music out there in the dark. I glanced back at Millie. I knew she'd guard my body forever. She was already curled up against me, whimpering in an attempt to wake me up.

"I'll be back, Millie!" I cried. "For the love of God, please don't leave!" Her ears twitched again, but she didn't look up.

CHAPTER 41

Off into the velvety fog I ran, chasing the ghostly music. I ducked beneath branches and leaped over snarls of roots. Disgusting fungal growths hung like vines from high up in the trees, battering me as I moved and stinking up my clothes. Some fell to the ground and exploded in noxious clouds. Awful noises pierced the mist all around me, and I didn't dare imagine what sort of ghoulish creatures they must have come from. On and on I ran, pausing only for a moment to locate the source of the noise.

Chattering voices arose in the distance: laughter, singing, cheering, and conversation all drifted to my ears in muffled fragments.

Faint yellow lights appeared in the distance. They glimmered through the fog like tiny lighthouses that guided my path. The voices and music grew louder. The distinct *clink* of champagne glasses and forks on plates rang through the night.

A cry for help rolled to the tip of my tongue. A split second before I could bellow out into the night, something moved behind me.

I stopped running and sank to a crouch.

A dreary melody reached my ears. Someone was humming in the dark.

Just beyond the fog's veil, the outline of a hulking man appeared. He lurked between the trees, and between his despondent hums he growled like a wolf. He stopped and sniffed the air in one great breath, then continued stalking in the opposite direction.

"*Rak...rak...rrrghh...*"

I crept toward the light, hoping that he hadn't noticed me.

When I was about a hundred paces away, I broke into a full sprint.

The man heard my footsteps and unleashed a mournful howl into the fog. The sound conjured images of a monstrous creature in my mind. I screamed. An explosion of terror propelled me toward the distant lights like a meteor. I flew over moss and roots and puddles of black water. Twigs slashed my face. The thing barreled after me, snapping twigs and branches as it charged through the woods.

The lights were just ahead now, and I could see the great shape from which they radiated.

A house.

It wasn't like Magnus's shack, but rather a huge manor, standing alone out here in the swampy overgrowth. No roads led to it. A piano and violins trilled inside, and I could make out dozens of people through the windows. An ornate front door towered over a garden out front, which seemed to thrive merrily despite the putrid ecosystem in which it lived.

I slowed to a dizzy stumble. The contrast between the rotting forest and the elegant house within it confounded me. When a branch snapped just behind me, I staggered to the door and slammed into it with my arms and screamed at the top of my lungs.

The music ceased.

The heavy door opened.

"Oh my! Are you alright?" asked a short, chubby man. He was very well dressed and wore a white mask on his face. I opened my mouth to respond, but couldn't find any words. Similarly dressed people gathered behind him, peering out at me with curiosity. Many wore brightly colored, ornamental masks. Some donned face paint.

It was a masquerade ball.

I drew my eyes back to the short man and began to cry.

"I'm lost!" I sobbed, "And I think I might've hit my head, and someone's following me!"

The man took my hand and pulled me inside, then locked the door behind me. Just the sound of the locks falling into place instantly relieved me, as did the chatter of all the concerned partygoers. They flocked to me by the dozen.

While the crowd fussed over the cuts on my face, I watched the pianist resume his playing across the room. He was tall and thin, and donned an elegant white vest and pants. White gloves covered his hands, and his fingers danced across the keys. His mask was simpler than the others, hiding only his eyes and forehead. He smiled warmly at me, then closed his eyes and became lost in the music.

Someone guided me to a big chair with uncomfortably stiff cushions. As I looked around, I took note of the opulent décor: expensive throw rugs and paintings and exotic furniture graced every inch of the house. A ballroom floor lay next to the pianist, and several couples danced on it. Everyone had drinks in their hands and wore strange costumes.

A man wearing a military uniform knelt down beside me.

"Poor thing!" he said. "What ever happened to you?" He produced a handkerchief from his coat pocket and matted it down on my bleeding knee. I must have fallen. I couldn't remember. My memories blurred together. By his age and the look of his uniform, I could tell that he must have been a high-ranking officer.

"Yes, tell us!" said a woman with a shrill voice.

Tears dripped down my face, and my hair must have been a fright. I looked up at all the strange masks, which peered back at me lifelessly, and I blurted out whatever I could remember.

"I…I woke up like this. I mean, I don't know if I was asleep or what, but it was so dark… I might have fainted, and…and I could, could see myself, like I was dead or something! So I ran away, and I heard music, and…and I followed it, but there was something in the woods…something wandering around in the dark, and I—"

Another woman interrupted me, turning to the group and saying, "Isn't that forest just a nightmare? Where I'm from we don't have anything as savage. I prefer the city!"

Guests began to chatter in various languages, some familiar to me, and others utterly foreign. A man and his wife paused their conversation and looked at me. The man asked in a thick accent, "What was this thing you saw, out there in the fog?"

Before I could respond, I was bombarded with several more questions.

"Was anyone else with you?" asked one woman.

"Are you hurt anywhere else?" said another.

Before I could answer, my hand was taken by a young man in a ruby red mask. He stepped between me and the other partygoers.

"Well, now she's here, and that's all that matters!" he announced in a grandiose voice. "Let's give her some air, friends! Laugh, dance and be merry!" He raised a glass of wine to them. They obliged, and slowly dispersed. The man turned and implored me to walk with him.

"I'm sorry," he smiled, "we all love meeting new people, and sometimes we forget our manners. I'm Ivan. Welcome to the party!"

His wavy blond hair and strong jawline made him look rather dashing. Unlike most of the other guests, he wore a tuxedo. His mask spanned his face from forehead to chin, except for a thin slit in the shape of a smile. It had arched eyebrows painted onto it, complementing his friendly demeanor. Ivan looked young, maybe in his early twenties, but I got the impression that this big house belonged to him.

He never let go of my arm, which was interlocked with his, and we paraded slowly around the bottom floor of the house. He introduced me to some of the guests, always speaking with the formality of a cultured gentleman.

"What is this place?" I asked as he handed me a glass of champagne.

"Just a party," he replied. "It gets so lonely out here, so I like to spice things up now and then. I can't remember the last time I had anybody over. In fact, I can't remember anything!" he laughed heartily and swirled the wine around inside his glass, then took a big gulp. We promenaded through halls and rooms filled with drunken, happy people.

"Does a girl so beautiful have as nice a name?" he asked.

A smile spread over my face. I looked into his eyes and felt taken by his charm, but I had not yet lost my wits. I dropped my gaze to the floor.

"Emma." I lied.

He smiled and said, "Emma and Ivan. Rolls off the tongue, don't you think?"

I nodded shyly and took a sip of my drink. I'd never tasted champagne before, and it took great effort not to spit it out. We set our glasses down and strolled into the ballroom, where he led me through the steps of a dance.

"You're very good at this," he joked. "Did you take lessons?"

I stumbled to keep up, privately regretting all the years I'd spent climbing trees instead of learning to be a lady.

"Ivan," I said, looking around the room, "I didn't see any cars outside. How'd all these people get here?"

He took a deep breath and continued dancing, and after a few moments, offered simply,

"Oh, they find their way easily enough."

I hung my chin over his shoulder so he couldn't see my confusion. After a while, I asked,

"Do you have a driver?"

Ivan laughed and brushed his fingers through my hair. He shook his head and looked into my eyes with a stern gaze.

"Wherever would you go? Fog's too thick. And you've only just arrived!"

A cold feeling crept over my skin. I tried my best to stifle it, but he could see the worry in my eyes. I swallowed hard and looked at him as bravely as I could, and demanded,

"Ivan, how did all of your guests arrive here?"

He smiled.

"The same way you did."

I took a step away from him. He laughed and looked over his shoulder, embarrassed.

"Please," he whispered, "don't cause a scene. It's such a nice party." He grabbed my wrists and yanked me back toward him. He put his lips against my ear.

"We're all trapped in this nightmare," he said, "and this is the best place to be, far as anybody's concerned." Ivan then began to hum along with the music. I danced with him, terrified to break away. I considered bolting for the door.

"Let me explain, Emma, and you won't be so upset." He stroked my cheek with the back of his hand. "But first, I want to see your face," he said. "Take off your mask."

I tried to pull away from him, but he clutched me with his other hand. His strength felt inhuman.

"Don't be nervous," he continued, "we've all seen each other. Here, I'll even show you mine."

Ivan peeled off his mask, revealing a putrefied face. His eyes had sunken deep into the pits of his decayed skin, and his nose was rotted nearly to the bone. A little hole pocked the center of his forehead; it almost looked like he'd been shot. A faint stench emanated from his skin. I almost puked all over his tuxedo.

I fell back onto my butt and scrambled to get away from him, slipping around helplessly on the dance floor. The music stopped and other guests began to take notice of my behavior.

"It's okay dear, don't be afraid!" a woman beckoned while removing her mask. She and other guests had similarly disfigured faces, and it dawned on me then that I was in a room full of dead people.

"Show us how it happened!" Ivan shouted, stepping forward and reaching for my neck. "Don't be such a difficult little imp!"

I swatted his hand away and screamed. A group of male guests advanced on me. I clambered to my feet and dodged several of them, almost knocking a woman over in the process. In my frantic hurry, I rushed headlong into the arms of the pianist. He wrapped me in a protective hug.

"Enough!" he yelled at the other guests. "Leave her alone. Let her go." He still had his mask on, and took my hand as the room fell to a hush. "Are we animals?" he said. "You forget! Where will she go? We'll see her again soon." The pianist put his hand on my back and escorted me to the door. He opened it and gently nudged me out. I turned back to him, seeking answers, but he interrupted me.

"We're only victims. Please forgive us."

With that, he closed the door, and the music resumed moments later. I stared at the house for a few seconds, and then scanned the woods for the creature I'd spotted earlier. I raced off into the night, never wanting to return to that awful place again.

CHAPTER 42

Orange moonlight came through the branches and lit up the fog in certain places, casting the illusion of ghosts drifting between the trees. I looked down at my wrists as I moved, watching the bruises form and feeling the ache of Ivan's grasp.

"What a horrible place," I mumbled. I slowed to a walk and tried to fight off the dread that had settled over me once again. I was desperate to find a landmark that might help me find my way back to Magnus. Everything had shifted. The earth had moved. The hills, the color of the tree bark, the sounds of the forest – it had all changed. I whirled around, trying to find my way, when suddenly I heard the sobbing of a man in the distance.

I listened carefully and crept up between two trees.

"Hello?" he whimpered. "Is anyone there?" He was speaking English. I was suddenly grateful we'd learned it in school.

A lost traveler? I thought.

The man sounded pathetic and miserable. I listened to the crackling of the leaves under his feet, then decided to follow him as quietly as I could. I kept far enough back that I could only make out his movements through the fog.

Then, I lost sight of him. Desperate to not be alone, I broke into a dash and searched the area. It was as if the man had simply vanished. Growing frantic, I called out to him. Only my voice echoed back to me, along with the angry shrieks of a crow.

I sank down against a tree, crying pitifully for help. I crunched up in a ball, laid my head onto the stinking soil, and shut my eyes. I wanted to leave this place. I wanted it all to be gone. I wanted my dad.

Between sobs I realized that I was laying on something

hard.

I sat up. The dirt beneath me was compacted, as though it'd been walked on a hundred times.

A trail!

It was a narrow footpath, just like the one leading away from Magnus's shack. Hope took hold of me. I looked both ways and chose a direction at random. I didn't care. I'd run a thousand miles up or down it to find help.

Eventually, the trail ended at a small clearing whose entrance was obscured by gobs of dangling fungus. I had to force my way through it. The growth was warm and rancid, and dripped unspeakable slime on my clothes as I passed.

As I came out the other side, I gasped.

A lake with a sandy shore lay before me, and beyond it, a big town. *My* town, ablaze with light. My heart swelled. I leaped over a fallen log and raced toward the lake. I intended to follow the water's edge to the other side and try to find help in town. I prayed they'd be able to see me.

"Wait," a familiar voice called out from behind me. I spun around and saw a shadowy figure standing near the fungus I'd pushed through.

How could I not have heard him? I wondered.

I froze, trying to make out who it was, when he began to approach. I took a step back. My foot sank into the wet sand.

"Who's there?" I called out.

He continued to advance, slowly, with his arms up to show that he meant no harm. I continued to back up. The icy water stabbed at my ankles. As the man approached, I saw that he wore a gaudy outfit, and then realized that it was a guest from the party. He had a blanket wrapped around his shoulders.

"Get away from me, you freak!" I shouted, ready to claw his eyes out.

"Don't go," he called out softly. "You can't leave."

The man stepped into the pale glow of the city lights. His white gloves and mask lit up.

It was the pianist.

My nerves calmed a little, but I was still ready to dash away.

"You…what do you want?" I asked. "How'd you find me?"

He ignored my questions.

"Please," he begged, "Go back. There is nothing for you out there."

I looked over my shoulder at the town, and again felt the urge to run toward it. I wanted to run home squealing for my mom.

"You're not finished here," he continued. "I know your plight. I've been in your shoes myself. That's not the way out." He pointed a long finger at the lights.

Baffled, I searched for words, but nothing came out. He took a step toward me and removed the blanket from around his neck. I felt soothed the instant he wrapped it around me. He gently pulled me toward him. I still couldn't speak.

"This is for you," he said. "Keep it. I know you'll make good use of it, even if you won't listen to me."

I finally found my voice and crumbled like a river dam.

"But how'd you find me? What do you mean, you know my plight? What is this place? Please, I'm lost. I think something terrible is happening to me. I just want to see my family again. God please, help me get out of here!"

Before he could answer, a tremendous roar erupted in the distance. It was the same terrifying sound I'd heard twice before. The pianist and I both jumped.

"Run," he whispered. "Go back the way you came. If you try to escape, you'll only make things worse." And with that, he turned and walked away briskly in the direction he came from, vanishing into the fog.

I stood abandoned, shivering beneath the blanket and too distraught to think. I considered the pianist's warning but ignored it. Nothing was going to stop me from getting home.

I trudged on, my feet soaked up past my socks. Damp and heavy sand clung to my shoes, and the black, starless sky loomed just over my head, weighing down on me with its profound darkness. The lake, just to my left, sat as still as a corpse. The water looked black as oil, and lifeless as hardened clay.

The wind picked up as I continued toward the town. The closer I drew, the louder it howled. The lights in the small houses and shops seemed to dim, like candles burning out, and appeared to recede into the distance as I walked toward them.

Something was wrong.

As I made my way toward the town, the lake began to stir and bubble. A giant whirlpool formed and churned at its center. The wind kicked up mounds of sand that cascaded against me, and the entire beach came alive in it. Sand leaped into the air all around me.

Suddenly, the sand took the shape of human bodies. The figures rose from the beach, trying to escape it. At first, they groaned in misery and could only pull themselves out up to their chests and waists before collapsing back down into nothingness, but their attempts grew more fruitful as I broke into a sprint. All around, beings made of sand clambered to their knees, sometimes to their feet, and walked a few paces before their shins broke away, sending them hurtling back down to explode into puffs of scattered granules. They screeched and beckoned for me with outstretched hands, but they were too slow. I darted between them and raced down the shore toward the town.

The blanket fluttered around me. The city lights grew dimmer and dimmer, and in another few steps, they completely disappeared.

I stopped in my tracks, perplexed and disheartened. I could no longer make out where I was, or where I was headed; nothing was visible spare the black lake to my left and the plagued woods to my right.

"Shit!" I screamed at the top of my lungs, hurling my blanket to the ground and kicking the sand.

I grabbed the blanket and marched into the woods in a random direction. The wind calmed. Crows cackled far off in the distance, mocking my frustration. They'd probably be feasting on my body by the time I got back to it.

My stomach began to hurt again, and my head felt heavier as I moved. It took all my strength to keep my legs working, as though I walked underwater. My vision darkened. Ominous squeals and growls erupted from every direction. I feared I'd soon be a meal for some ghastly creature.

An unseen force yanked me backwards and down to the ground. The canopy above me melted away, and the darkness of the sky swallowed me up.

CHAPTER 43

I cracked my eyes open. Waves of dizziness washed over me. I tried to remember where I was, when suddenly a warm tongue slid across my face. I summoned all of my strength to turn my head, and a relieving sight lifted my heart right out of my chest.

Millie!

It was my dog, my sweet dog, barking in joy at my awakening. Still weak, I reached up and hugged her.

"Oh Millie, thank God. How long have I been here?"

I noticed a blanket draped over my body.

"Did you see...someone..." I tried to ask the dog. Dizziness washed over me again, this time much stronger, and pulled me back to the grass. My head spun, and my eyes would not stay open. I tried to scream in protest, but to no avail. The darkness sucked me right back in. The last thing I heard was Millie's frantic barking.

When I woke up again, Millie wasn't licking me anymore. She lay a few feet away, staring at me with an extinguished look in her eyes.

I sat up and called out to her. Her ears jumped, but did not seem to locate the source of my voice. I called her again, but got the same reaction, so I crawled over to her. But then I looked behind me, and as before, I saw my lifeless body alone and cold.

"What have I done?" I pouted, wiping my face with dirty hands. I wanted to give up, but I thought of Gabriel. I thought of my parents. And I thought of the sunny pastures around my home. I wanted to see them all again. I remembered the pianist's words then, and saw the blanket still wrapped around my motionless body.

The forest had changed again. It was worse now. The fog was so thick I could not even see ten feet into it, and the fungus that dangled from the trees was gone. The trees themselves were dead and bone-dry; sometimes their branches broke off and fell to the ground. The earth no longer felt cool and damp. Shriveled leaves crackled beneath me, and ash drifted on the air.

I sat and listened. I carefully sifted through everything the pianist had said. He had made it seem like I was here for a reason.

Before long I heard humming in the dark. It was the same song hummed by the creature that had chased me into Ivan's house: beautiful and sad, like a song at a funeral. This time, however, it sounded like a woman with a deep, raspy voice. The hair on my neck stood up.

The woman giggled. She moved quickly through the foggy darkness. Her footsteps were soft, not like the monster's.

Not knowing what else to do, I took the risk of talking to her.

"Hello?" I called out. "Is someone there?"

The humming ceased, and a breathy voice responded, "Have you found it?"

She spoke English, just like the lost traveler I'd heard earlier. They must have gotten separated.

"I'm over here!" I replied.

The woman appeared from the mist. She strode toward me at first, then wavered, as though she didn't see me. I hesitantly approached her. We stood in a tiny clearing flanked by a ring of tree husks. The woman scanned the area, but never looked right at me. Her yellow eyes reminded me of rotten milk.

I tried to speak.

"Excuse me, miss, I'm—"

"No, you're not," she said. Her voice was so abrasive it felt threatening. I struggled to understand how such harsh sounds could come from a woman so beautiful. She glanced at me dismissively. "I'm still looking," she continued. Jet-black hair drooped from her head and framed a pale face. Her petite body stood rigid, coursing with a rage she could barely contain. Deep scars crossed her arms and face. I guessed she was in her thirties, but wondered if she, like the others, was dead.

"What…are you looking for?" I asked, taking a step backwards.

In one impossibly great breath, she smelled the air with her eyes closed. When she reopened her eyes, they darted back and forth, toward and away from me. As she moved, all of her muscles tensed rhythmically, like those of a feral animal. Her strained body prevented her from walking normally, and her jaw clenched between sentences. She grinded her teeth and her face twitched.

"I lost something," she replied. "It got out again, out into the world. Probably wandering around crying, begging for its mother." A thick, wet chuckle gurgled up from her throat.

"I'm sorry, I don't understand," I said politely. "What do you mean? What is it?"

"Like a ring," the woman trailed off, looking all around, "so important, so easy to lose. I can't seem to take better care of my things. And look how much we argue." The woman examined the scars on her arms. She turned away and stared at something through the fog, but I couldn't see what.

I knew the woman was insane. I knew I had to get away from her. But I had to find out if she knew anything that could help me.

"Miss," I said in a meek voice, "do you know what's happening here? What is this place?"

Without turning to me, she whispered, perhaps to herself, in the same revolting voice.

"I've asked myself this. I can dream up with a thousand explanations. But I'm not—"

A twig snapped in the distance, and the woman's head cracked like a whip in that direction. She issued a low growl and began to walk in the direction of the sound.

"Wait, please, I need your help!" I begged, storming after her. "Tell me where to go! How do I get out of here?"

"Get out of what?" she snapped, looking over her shoulder at me. "This is *all*." She kept walking. I barely heard her say, "I'll find it. Don't you worry."

"What is *it?*" I demanded.

"It's *mine!*" she screamed. Her voice thundered through the woods and must have gone on for a hundred miles. Crows screeched in reply, and then everything went silent. She snickered and walked away.

Entirely shaken up, I ran away as fast as I could. From far off, I could hear the woman's inhuman voice, humming a song of despair once again. The dreary melody repeated over and over in my head, and made me feel lonelier than I'd ever felt.

CHAPTER 44

I had no idea where to go, but I ran as fast as my legs would take me. Everything looked the same. But as I moved, I came to a place where the canopy thinned enough that I could see a bit of the sky. It remained lifeless and infinitely dark without the twinkling stars. I never thought I'd miss them so much.

When I stopped to catch my breath, I heard the crackling of twigs underfoot, and the voice of a man.

"Is someone there?" he called out in a timid voice. "Mom? Is that you?" He spoke English. He must have been the lost traveler from before.

My urge to flee battled with my desperation for human contact. My reason told me to avoid all the strangers I came across in these woods – but then I remembered the pianist. Not everyone out here was wicked.

"Hey, I'm here!" I called, squinting through the orange gloom. "Where are you?"

I came upon a fallen log and saw a man leaning against it, clutching himself. Mud caked his shredded clothes. He wore no shoes.

"Oh, thank God!" he said, his eyes lighting up as I approached. "I lost the road. Do you know a way out?" The timid look on his face relieved me in a way. It felt good meeting someone who was just as scared as me.

"I'm sorry, but I'm also lost," I responded. "How'd you get here?"

I moved closer and sank down next to him. A bloody cut stretched across his arm.

"I…" he looked around apprehensively, "…I'm not sure. I woke up here. I mean, I woke up inside my own house. But I ran away, and everything was different. And there was this car accident..." he paused, then shook his head in defeat.

"Do you know how long you've been here?" I asked. With a motherly impulse that surprised both of us, I reached out and examined his injury. His eyes met mine. I saw oceans of sorrow in them.

"I don't know," he said. "It feels like days. But there's no sunrise, only dark. I haven't had to eat. I don't feel sleepy. It's like...time has just stopped."

"I imagine this is what being dead feels like," I replied.

His eyes darted all around the nearby woods, scanning for danger. When he was satisfied that nothing lurked nearby, he studied my face.

"You're so young," he said. "What are you doing out here all alone?"

I looked away and combed the dead leaves from my hair. I couldn't bear the sadness in his eyes. The soupy mist thickened around us.

"The last thing I remember was falling," I said, struggling to remember my English. I rarely used it anymore.

"Falling?" he asked.

I tried to explain to him what had happened, how I'd woken up here. I told him about the masquerade and the corpses attending it. I told him about the large figure that had chased me through the fog. As I spoke, the man's face paled, as though I'd just read him a death sentence.

"It hummed a song, didn't it?" he asked. His words barely left his mouth.

He read my response in my eyes, and dropped his head back against the log. His movements revealed another gash on his neck.

"Something's after you, isn't it?" I asked.

"I tried facing him," he murmured. "It was the first thing I tried. I've run from my demons before, when I was younger. I know you have to face them. But this...thing...he's different. He's hunting me, and no matter how far I run, he always finds me. It's why I'm out here in the first place."

"What is he?" I asked.

He looked at me and said simply, "The devil."

My mouth went dry.

"What does he want with you?" I asked.

He picked the dirt out of his fingers.

"He won't tell me," he replied. "Believe me, I've asked. He told me that he'd put me out of my misery soon. He says he can rescue me, but needs more time."

The man saw the puzzled look on my face.

I'm the mouse, you see. No fun if the cat kills me quick."

"I escaped it!" I said, trying to cheer him up. "There is hope."

He scoffed at me.

As we spoke, I considered the idea that just being around this man put me in danger. I had to make a decision soon. Should I abandon the only friend I'd made out here?

We talked for a few more minutes. The man told me about his mother's disappearance, and I told him about the creepy woman I'd met. I told him how she walked, and how she mumbled like a crazy person. The man seemed even more interested in her than in the monster that stalked him.

Suddenly, the man shot out his hand to quiet me.

A distinct humming radiated through the fog in short wisps, drawing nearer every second. The song reminded me of one of Mozart's eerily cheerful works.

My heart thundered in my chest. I glanced up and saw my new friend's eyes screaming in fear. We peered over the log and saw only the closest trees. We both waited, breathless.

Twigs snapped nearby.

"He's coming," the man choked out.

He grabbed my shoulders and spun me toward him. Despite how warm it was, his fingers felt like ice. I'd never seen anyone so afraid in all my life, and it terrified me. What unspeakable things this creature must have done to him.

He told me to run.

"No," I responded.

I couldn't understand why I felt obligated to stay. Maybe on some level, this moment paralleled my desire to stand with Gabriel as he fought for his life. Maybe it was a morbid fascination with what might happen.

"He'll kill you if you get in his way," he whispered, and again, implored me to leave.

The humming ceased, and we both froze in the silence.

Maybe it didn't hear us.

I held my breath. My hands ached. I realized I'd been gripping the man's arm so hard I was causing his wounds to bleed even more.

A voice came from behind us. It called out a name I couldn't quite hear, but it was the same throaty, brutal voice the crazy woman had spoken in.

"Please! Please, come back to me!" she cried. "I'm sorry! I'm all alone and afraid!"

"It's him!" the man pointed, as a large, burly shadow fell over the fog.

A fear surged through me then that I'd never known, even in all my time in this otherworldly place. The shadow was massive.

"Filthy rat!" she screamed. "Hope has *forsaken* you!" The shadow receded, and a slender woman emerged. She strode directly toward us.

Whatever this lady wanted, I remembered her disinterest in me. Maybe she'd be reluctant to harm a stranger. I scrambled between her and the man, wanting to prevent a confrontation.

"Leave him alone," I said. Her sallow eyes burned away the courage I'd mustered. The woman bounded up to me, stopped right at my face, and looked over me with outrage. Hideous scars now crisscrossed every inch of her face.

"Don't hurt her!" the man yelled behind me.

"Professor, come home!" she said to him. "We must leave *now*. I can still save you from this place!"

"Run!" the man pleaded with me. "Just get out of here!"

"Listen to the rat, child," the woman said to me with a smile. A maw of jagged teeth erupted from behind her lips. "Flee, or I'll rip this pretty mane off your head." She ran a gnarled hand through my hair. A thousand tingles danced across my neck. I shuddered in revulsion.

"Don't touch her," the man said in a threatening voice.

"You owe me in blood," she replied, pointing a finger at him.

The woman shoved me aside with little effort and strode up to her prey. She seized his head with both hands and ripped him from the ground. She pressed her mutilated face against his and inhaled.

"Fight her!" I yelled, not knowing what else to do. "Don't let her do this!"

The woman didn't seem to want to hurt the man, even as he struck her repeatedly. She lusted for something else. I watched as he writhed in her claws; the monstrous woman easily deflected or absorbed every blow while holding the man tightly in place. Eventually he went limp, and she threw him to the ground.

The man shrieked in pain as he collided with the stinking soil.

"Are you okay, little one?" she asked with mock sympathy. She poked a finger at me and whispered something into his ear. They argued for a moment, but the language and my terror smeared all the words together.

The woman bent down and grabbed the man's ankle, then looked right at me.

"Do you want to watch?" she asked. Her expression radiated a twisted joy.

I tried to speak, but my lips wouldn't move. My mouth hung open, unhinged with fear.

"Run!" the man screamed from down on the ground. "For God's sake, run for your life!" The woman turned and headed for the woods, dragging her victim behind her. Before they disappeared completely, I heard her cackling.

And then, something else caught my eye through the fog. A hunched figure wandered into view for a moment, then vanished.

Magnus.

"Hey!" I shouted, dashing toward him.

"It's okay, dear," he said, his voice wafting from the distance. His ghostly image faded from sight. "Everything's okay."

"Where are you?" I called out, spinning around and scanning the woods for him.

"Here."

I stumbled toward the sound. The fog grew thicker and thicker. It left me stumbling through an ocean of gray. The air became water, and I coughed and choked on it. I stumbled around with my hands out, on the verge of passing out.

Then, a blinding sword of light plunged through the trees and burned away the darkness.

CHAPTER 45

A sundrenched meadow lay before me. Lush trees encircled it, their trunks shivering and bending with each breath I took. The grass gleamed in a warm blanket of light, and neon colors radiated from every object. Birds fluttered overhead, cheering the day with their songs, and butterflies drifted whimsically from flower to flower. A lazy breeze set the entire scene dancing. Whenever it blew, it filled my lungs and electrified my senses. High above, the sun blazed with heavenly fury, chasing off the gloom that had swallowed the Southeast Woods.

The meadow felt old and sacred, far out of place in my familiar homeland. I stood like a marble statue, ensorcelled by beauty and wonder and pleasure, taking in every sight and sound and becoming a part of the landscape. All of nature's vibrant colors washed together in a fantastical blur, and it became clear to me that my perception was still wildly distorted.

After my shock waned, the memory of everything I'd been through returned. I looked over my shoulder to see where I'd come out of the woods, but a motionless wall of fog concealed it, obscuring the wretched things that lurked within. Dead tree limbs jutted out of the gray like desperate hands grasping for help.

I turned and wandered through the meadow, feeling my worries melt away. The sun doused me in its warmth like the embrace of a loved one. A small pond lay ahead, secluded by a ring of trees. The sound of its water lapping beckoned me closer.

I couldn't resist. I strolled to the edge of the pond and clumsily removed my shoes and socks. The moment I dipped my feet into the cool water, a fresh torrent of pleasure ran through me. My head spun in ecstasy. I hummed along with the birds and watched them as they jumped about on the branches, studying me. I touched the water and felt the urge to swim.

There was no one around. I took my clothes and put them in the nearby grass, then waded into the water.

Am I dead? I wondered. The thought drifted through my mind like a cloud through the sky, vanishing into the distance. For some reason, where I was, or how I got there, no longer mattered to me. I even began to laugh at all the things that had ever worried me.

My eyes were suddenly drawn to the dark part of the woods.

Did I just hear a voice?

I tossed my wet hair back and listened. The birds made it tough to hear anything else, but I was sure I'd heard a voice. The fog still loomed in the same place, right where the trees began to die, never drifting or receding.

"Hey!" someone cried out from far away. "Help me! Up here!" The voice echoed through the nightmarish woods and poured into the meadow, warped and dissonant.

"Up here! Please, help!"

It was the voice of a man, gruff and deep and unfamiliar. His plea struck my heart. He sounded terrified. I scanned the fog's veil, but found no one. Was it a trick? Was someone trying to lure me back in?

The voice never called out again. I couldn't tear my eyes away from that wicked place, but I believed that as long as I stayed out here in the light, nothing could harm me.

Then, someone spoke from behind me.

"That's the Nightmare."

The voice was familiar. Standing there at the pond's edge was the pianist, still in his mask and suit.

Realizing I was exposed, I dropped back into the water until it came up to my chin.

"Please," he said, chuckling, "there's no shame here. Look around you. It's a bit like Eden, isn't it?" His words sounded as melodious as his playing. It was hard not to like him; he had a warmth that made him feel like a bit like family.

The pianist reached his hand out. I watched him for a moment, and when I decided he meant me no harm, I waded over and reached back. My hand slipped through his, as if I'd tried to grab smoke. Then he pointed at my clothes. I moved to the shore and picked them up, never taking my eyes off him.

"You touched me before," I said. "At the party. Why can't you do it now?"

"You're leaving," he replied. I had no idea what he meant.

"What are you doing here?" I asked. I began to dress, still sopping wet. He ignored the question.

"You've found your way out," he said. "Well, out of the Nightmare, I should say. Yet you're still here."

"How'd you find me?" I pressed, walking over to him. "Have you been following me?"

The pianist smiled, and looked to the sky, searching for the right words.

"I didn't need to."

"I don't understand," I said.

He sat down in the grass and gazed out over the pond. I sat beside him, still peering at his mask with curiosity.

"The Nightmare isn't a place," he began. "You can't find it or run away from it. It's sort of...an experience. It exists beyond the space and time you live in. It's a flicker of a moment, and an eternity. A home to people with scars on their souls."

"Like the people at the dinner party?" I replied.

"Victims, yes," he said.

"Something can't last a moment and an eternity," I said.

The pianist laughed. His white mask glinted in the sunlight.

"What not? Because that sort of thing doesn't exist in your world? How similar is this place to your world anyway?" He moved his fingers across the grass. It changed colors in response to his touch: blue to yellow to red, then back to green. "Memories are like that too."

I reached over to touch his hand, but again I was unable. My fingers simply met with the grass. Its color rippled.

"What do you mean by 'victims'?"

The pianist drew a sharp breath.

"The noises you've heard a few times today – the rumbles and screeches in the distance – do you remember?"

"Of course," I said, recalling the awful sounds.

"They're the sounds of metal creatures, crawling and flying. Built for the purpose of destruction." His emerald gaze lanced through me.

"Planes and tanks?" I asked. I'd seen photographs of war machines in my father's newspaper, but never in real life.

"The roaring you hear is the sound of the greatest monster the world will ever know," he continued. "It will level cities and end millions of lives. Its shadow will fall on all of us, and it's already begun. Those party guests were the some of the first who quenched this monster's hunger." He tapped his cheek with a finger.

"Their skin…those masks," I said, "they were all dead?"

"Yes," he answered. "Soldiers, civilians, all from different parts of the world. All victims of the war. But not all who walk in the Nightmare are dead."

My heart fluttered at the idea that I was still alive and breathing. I remembered my body. I remembered Millie. I thought of my parents, and felt the ache in my heart returning.

"Then why am I here? And why'd I get to leave?" I pointed at the fog.

The pianist again fell silent, searching for a way to explain his world to me.

"We come here to learn from our pain," he said. "The Nightmare is the realm between awake and asleep, between reality and dream. And to unweave it is to find the way out."

"Nightmare," I echoed, pouring over my experiences here.

"What are you learning here?" he asked. "It unravels differently for everyone."

I considered his question for a moment, but only thought up more of my own.

"How do you know all this?"

"I had to figure it out myself."

"Then why are you still here?"

"I'm…caught up here," he said hesitantly, "…waiting to

be set free." He looked away.

"How?"

The pianist sighed.

"Did you die in the war too?" I pressed.

"No," he said. "I got sick."

"How long have you been here?" I asked.

He swallowed.

"A few days, a few years. I don't really know."

I shrugged in confusion.

"I need to tell you something," the pianist said, leaning in closer. "And I need you to hear me."

I nodded.

"When you leave this place," he said, "the real nightmare will begin."

Goosebumps popped up all over my arms. I imagined the foggy darkness of the Southeast Woods reaching out and covering my home, my town, and everyone I'd ever loved.

"Soon it'll be up to you to lead your family," he said. "To be strong for them. They'll fall apart without you. I've seen it."

I didn't blink. I just stared at him.

"And to complicate things," he continued, "the rest of the world is about to fall apart too. That shrieking beast you heard moves slowly, but it'll be here, in your land, even in your town soon enough."

"What's going to happen to my family?" I asked, terrified of the answer.

"Gabriel is dying," he replied. His expressionless mask made the words feel like a slap in the face.

Tears forced their way up and blurred my vision.

"How do know about Gabriel?" I said, trying to stifle the whimpers I felt lining up on my lips.

The pianist straightened his vest and looked around, then back to me.

"You'd be surprised what you can learn from other people's nightmares," he replied. He reached out to put a hand on my shoulder, but then receded. "I'm sorry, dear. I'm so sorry. Gabriel will die."

It suddenly felt like the air had rushed out of the meadow. I couldn't move or think or breathe.

"You already know this," he added, "and it tears you apart. It haunts your dreams, and forces you to stand at the edge of the world of the Nightmare. You've peered into it before. But now, you're here."

The tears wandered down my cheeks. My hands felt numb. The pianist's voice softened.

"I believe that even with your despair for Gabriel, you weren't damaged enough to fully enter this world," he said. "But then you did something. Something brought you here, artificially. Temporarily."

I brushed my wet hair back and looked at the sky. Chubby clouds hung on the blue and seemed to breathe in and out. All around me, the forest wiggled, and the meadow danced.

"I ate a mushroom," I replied. "Stole it from a hermit. I'm...an idiot."

The pianist let out a hearty laugh. His smile was contagious, and I felt one spread across my face. I laughed and cried at the same time. My face was an ugly mess.

Again, he paused, deep in thought.

"And so you came," he said, "to contend with your fear of losing Gabriel. It was just enough to send you over the edge. And now the poison is thinning in your veins, so the Nightmare's hold on you is weakening... which is why you're *here*." He opened his arms and beheld the pond before us.

"You're floating back down," the pianist said. "Back home."

I remained silent, baffled by everything he'd told me. A million thoughts swirled in my mind, but like the colors that rippled in the grass, they went in every direction and were too quick to follow. To perplex me further, the pianist added,

"Gabriel's freedom is in your hands."

The pianist reached up and removed his mask. I braced myself for a gruesome sight.

His face had not putrefied like the other faces I'd seen at the party. It was the face of a young man, healthy and full of life.

Perky cheekbones rose over a warm smile, and a strong chin and brow framed his features. His eyes were like chips of jade, their shapes unmistakable. I'd know them anywhere, even when set in a face I did not recognize.

They were the eyes of my little brother.

CHAPTER 46

"How…how can…" I stuttered.

"Hello sister," he said, gentle as a lamb.

The paltry dams at my tear ducts broke again, and a waterfall came gushing down.

"I told you," he said, "Time is irrelevant here. Two people who dream a thousand years apart can be united here. That lonely man you met, and the creature who followed him – I can only imagine where they came from."

Gabriel stood up. I jumped to my feet, still entranced by his face. I couldn't stop looking at it. He took a step closer to me.

"I've aged here," he said. "I remember you looking down on me in my cradle… it feels so long ago. I've been here for an eternity, and all I can think of is death and escape."

"I was with you this morning," I replied, my voice breaking with sorrow. "I came here to help you!"

"But this is your dream," he went on, ignoring my protest. "You see me now the way you imagined me all grown up. I wonder, if Mom and Dad were here, would I look any different?"

"Gabriel," I said, reaching out to touch his face. They slipped through him.

"No," he said flatly. "Not any more than everything else you've created here. Gabriel is all around you. You saw his withering body in the dying trees. His will to live, those people in the sand. His illness—"

"The fungus," I interrupted.

"But his spirit lives!" he boomed. "Can you feel it? The breeze, the birds that serenade you – his innocence remains, no matter the ravages of the Nightmare."

I looked around at the grove.

"He saw all these things whenever I took him outside," I said. "Is this how he feels for us? For his family?"

"Especially for his sister," the pianist replied.

I smiled.

"It is a terrible thing," he said, "to be bound here forever, after the body passes on. Gabriel will be trapped here like the guests at the party. But...you can still save him."

"How?" I asked. The thought of my brother becoming one of those wretched things was unbearable.

"Let him go," the pianist said. "He's imprisoned here because he doesn't want to leave you. But he's too far gone to come back. You and your parents bind him to this place, depriving him of the blessing of death."

"Let him go," I said to myself. The words stung, but they felt like the truth.

"You *must*," the pianist stressed. "Gabriel has little time left."

I sat back down, clutching myself. The pianist's words pulled me in one direction, and my reluctance to say goodbye pulled in the other.

"Why does it have to be him?" I asked. "Why someone so young?"

The pianist crouched in front of me and looked into my eyes.

"You forget all he's done," he said. "Little Gabriel was an unexpected surprise, that's for sure. But he united your family on the day he was born. Now leaves you together, stronger. Maybe he's just an infant, but he did something remarkable. He taught you about love and responsibility, didn't he? And devotion to your family?"

I smiled and nodded.

"He did."

Gabriel didn't just teach me how much I could love a person. He taught me how much my parents loved their children. I never got sick, so I never saw how easily their hearts broke.

"That's pretty amazing for a baby," the pianist said.

I nodded.

"And you vowed to save him, didn't you?"

I nodded again, and sniffled.

"Help him by loving him," the pianist said, "and by releasing him. Don't be afraid. Celebrate his life and his impact on yours. Cherish his memory, and be thankful he was here, however short his stay."

I sat in silence for a while, contemplating everything. The world fell still. The clouds departed from the sky and left the bright blue uninterrupted.

It was simple. I had no choice. I knew what I had to do.

"I'd do anything for him," I said.

And with that, the pianist faded away. When I looked up again, he was gone, and a lively breeze came rushing through the meadow. It blew life into the earth and set everything shivering and dancing again.

If it meant that Gabriel would never have to set foot in the Nightmare again, I could let him go.

CHAPTER 47

I sat there by the pond for a while. The sun moved to the horizon, casting everything in orange light. All around me, fireflies twinkled. The trees did not bend and sway as they had before, and the exaggerated manner in which colors had glowed seemed to wane with each passing minute.

With a calmness I'd not felt in months, I hummed what I could remember of the birdsongs that had faded away. I closed my eyes to play out the final scenes of my brother's life in my head. I held him in my arms, I kissed his face, I talked to him. I saw the glimmer in his eyes, heard his little coos, and watched him fall asleep. It was as if no harm had ever come to him, as if none of this had ever happened. I hugged him goodbye.

A noise interrupted my reflections.

Leaves rustled behind me. Footsteps crunched – fast and light.

I didn't see who approached until he blew right past me: a little boy, maybe only four or five years old. He scurried so fast I couldn't make out his features. He'd come from beyond the bright woods beyond the meadow, and was heading straight toward the foggy wall of the Nightmare.

His sudden entrance left me frozen and unable to react. As he passed into the embrace of the soupy darkness, I collected myself enough to cry out,

"No! Wait, come back! Don't go in there!"

It was too late. The fog swallowed him up.

"Shit!" I yelled. I thought about letting him go, but Gabriel returned to my mind. I gathered my courage and broke into full sprint after him, trying not to imagine what cruel fate he'd meet there.

Into the fog I ran, but it slowed me, and grew thick around my body. I pressed on blindly, choking and wheezing on the heavy moisture. In a few more steps, the wet feeling in my lungs turned to fire. The fog became smoke, and my legs collapsed beneath me. I was fading away again. A gale of boyish screams echoed through the dark, and then I lost consciousness.

Cool air washed into my lungs and awakened me.

I had no sight for a few moments, but the gentle songs of crickets wafted on the breeze. My skin felt cool against the damp grass, and the spring air smelled fresh. I felt a long, wet tongue slide across my cheek and nose, and immediately recognized it. As my vision returned, a blurry, overjoyed Millie bounced up and down beside me. She barked and sniffed and wagged her tail furiously. I threw my arms around her.

"Millie!" I yelled. She licked my face. The slobber didn't bother me at all.

When I looked up, a million stars glittered in the sky. Familiar, healthy trees loomed overhead, devoid of the horrid fungus that once clung to their branches. Best of all, no fog crept through the woods. I didn't hear the cries of the damned, or the growls of monsters. I was back in the familiar grove at the edge of the Southeast Woods. The Far Fork lay just ahead.

I threw the blanket off and stood up. Relief flooded through me when I saw that my body was not left behind. My journey of terror and illumination seemed to be over, and I took off running into the night. Millie raced just ahead of me. She knew the way home.

CHAPTER 48

It took little time to get back home. I didn't stop for a single moment to catch my breath. I didn't care if I dropped dead on my doorstep. I wanted to see my family again. I had to see Gabriel one more time.

We leaped over little stone walls and crossed through moonlit fields. When we reached the top of a grassy hill, I could see our cottage in the distance, nestled against the woods at the edge of a little meadow. Warm yellow light glowed from inside. My parents were still awake. I dashed toward my house in a frenzy of tears and laughter.

I threw the front door open, nearly breaking it in half as I did.

"Mom? Dad?"

I caught my breath. My eyes adjusted to the bright light.

My mother sat motionless in her chair with a handkerchief and a vacant gaze. My father was in the kitchen, tending to the cuts and bruises of a little boy – the same boy that had run past me in the meadow. When our eyes met, I knew he'd seen the Nightmare too.

"I found him outside," my father said without looking at me. "He speaks Polish, but he can hardly talk. Poor thing is petrified. I can only understand a few words he says, but none of it makes any sense. He—"

"Gabriel is dead," my mother interrupted.

A tear dripped off her cheek onto the floor. I stared at the little pool it left on the wood, unable to look into my mother's eyes. My heart crumpled like a piece of paper.

My father walked over and gave me a big hug, then said,

"All this nonsense, all this chaos. Have you heard what's

happening? What they're doing? The riots…even the police! And the filth they're trying to teach you in school! This whole country has lost its mind. Your mother's finally convinced me. She was right all along."

I looked up at him, confused and afraid, but said nothing. He clutched me by the arms and gazed into me.

"Ready some clothes, Anja. Tomorrow we're leaving Germany."

PART **IV**

I'm sometimes weak, but in the end, our memories make me strong.
You know that I'll still love you so, however long you're gone.

CHAPTER 49

My name is David Petri Cadler, and this memoir is to serve as a window into my final thoughts, should I decide to take my own life. I don't know for whom I write these words, nor who would care to read them, but I want someone to know what happened. I want someone to know what was done to me.

I haven't written in years. It's a shame that I've only started up again while on the run from the ghosts of my past. I've been sleeping in seedy motels (or trying to sleep anyway), on the couches of friends I no longer deserve, and even in my car. I've been running all my life, and I'm fed up with it. The time has come face my demons. Perhaps I should begin my story where they were born – in my dreams.

When I was little, my mother used to tell me Yiddish and Hebrew folktales at bedtime. I was especially fond of the mythological creatures: the Leviathan, the Qliphoth, the Dybbuk. But my favorite tale, ironically, was the one that always gave me nightmares: the story of Rabbi Loew and his experiment with a golem built from clay. The rabbi's massive creation broke away from his control and terrorized the local townspeople. For years, the expressionless monster pursued me in my dreams. But I never found out what it wanted to do to me. Right before it could snatch me up, I'd be jolted awake by my own screams.

My father always chastised my mother for filling my head with "that mythical nonsense," but I would beg for more of it each night. Because of my obsession with fear, I'd spend countless nights trying to evade the nightly grasp of sleep, and with it, all the horrible creatures my imagination could conjure.

One night, however, I saw those creatures while I was

awake. I was standing in the kitchen, begging my mother for another story from the Talmud. After enough prodding, she reluctantly agreed and set off to prepare me for bed. I said goodnight to my father, who was sitting in the living room, reading the newspapers with visible disgust, as he did every night. Although he wore a gloomy expression in nearly all of my memories, this evening's was especially morbid.

As I stood in the kitchen, a noise came from outside. As long as I live, I'll never forget that sound: boots – hundreds of boots – clomping down the road outside my home, smacking and splashing in the rain. All three of us fell silent. My mother told me to wait in the kitchen, and then joined my father at the living room window.

The front door to our house flew open with a deafening crash. A moment later, I heard my mother's cries and my father's shouting. I ran to the hallway, but as I rounded the corner, I saw the manifestation of my darkest dreams. There, lumbering in from the storm, were three massive entities. I immediately recognized them as golems.

They looked exactly as I'd imagined them in my nightmares. The creatures towered over my parents and seized them by their throats. One of them easily lifted my mother off her feet and gazed blankly into her eyes.

They didn't spot me at first, but as I turned to flee, I gave myself away. One of the golems hurtled after me, knocking over a vase and barreling down the hall like a wild bull. I darted up the stairs and hurried into my parents' bedroom. There, I slammed the door and hid myself as best I could in my father's oak wardrobe. My pursuer effortlessly splintered the door with a kick and ripped open the wardrobe. It rifled through my father's hanging clothes until its cold hands came upon me, then it ripped me out from my hiding place.

I was a worm in the golem's death clutch. I went limp and squeezed my eyes shut, awaiting the end. After a few uneventful seconds, I risked a peek at the creature. Then, something curious happened.

It studied me briefly, and although its face was obscured in the gloom, I could feel my gaze being returned to me. The golem hoisted me up under its massive arm, trotted to the large window on the other side of the bed, and quietly pushed it open. To my amazement, the golem carefully lowered me out the window, dropping me onto the grass below. As I lay there in pain, I looked up at the window, and saw the being watching me from the dark. I still couldn't make out its face, and I couldn't understand why this shadowy thing had crawled out of my nightmares to spare my life.

I regained my senses just in time to hear more screams coming from the front yard. The golems dragged my parents out of the house. They had come to take us away. I stood up on my cold, bare feet, and ran full-sprint into the woods behind my house. In a few moments I was engulfed in a sanctuary of pitch black, and although I didn't know where I was going, I did not stop running.

I came upon a stream and cut my feet on its rocks while crossing it. Only then did I realize how exhausted I was. My pulse boomed in my head, my ears rang, my lungs burned. I stood there on the wet bank, trying to figure out what to do.

The world began to spin around me and withdrew from my grasp. I suddenly didn't feel so cold, or so afraid, or so agonized by my wounds. I felt nothing. The last thing I remember was the sound of my little body smacking the mud.

I don't know how long I slept.

Classical music drifted around in the musty air, beckoning me awake. The mud that had swaddled me was now dry and cracked, caking half my body and clinging to my night clothes. Pins of faint light pierced the canopy of the thicket I laid in. Whether it was dusk or dawn, I couldn't tell.

"Mamma?" I called out.

Nobody answered me. Nobody except distant animals, who croaked and sang dreary melodies.

I stood up and tried to brush off the dried mud.

Where am I?

All around me, the forest heaved and swayed with unnatural life. The spindly fingers of the trees wiggled and slithered above me. Their trunks throbbed, like they were drawing in huge breaths and blowing them out into the sky, causing a hot breeze to shake their leaves. Now and then, a tormented animal's cry echoed through the woods. The stream was now bone-dry, and so was the mud along its banks.

I'd never been so afraid. I couldn't remember where I was or how I'd gotten there. I didn't remember the golems, or what had happened to my parents. Instead, I just sobbed and wandered around, looking for my mom.

The forest seemed intent on doing everything it could to hinder my steps. It tripped me with branches and roots, and sent shrieking bats and crows overhead each time I called out for help. The music echoed through the trees in swells, but it was impossible to follow. Each time I headed toward the noise, it either fell silent or came from another direction. I heard jovial laughter and clinking glasses, the soundtrack to a fancy dinner party. But each time I tried to chase them, the sounds faded like ghosts in the mist.

As I waded through the forest, the darkness grew. The trees vanished with the light, and the world became a black hole that swallowed me up. I could no longer see, so I felt my way around. Everything I touched felt unnaturally warm, and the moss beneath my feet smelled rotten. A jutting root caught my foot and sent me careening to the ground.

I cried hard and loud. My pants were ripped, my feet were bleeding, and worst of all, I was lost. I curled up into a ball, praying that by the grace of God, my mother would come running out of the darkness and sweep me up in her arms.

But then I saw a light.

A dim glow drifted from up ahead. I stood up. It was a single, silver ray of moonlight, and it fell on the ground next to me. I followed it. I could barely see anything by it, but it was just enough to take me to the edge of the forest. As I approached the tree line, I realized I'd found my way back to the stream.

While pondering how I'd managed to walk in a big circle,

a cacophony erupted somewhere nearby.

Screams.

Not frightened screams, but angry ones, deep and hoarse. They didn't sound like people. The words were indecipherable, as if spoken underwater. I suddenly remembered the golems and imagined them calling out to each other, searching the woods for me.

I dropped to my belly and cowered there beside the bank, praying I wouldn't be found. I prayed the way my mother had taught me.

They were all around me. Dozens of them. I couldn't see them, but I could hear their huge feet as they stamped through the dirt and leaves. They shouted to each other and surrounded me, scouring the woods to find the pitiful child who'd escaped.

I held my breath so long my head spun. My heart flitted in my chest like a caged hummingbird. As the pack moved away from me, I crouched behind a fallen log, hiding as best I could. I stayed put until I couldn't hear them at all.

I'm not exactly sure when that moment came. I fell into a dreamless sleep.

CHAPTER 50

When I awoke, the sun was shining down on me. Puffy clouds meandered across the sky, and birdsongs filled the air. It must have been midday. My empty house sat a few dozen steps away. Some of its windows had been smashed, and many of our belongings lay strewn across the lawn.

I decided to look for help instead of returning home. I climbed up the far side of the stream bank and found a trail that led through the woods. The closest houses outside of my neighborhood were a few minutes' walk southeast, so I headed in that direction. I knew of a farm somewhere out there too; my parents had taken me there a few times for dinner. I suspected those folks might know what was going on.

I followed the path for a minute or so, passing under gigantic trees as I did. Little streams trickled all around me. Frogs and butterflies darted here and there, and birds warned each other of my presence from high above. I might have reveled in the serenity, but the thought of my parents and the monsters who took them gnawed at my mind.

Leaves crunched behind me.

I whirled around.

A huge figure stood there in the distance, staring at me from between two trees.

It was one of them.

The golem stuck its gray arm out and pointed a finger at me. It shouted something, but the words were muffled by the stone mask it wore over its face. Or maybe the stone was its face.

I screamed. It leaped over a dead tree and bounded through the stream, its giant feet sending water spraying in all directions. As I'd practiced so many times in my nightmares, I turned and fled as fast as I could, racing up the trail toward the sunny pastures on the other side.

Branches flew past my head as I ducked beneath them. I jumped over little brooks and cut between trees, but my tiny body was no match for the golem, and the cuts on my feet slowed me.

A hundred paces away, the trees opened up to a bright meadow. And there, where the woods met the field, stood a man in a brown coat. His face was full of rage, and his hands clutched a rifle. I nearly fell over trying to stop in my tracks. He sank down, took the gun in one hand, and beckoned me with the other.

I dashed toward him, tears blurring my sight. He called out in an unfamiliar language. I could hear the golem just behind me, panting like a hungry wolf.

The man aimed his rifle, and as I passed by him, the shot went off like a bomb. Its thunder shook the forest and sent birds flying in all directions. As the explosion faded into the distance, dead silence echoed back. Not a single sound came out of those woods for minutes. I couldn't hear the golem anymore.

I fell to the ground, gasping for air through a cascade of tears and snot. The man in the brown coat approached, looked over my cuts with his emerald-green eyes, and picked me up. He said something to me that I couldn't understand and placed me on his shoulders. We headed into the sunny field.

CHAPTER 51

Our walk was a solemn one. The man's footsteps crunched against the dirt path, and a breeze pushed the golden wheat around. No words were spoken. In the distance, the forest wrapped around the fields and swallowed them up on the other side. Behind it, the blue sky climbed up to infinity.

We came to a cottage that rested against the edge of the woods. It was warm and inviting, a lot like my house. I wondered if the golems had found this place too. The man set me down on my feet and patted me on the head, again speaking to me. Whatever he told me was very important; I could tell by the look in his eyes. But his words were lost to history, and I know I'll never get them back.

As we walked up to the door, a woman opened it from inside. She was crying and babbling in their language. In her arms was a baby wrapped in a white blanket. The man set his rifle down and rushed past me to examine the child. He began to hyperventilate, and paced around on the porch, pulling his hair with his fingers. He rocked himself back and forth, then turned and looked at me. His eyes welled with tears. I already understood.

"Gabriel," he cried. *"Warum? Warum, Gott?"*

We headed inside. The woman put the baby back inside a wooden crib and covered it with the blanket. The man wrapped his arms around his wife, kissing the side of her head and holding her close. They both sobbed. I cried too.

The hours passed. The man tended to my wounds with a wet cloth and a bottle of stinging liquid, which he occasionally drank from. He and the woman bickered, probably about what to do with me. The man kept shouting and motioning an open

Felix Blackwell

hand at me, probably asking, "What else are we going to do with him? Leave him out there?" The woman just kept crying.

Suddenly, the front door flew open, silencing their argument. I nearly jumped out of my skin, terrified that the golems had found me. To my relief, a disheveled-looking girl stumbled in, followed by a big furry dog. She halted at the sight of me, and her eyes darted back and forth from me to the couple. Her eyes were the same bright green color as the man's.

The following night, a car arrived at the cottage. The family loaded a few suitcases and we all squeezed inside. We stopped at my house and found it still vacated, and the woman tried to explain something to me. I knew my parents had been taken, but I couldn't understand why.

We stuck to back roads. For most of the drive, I could see only the stars. As the road climbed and descended the hills, I could make out lights in the distance – small towns like my own, and huge cities, places I'd never been. The man pointed at each of them and told me its name. I couldn't even pronounce them back to him.

The man reminded me of my father. He was loving and protective, and his eyes conveyed the heaviness in his heart. It was obvious how much he cared for his family, and he extended that care to me, a strange runaway. He comforted me throughout the trip; I wondered if I reminded him of the baby he'd buried hours before. Only by listening closely to the family's conversations did I learn that the man's name was Dietmar. I can't recall the names of the wife and daughter, but they all learned mine.

We boarded a train and travelled for many hours. Late the next morning, we arrived at a dock. I'd never seen a real ship before, and they were bigger than my tiny brain could have imagined. We waited a whole day to board. I passed the time watching the ships pull in and out of port, wondering if I'd ever see my mom again. Back then, I didn't know I was looking at warships.

At this point, my story becomes even more confusing. We

crossed the sea to a faraway place, then boarded another train. We arrived in a small town, but as we exited the train, we were stopped by soldiers and police. Dietmar had an argument with the men. He showed them a mess of papers, but they kept pointing at me. One of the soldiers went to grab me, but Dietmar shoved him away and stepped in front of me. Then things got ugly.

Two soldiers attacked him. One tackled him to the ground and the other beat him with the butt of his rifle. Dietmar's wife and daughter began screaming and rushed to his aid, but they too were seized. Another soldier grabbed me and picked me up. I tried to fight against his grip, but he hauled me away.

Dietmar shouted something to me as he disappeared from sight.

"Pine Rest, David!" he said. "Pine Rest!"

He shouted it a dozen times. I swore to myself I'd never forget those words, even though I didn't understand what they meant.

I was brought to a huge building. Several people talked to me until they finally determined what language I spoke. A man with a thick moustache and little brown eyes told me, in broken sentences, that they'd be "sending me back home." I tried to tell him what had happened, but he either could not understand or refused to listen.

"Home," he kept saying. "You're going home."

I was loaded onto another train, then a ship, and a week later, I arrived wherever they thought "home" was. I spent the next eight years there, a thousand miles away from Dietmar and his family. I never saw my own parents again.

Those eight years were important. They are a tale worth telling, and I will tell it. But before I do, I want to skip ahead and explain how I defeated the golems. I want to tell the story of how I met Trent Cadler.

CHAPTER 52

I was four years old when I first traveled to Pine Rest, and twelve when I finally returned. I still hadn't learned a word of English, but nothing was going to stop me from finding Dietmar – the man who'd saved my life.

The nightmares had come back. For years I'd been free of them, but the moment I set foot in Pine Rest again, they resurfaced in my sleep. The line between reality and the dream world blurred more with each passing night. I couldn't tell what was real anymore.

Then the worst night came. It was pouring outside; the rain was heavy even for England. Its spatter against the ground outside reminded me of boots. It conjured thousands of golems, stomping around in the darkness of my mind, searching for children to snatch.

I cowered in the rickety old bed they'd given me. The beds to my left and right were empty. Only a few children remained in the orphanage now, and none of them liked me. Due to my incessant night terrors and the language barrier, nobody bothered reaching out to me, so I kept to myself as much as I could. Lightning crashed outside every few minutes and lit up the huge stone room, illuminating stained-glass images of Jesus and the saints as they glared down at me. We were housed in an old church on a hill above the town.

My sweat soaked the dirty mattress. My heart thrummed in my chest. I knew that sleep was drawing near, and with it, the monsters that lurked on the other side. In my desperation, I recited the prayers I'd learned from my mother, but the thunder roared with such power I was certain God couldn't hear me.

It must have been the constant drone of water that lulled

me to the edge of sleep. I blinked my bleary eyes, struggling against the darkness that sucked me in. My body felt heavy and numb. The lightning crashed relentlessly.

Then the room changed.

I could barely see, but whenever the bolts struck outside, they revealed a gruesome scene in the church. The colors of the windows smeared together, and the heavenly saints had melted into wicked mockeries of themselves. Beds had become malformed and crooked. Sheets were stained in rancid fluids. The candelabras at each corner of the room drooped and wilted like dying flowers.

And then, they came.

The sound of raindrops exploding against the stone walls swelled and became the sound of boots pounding the old wooden floors. All around me, I heard the golems rifling through wardrobes and ripping doors from their hinges. It was only a matter of time until they broke into our sleeping quarters and found me.

I threw the sheets from my body and leaped out of bed, scampering toward the bathroom to hide. I darted past the other children, who slept blissfully in their rotten beds. My bare feet hardly made a sound on the floor as I moved. Maybe I had a chance. Maybe the golems wouldn't hear me.

Clunk! Clunk! Clunk!

A boot smashed against the bedroom door. I slid into the bathroom and closed the door behind me. They'd found me. They knew I was here. The world spun, and the room shrank down on me. I tried to look for something to hide behind. Whatever strange force had warped the bedroom had done the same to the toilets and sinks in here.

The window.

I climbed up onto a crooked toilet to reach it.

The bedroom door burst open. Its metal knob pinged against the stone wall as it swung. The creatures stormed in.

I threw my weight against the window frame, trying to dislodge whatever had jammed it. The creatures lumbered straight for the bathroom. The sound of beds being thrown around echoed throughout the building. Children screamed and whimpered.

The window wouldn't budge.

I looked outside into the storm, then over my shoulder. A golem lurched into the bathroom, barely fitting through the door frame. It was impossible to tell if its gray skin was really skin at all – it looked more like cement. A slab of clay or stone covered its face, leaving the golem without any identity at all. It looked exactly like the others in every way.

Despite its lack of eyes, the creature spotted me. A deep and rumbling groan escaped from somewhere inside its head, and came at me, intent on grabbing my little body with its bone-crushing hands. Electrified with fright, I balled my fist and smashed it through the window. Little shards dove into my knuckles, and my scream attracted more golems to the door. I clambered out the window and fell six feet to the asphalt below. The golem thrust a huge arm through the window after me, grabbing at the air.

No one could hear me now. An endless waterfall of rain poured down from the sky and crashed all around me. Thunder cracked and rolled across the night, masking the sounds of my footsteps and sobs.

The narrow road out of the orphanage snaked down the hill into the woods. The lights of a small town twinkled nearby. I had no idea where to go; Pine Rest was totally foreign to me. All of the signs were gibberish to me.

I sprinted down the hill. Nothing followed me.

The road was empty and seemed to go on forever. Street lights flickered as I passed beneath them, but they lit my way well enough. From the road, In the distance, the town was flanked on all sides by forested hills, and high above, a patch of storm clouds loomed. At the town's center stood a huge, well-lit building. New energy coursed through me. People would be awake there. Lights would be on, and I wouldn't have to be alone.

As I crossed an overpass, I found a narrow metal staircase leading down to the city streets. The storm intensified, pelting my face with rain and blinding me. The sound of boots swelled behind me. It sounded like a hundred golems jogging in unison.

Time to go.

I bolted down the stairs, not anticipating how slick they'd be. The moment my feet slid out from beneath me, I remembered what it felt like to walk across a frozen pond – a feat almost impossible to do with any grace. Before the thought dissipated from my mind, I smacked hard on the steps and tumbled. My elbow caught the first impact, then my side. A sickening pop resounded as my rib cage connected with the metal. It probably would have hurt too, if the final stop hadn't knocked me out completely.

I must have lain there for some time, because when I regained consciousness, the rain had lulled. The overpass spun in dizzy circles up above. The sound of marching golems grew louder.

Get up.

I tried to force myself up with both hands, but my fiery pain seared across arm. I tried to scream, but bruised or broken ribs silenced my voice. I drew only shallow breaths, and the air came with such labor that I nearly blacked out again.

An image of Dietmar and his lovely family came to me then: his aging face streaked with worry, his mournful eyes looking onto me with pity. I saw him there in my mind, clutching his wife and daughter, mouthing something to me.

Pine Rest, David.

Somehow, I found the strength to get up. With the last of my energy, I hobbled across the empty street, leaning against the sides of buildings for support. The well-lit building was so far in the distance I knew I'd probably give out before getting there. I inched along, blood trickled down my neck. The back of my head swelled.

The world spun like a top. The ground swayed and rolled. My legs wobbled as I moved, and a numb feeling crept down my neck and spread across my back. It crept toward my legs, and everything went tingly, like my limbs were asleep.

I stumbled and fell against a parked car. As I pushed myself away from it, I noticed a horn and light on its hood.

Police car, I realized.

I looked past it. More of them lined the parking lot in front of a gloomy old building with big double doors. I staggered up the steps. The rain returned with force, and lightning blasted a nearby street light. Half of the lights on the entire block went out. With all of my might, I pushed against the doors. They opened with a tremendous groan.

It was dark inside, but I heard people running around and talking. I took a few steps into the building, my wet feet slapping on the floor. A figure emerged.

He was a huge man, taller than six feet with a muscular physique. He was almost as big as a golem. His hand flashed to the pistol at his hip, and his other hand shot out in a *halt-right-there* gesture. He yelled something I couldn't understand. The power in his voice hit me like a tidal wave. I froze.

Lightning crashed nearby and lit up the department. A terrified woman stood at a desk a few feet away, and another man behind her. They vanished into the dark a second later, and a numbing cold swept across my limbs. I slumped over like a scarecrow without a pike.

I resigned myself to the sting of the hard floor, but someone caught me.

CHAPTER 53

"Get up, get up," someone whispered in the dark.

My eyelids felt like they'd been glued shut.

"We don't have much time," he said. His accent was unlike any I'd heard before.

A gentle hand gripped my shoulder.

My eyes cracked open.

A blurry image of a man in a white coat came into view. He was looking over me, but the lamp dangling above his head cast his face in shadow. Its harsh beam did little to chase away the darkness from the rest of the room.

"Good," he said. "Up, up. Come on now."

His hand found its way around my back and pulled me forward. Blue sheets slid off me as I moved. The man propped my weak form against his chest. The lamp's bulb flickered.

I was in what looked like a hospital. A lone window sat on the wall, crisscrossed with metal bars to prevent escape. A bright, moving light filtered in from outside the glass, perhaps from a spotlight or distant lighthouse.

"Can you walk?" the man asked. He was old, judging by the wear in his voice.

"What...h..." I tried to speak, but my brain couldn't put together the words.

He patted my back.

"Don't worry, my boy," he said. "I'll take care of it."

The lamp buzzed and brightened suddenly, banishing the darkness around us.

Now I could see the man better – he was a doctor. Wild gray hair stuck out all over his head, and blue eyes examined me through a pair of cracked glasses. I saw the name emblazoned on his medical jacket, but I couldn't read it.

"How'd I get here?" I finally managed to say.

The doctor spun around, me in his arms, and poked his head into the hallway. He hastily retreated and put me back down on the bed.

"Just a moment," he said, returning to the door and listening carefully. He clutched the knob tight, ready to stop someone from trying to enter.

Beside the bed sat an empty chair.

If I still had a mother, she'd be sitting right there, I thought.

The doctor looked at me and straightened his coat.

"A police officer," he said.

"What?" I asked.

"The man who brought you here," he explained. "A detective, actually."

I suddenly remembered being inside the Pine Rest Police Department. I remembered the look on the big man's face. I thought I remembered him dashing to my rescue as I blacked out…but I wasn't sure.

"Where is he?" I asked.

The doctor looked at the empty chair and brushed his hair back.

"Oh, he'll be here any minute now, I expect," he said. "But we don't have time to wait."

After a few moments, the doctor threw the door open and hurried back to the bed. He hoisted me up in his arms and stepped out into the hall.

It was dark.

Water dripped somewhere off in the distance. The sound echoed on forever, filling every black corridor of this place with ominous noise. The doctor's footsteps filled the empty spaces. The air smelled of wet clay and stone.

"What is this place?" I whispered.

"The medical wing," he responded.

We shuffled past arrays of doors. A barred gate awaited us at the end of the hall. On the other side, a dim light popped on and off, throwing long shadows in every direction.

"The medical wing of what?" I asked, clutching the doctor a little tighter.

He plopped me down on my feet and fished through his jacket for a key. My legs wobbled a bit, but I stood. My bare feet immediately registered the unusual warmth of the ground. My arm didn't hurt anymore, and my ribs felt fine.

The overhead lights crackled and buzzed, briefly illuminating a door to the right side of the gate. I looked up at it.

The silhouette of a person's head loomed in the window.

I froze in the darkness, waiting for the light to flicker back on.

It flashed again.

I tried to understand what I was looking at. It wasn't a face peering down at me, but a hairless, featureless head. It had no eyes or nose or mouth – just a mottled pink and white head. Its chin wiggled a bit, and the head cocked to one side. It knew I was there.

The gate lurched open with a metallic clink, then a deep groan. The doctor's hand fell on my shoulder. I jumped.

"Come," he instructed.

I looked back at the head, but the light had gone out.

We made our way across another hall, through another locked gate, and down a staircase. Halfway down the stairs, we came to a door marked with the number 2 and some other writing I couldn't read.

Before opening the door, the doctor looked down at me.

"Be as quiet as possible," he whispered. "They'll be looking for you."

I felt my face go cold, and probably white.

He pushed the door open.

I stared down another hall, this one narrower and dressed in red carpet. Several dim lamps hung from the ceiling, glowing with steady light. A few wooden doors lined the hall, but none of them had windows. Huge elevator doors stood at the far end; their buttons gleamed softly.

The doctor stepped out in front of me and hurried down

the hallway. I followed him, noticing that some of the knobs on the doors had been torn off. He stopped at one of the doors and looked back at me. He took out his key ring, flipped to a key, and shoved it into the lock.

The door creaked open. It was pitch black inside, but the doctor entered and told me to follow. He closed the door behind me and flipped a light switch. The light popped on after a few crackles.

We stood in a little office. A massive desk sat in the middle of the room, its surface littered with dozens of files. Huge stacks of documents covered most of the floor; some of the piles were as tall as me. I plucked a file off the nearest stack and examined it. The words meant nothing to me, but my eyes were drawn to the bright red stamp at the bottom – an eagle clutching a symbol. I recognized it but wasn't sure what it was. From where I stood, it looked like every document in the room bore the same eagle stamp.

The doctor went to his desk and rifled through its drawers.

"What are these?" I asked.

He paused to look at me, then quickly returned to his search.

"Prisoner files," he said hesitantly. It sounded like an admission.

"Prisoners?"

"It's funny," he said, giving up on his task and dropping down into his chair. "They think they've got everything in perfect order. So meticulously organized and planned and executed."

I put the paper down where I found it and walked up to the desk.

"But they're prisoners," he continued. "They don't even know it."

His gaze fell on the stack in front of him.

"*A-hah!*" he said, carelessly pushing them off the desk. They flitted to the floor like dead leaves. Hidden beneath the pile was an old leather journal. The doctor seized it up in his hands and opened it. He flipped through its pages.

"What's that?" I asked, wondering what we were doing

here.

He set it down on the table.

"That, my boy, is the medical journal of César Arturo," he said, his voice beaming with excitement.

I stared at him blankly.

"He was a great man, a doctor from Spain. They brought him to England to help the soldiers coming home from the war. He was an expert in combat stress." The doctor opened a nearby file folder and searched through it, muttering to himself.

"England," I said, remembering a little more. "Are we still in Pine Rest?"

His expression went grim.

"Couldn't be further from it, I'm afraid," he replied. He seemed preoccupied with his thoughts and continued rambling. "Arturo became obsessed with nightmares. It's all he wrote about, toward the end."

I skimmed through the journal. I couldn't read it, but the writing was beautiful.

"I think it can help me get out of here, once and for all," he said.

I examined the man with suspicion.

"Who are you?" I asked.

He closed the folder and glanced around the room. His bushy eyebrows wiggled like caterpillars as he searched for a way to explain himself.

"Just one of the lucky ones, like you," he said with a sigh. "But I have this." He tapped the journal in my hand.

I opened my mouth to question him but was interrupted by a deafening metal screech. We both jumped at the sound of it.

The doctor and I held still, hardly breathing, just staring at each other. The noise came from outside the office, somewhere down the hall.

"The elevator," he whispered, scurrying out from behind the desk. "They're coming for you." He grabbed me by the arm and yanked me to the far corner of the room. "Hide!"

Without protest, I squeezed between the file cabinet and

the wall. I crouched down, mostly concealed by a large stack of papers, and held as still as I could.

Heavy boots stomped down the hall, the carpet doing little to muffle them. I didn't have to wonder what it could be. They sounded like a small group, maybe four. The doctor rushed over to his desk and pretended to review files.

"Farmer!" a man yelled in a shrill voice.

"Wo sind Sie?!" he screamed, his jagged voice lacerating my ears.

I peeked through a little space between the stack and the cabinet. The doctor simply held a finger to his lips, hushing me.

The man outside grabbed the knob and found it locked, so he slammed a fist against the door. He sounded so angry I feared he'd break it in half.

"Farmer!" he shouted again.

The doorknob rattled.

"Jawohl!" the doctor responded, leaping up from his chair and scurrying for the door. He stopped just before opening it and shot a concerned look at me.

"Aufmachen!" the man screamed. *"Schnell!"*

The doctor straightened his medical jacket and reached for the knob.

CHAPTER 54

The doctor didn't have time to pull the door open. The moment he unlocked it, the door swung at him and clattered against the wall. He stumbled backward as a man in a bloody surgical apron stormed in. Three golems followed behind, crowding the tiny office with their massive forms. They surrounded the doctor, who now looked even shorter than before.

"*Warum sind Sie noch hier?*" the man asked. A surgical mask dangled below his chin and bobbed around as he spoke.

The doctor did not respond. I couldn't see his face, but he cowered before the golems and lowered his head. The salt and pepper hair that once jutted in every direction now drooped with nervous sweat.

The surgeon took a step forward, his face full of rage.

"*Wo ist der Gefangene, Farmer?*" he asked, staring directly into the doctor's eyes. He never blinked.

"I...I don't know," Dr. Farmer replied. His little hands shook at his sides. "If...if you please, Herr Doktor—"

The surgeon glared.

"How *dare* you speak Polish to me," he whispered, sticking his face close to the doctor's. "If the Kommandant heard us…"

"I apologize, Herr Doktor," said Farmer, "but I must tell you something, and I don't want them to know."

The golems looked at each other. Their metal heads glimmered in the soft light. The stone slabs over their faces gave them a look of eerie calmness. One of them shifted its bulk, crunching a boot down onto a helpless sliver of paper that had fallen off its stack. Its entire body was the color of clay, as though someone had dug the foul creature out of the earth. They all looked exactly the same, down to the tiniest detail.

"Speak then," the surgeon replied, his voice flat with annoyance.

Dr. Farmer straightened up.

"I think one of your men is helping patients escape—"

"Prisoners," the surgeon interrupted.

"Yes, of course, my apologies, Herr Doktor," said Farmer, collecting himself. "Two prisoners have gone missing. We found the first in the barracks. How could she have gotten there—"

"*It*," the surgeon interrupted.

Farmer hesitated.

"How could *it* have gotten there."

"Yes, of course, Herr Doktor. I'm sorry, my Polish is not as elegant as yours. But how could *it* have gotten down there without assistance? After all, the tunnels to the barracks are locked, and only a few of your men have the proper keys."

The surgeon never took his little rat eyes off Dr. Farmer. He considered his subordinate's words.

"A second prisoner has escaped – the new arrival," Farmer added. "And his – I mean *its* – room was supposed to be guarded."

The surgeon pursed his thin lips. His face was sharp and rigid, as if cut from marble with an axe. He backed up a step from Dr. Farmer, and both men drew a breath.

"I'll need access to the upper halls," the surgeon said, breaking the silence.

"Of course, Herr Doktor. I have access, but I—"

"You will transfer your keys to Steiger," the surgeon said, voice taking on a professional firmness.

Dr. Farmer paused for a moment. Another golem shifted in place.

"The janitor, sir?"

"Then you will report to medical reception," the surgeon continued, ignoring Farmer's confusion. "Don't let me find you in your office again. There's work to be done."

"Of course, Herr Doktor," said Farmer, straightening up once more.

The surgeon moved between the golems and stepped into the hallway. The giant creatures followed obediently.

"Farmer," he said, turning back toward us.

"Herr Doktor?"

"Find the prisoner. I have operations to perform. I cannot reschedule them."

"It will be done," said Dr. Farmer.

The surgeon looked over him suspiciously, then nodded with approval. The group stomped back down the hall. A door opened and closed in the distance, and then there was silence.

I stood up and tried to squeeze out of my hiding place, but I knocked over the stack of paper in front of me. It went to the floor with such a ruckus that Dr. Farmer and I both froze, expecting the golems to return. They didn't.

"Those monsters," I said, "I've seen them before. They even find me in my dreams."

The doctor leaned against his desk with a tired sigh. He removed his old glasses and rubbed his eyes.

"Awful, aren't they," he said.

His voice was so calming I wanted to hug him. I thought of my father in that moment, and of Dietmar.

"Most people have nightmares," Dr. Farmer continued. "Then they wake up, and thank God it wasn't real. But for people like you, it's different...Sometimes the nightmare just reaches out and takes you."

"Why am I here?" I asked. "Am I asleep?" I hobbled up to the doctor and sat down on a little pile of papers. He reached out and ruffled my hair.

"I haven't got this place figured out, my boy. Not entirely. It changes every time I come near another person. Their imagination...their fears and desires...their pain affects this world. The darkness here is like a canvas, and each man is an artist."

At age twelve, Dr. Farmer's explanation made little sense to me. As an adult, I understand it even less.

He pushed himself away from the desk and started for the

door.

"I want you to stay here," he said, his voice growing brave and resolute. "I'll come back for you. I promise."

I jumped to my feet. "But what if—"

"They won't come back," he interrupted. "Not for a long time. And if they do, you run down that hall and hide in another office. You'll hear them before they hear you. Do you understand?"

I shuddered at the thought. Then I straightened up the way he did in front of the golems.

"Okay," I said.

With that, the doctor marched out of the room. I heard him tap the elevator button and clear his throat. A deep hum issued from the lift, vibrating through the entire hall. An ominous ding rang out, and then he was gone.

CHAPTER 55

I sat at the doctor's desk for a long while, looking over his files. All of the documents were gibberish to me, but I was impressed with how methodically they were organized. Whatever the golems and their masters were doing here, they kept precise records.

After what felt like a half-hour of poking around the office, I realized that if I was in a dream, perhaps I could fall asleep and wake up in real life. I moved some of the paper stacks around and cleared a space to lie in, then curled up on the carpet. I covered myself with an extra medical jacket that had been dangling on a coat rack near the desk. Instead of closing my eyes, I stared at the rotting ceiling for a long while.

The lights flickered and went out. Darkness engulfed the room.

I sat perfectly still, listening for anything.

A piercing whine emanated from the vent on the wall, similar to the sound of a dentist's drill. The hiss then dipped into a low, crunchy buzz, as though someone were feeding logs into a wood chipper. Cold sweat beads formed on my face. My neck tingled until the sound abated, and the lights popped back on.

I leaped up and stood under the vent, listening for the sound again.

It did not come.

I lay back down on the ground, trying to put the awful noise out of my mind, but curiosity drove me to investigate. Against the doctor's instructions, I cracked open the office door, poked my head out, and looked both ways.

All clear.

I left the door open in case I needed to bolt back inside,

then trotted up and down the hall, listening for the sound again. There were no windows or vents, so it was unlikely that I'd hear anything out here.

The hall lights flickered and dimmed, then went off. After a moment, they came back on, but I didn't hear the sound. Frustrated, I went to the stairwell next to the elevator and descended to a door marked *1*.

This hallway was unlit, but a row of windows permitted me to see outside.

The first window was so covered in dust I could barely make anything out. I saw only shapes, slowly moving around.

Through the second window, there was darkness. It must have been night, but no stars twinkled in the black. A single guard tower stood a few hundred yards away, with a huge spotlight mounted on top of it. Though I couldn't make out who manned the light, I saw forms shifting about behind it. The light moved slowly through a dead field, over a barbed wire fence, and against the building I stood in. The milky beam poured through the window at the end of the hall and bathed everything in an eerie glow. As it moved toward me, I ducked. Finally, the light moved away and switched off. I could see nothing more through this window.

I scrambled down the hall, my feet gliding across the warm linoleum. I slid to a stop at the third window.

What is this?

The window overlooked some kind of internment camp. Rows of small buildings, probably bunkhouses, stood clustered together in a few empty fields. Barbed wire fences and guard towers enclosed the area, and golems stood watch at random positions near the fence.

And there were people.

Well, I couldn't tell if they were people, but they were living things. They shuffled around aimlessly in the fields. Some picked up rocks or searched for things on the ground. Others stood at the fence, gazing out into the distance.

They looked just like the creature I saw in the window after Dr. Farmer woke me up: no faces, no features, just pink, hairless bodies with splotches of gray and white. They didn't seem to communicate with each other, but it was clear that they suffered terribly. Their emaciated forms staggered and slogged. Many of them shivered or clutched themselves in sorrow and pain. Some were wrapped in tattered, striped jumpsuits, and others were completely naked. Those without clothes had no genitals at all.

Spotlights moved across the dark fields, illuminating the poor creatures in harsh light. One of the beings recoiled at being spotted, and attempted to limp away. The light fell on another, and another. All of them bore a similar marking on an arm, perhaps a brand or a tattoo.

One creature, cowering against a wall, seemed to lose consciousness and toppled over. It fell hard in the dirt and ceased to move. A group of golems stormed up to it, hoisted it in the air, and marched away.

The spotlights cut out, and everything went black.

I stepped away from the window. My mind raced in a thousand directions.

What is this place? I wondered. The fourth window was only a few yards from where I stood, but I hesitated to approach. An odd mixture of sympathy and fear washed through my gut. The feeling pushed its way up to my throat and became a dizzy nausea.

My breath quickened, and my feet began to move me toward the window.

"Hey!" a voice whispered.

I whirled around, but no one was there.

The voice called out again. It came from up above. I squinted through the darkness.

A large vent sat high up on the wall, and through it, I could barely make out a face.

"Who's there?" I called out. "Who are you? I can see you!"

The person shushed me, and again said something, but it was in a language I couldn't understand. Before I could say anything more, the thunderous echo of boots rose up in the hallway. The golems were coming.

I shot down the hall and practically dove back into the

stairwell. I wanted to get back to Dr. Farmer's office, but upon hearing movement at the top of the stairs, I went down a level instead of up. Behind me, the door crashed open, and the enormous things spilled into the stairwell. Panicking, I shoved open the door at the bottom of the stairs.

How I wish I could have read the sign on the door back then.

Another series of halls awaited me, probably designed to confuse escapees. The lights overhead jumped on and off, casting dizzying shadows on the walls. I wandered for a few minutes until I came upon an iron gate, just like the ones Dr. Farmer had opened. This one was unlocked, and there were slimy black footprints on the ground leading through it. They had been left by feet as small as mine, and glimmered like oil. As I touched one of them, a gurney squealed up ahead.

I crouched in a doorway and peeked at the source of the noise.

At the end of the hall stood a woman in hospital scrubs. Next to her was a small, featureless being, of the same kind I'd seen outside. It was about my size. The creature limped a few steps to the gurney and struggled to climb in. The woman helped it up. She wheeled the gurney toward me, but turned and moved it into a room. As she walked under the dim lamp that swung in the center of the hall, it lit up her face.

Her mouth had been sewn shut.

I gasped, audibly I'm sure, but she paid no attention to me. As soon as the woman closed the door to the room, I bolted through the gate and shot across the hall. I barreled down a wide set of stairs, then hid inside the only unlocked room I could find. The metal door screamed as I pushed it open.

The first thing I saw was a corpse.

CHAPTER 56

The stink of rancid meat assailed me. I choked back a volcano of puke.

Dozens of tables lined the room, a naked corpse heaped atop each one. I slowly paced down one of the rows, mesmerized by the sheer amount of death around me. These were prisoners too: they had no faces, no hair, no genitals. One of the bodies was smaller than the others, and its skin looked younger. On its arm, a crudely etched tattoo read *BW01413*.

All of them had been marked. It seemed to be the only way to distinguish one from another.

At the end of the last row was a much larger cadaver.

It was the corpse of a golem.

A bolt of panic arced through my body, compelling me to run, but a morbid curiosity anchored me to the scene.

I inched toward the body.

Its metallic head gleamed in the pale light. It lay flat on its back, its monstrous limbs dangling off the little table. As I approached, the smell of clay overtook the stench of death. With all of my courage, I reached out and poked the golem on its armored chest.

There was no give. Its body felt rock-hard, and probably weighed three hundred pounds. The front of its head was perfectly smooth, like marble. I had to know if it was a mask.

With a shaking hand, I reached out.

A pop echoed through the room, and the lights cut out. Everything went black.

The same grinding sound from earlier poured into the morgue, reverberating through the metal room like thunder. I clutched my ears in agony. I imagined my brain swelling up against my skull and bursting like a balloon.

Then, the noise cut out, and the lights popped back on.

When my eyes adjusted, a shriek escaped my lips.

The corpses – all of them – had vanished.

Before I could even guess where they'd gone, a door burst open somewhere outside the morgue.

Golems stampeded down the hall. They'd definitely heard my scream.

I glanced around, noting a small wooden door opposite of where I'd entered. I darted over to it, pushed it open, then ran back to the sinks on the other side of the morgue. I ripped open the cabinet beneath them and squeezed myself inside, barely closing it in time.

The horrible creatures barged in. They swept through the room like bears, turning tables over and making an awful racket. A heavy boot bumped into the cabinet door, nearly extorting a squeak from me. Finally, the golems charged out of the morgue through the door I'd opened.

I listened as their footsteps faded, then flung the cabinet open and spilled head-first onto the floor.

The lights went out, and the grinding came back. It came from the direction the golems had gone in. I sat up, dusted myself off, and squinted through the darkness. In a few seconds, the lights came back on, the rumbling stopped, and the building went graveyard-quiet once more.

I had to know what that awful noise was. Whatever the golems were doing here, whatever the purpose of this place, I didn't expect to discover the darkest secrets behind a brittle wooden door. Not with all the iron gates, the locks and keys, the guards and doctors. But behind that flimsy door I found the devil's throne.

The passageway beyond the morgue smelled wet and moldy. Green slime grew across the damp walls. Pipes jutted out and ran along every inch of the ceiling, dripping and steaming ungodly liquids. The path turned into a metal catwalk that led me over some kind of drainage system, with big pools of sludge and beeping machines.

The way was dark. A few old lights mounted high up on the walls guided me, as did the sounds of movement up ahead.

Footsteps echoed from beyond – softer than the boot crunches of the golems. Scraping sounds perforated them, as though someone were dragging burlap sacks of potatoes.

Tic tic.

Tic tic tic.

Tictictictictic.

A strange clicking arose, then died away before I could even guess what it was.

As I crept onward, the noises grew.

Soon I found myself above a humongous, well-lit chamber. Golems and nurses and other people ambled around down below. From my position I was able to lie flat on my belly and peer down at the scene without being noticed. I made sure to stay out of the light as best I could.

The room was organized into something like a factory line. A dozen secretaries and their typewriters lined one side of the room, and big machines with blades and presses lined the other.

My gaze fell on something in the corner – an enormous pile of corpses, all prisoners. They'd been carelessly piled next to a machine.

A *grinder.*

A trio of golems methodically picked up the sallow bodies and tossed them in. Once twenty or so had been loaded, the mouth was lowered, and the grinder whirred and turned on.

The sound of those poor creatures being blended and minced was more than I could bear. Bones crunched and snapped; skin flayed and blood spattered. Every light in the room dimmed as the machine drew power from the building.

My stomach churned too, like the grinder was mixing my guts into a puree. I gnashed my teeth in rebellion against the terrible noise. I buried my head in my hands. It was the only thing I could do.

When the machine cut out, a sigh of steam burst from the pipe above it. The liquefied remains of the prisoners pumped from a hose onto a conveyor belt. Another golem operated multiple presses, which flattened and shaped the white paste into thin sheets. A big iron pounded and steamed them flat, then a golem removed the sheets and hung them up to dry on the far wall.

They were turning the bodies into paper.

Sheets that had already dried were carried to a paper cutter, whose blades sliced them into smaller pieces. A nurse picked up the stacks and scurried over to the rows of typewriters, then handed chunks of paper to each secretary.

These women typed feverishly until the last cheery *ding* signified it was time for another sheet. They could not possibly see what they were typing; all of their eyes had been sewn closed. Maybe they weren't meant to see. Maybe they didn't want to.

Another nurse collected the finished work from each person and shaped them into neat stacks. She hurried to a doctor who sat at a big black desk and dropped the papers gingerly before him. He gave her a summary nod and reviewed the documents. After carefully examining each one, the doctor stamped it with a red rubber stamp, and then dropped it onto a huge pile on the floor near his desk.

Finally, another golem collected the stamped piles, waddled to an incinerator, and hurled them in. The kiln belched with fiery satisfaction each time it was fed. Smoke billowed through two stacks, up and out of the building.

Sweat dripped down my face. Bile crept up the back of my throat. I couldn't make sense of what I was seeing. I just knew it was wrong, more wrong than anything I'd ever seen, and I wanted to escape this awful place.

I pushed myself up with clammy hands and quietly returned to the morgue. I promised myself that no matter what, I wouldn't let that happen to me.

CHAPTER 57

As I exited the morgue through the main door, I reminded myself that I had to be dreaming. There was no way this could be the same world I'd grown up in. There was no way anyone would let this happen. I *had* to be dreaming.

I found my way through another door and down another series of sewer-like halls, rife with stench and rot and mold. The incessant dripping of leaky pipes camouflaged my footsteps. I moved up and over and across more catwalks than I care to remember.

I reached the top of a stairwell. At the bottom was a man, crouched down, peeking around the corner. His long coat looked vaguely familiar. Memories of the police department flickered in my mind. Was this the man who'd brought me here?

Against my better judgment, I sneaked down the steps and tried to get a better look, but he was too alert. He heard me a mile away and whirled around. His eyes met mine.

It was him – the detective. He reached out and grabbed me by the shoulders. Relief spread across his face. He smiled and said something I didn't understand.

"Trent," I said, pointing at him. I'd heard a woman say his name before I blacked out at the station.

His eyes lit up.

"What are you doing here? How'd you get here? I met a doctor, and he hid me in his office..." I babbled, forgetting that Trent probably spoke English.

He shook his head.

I knew he couldn't understand me, but I kept talking. Images of the macabre grinder clung in my mind.

"Trent," I said, feeling goosebumps ripple across my arms,

"they're grinding people up. I mean, these things that look like people. They're trapped here—" I saw the look on his face and gave up mid-sentence.

I moved to the last stair, curious about what he'd been watching. From around the corner, I could hear the familiar screeches of an angry man, and the scrape of a saw on wood – or bone.

I pressed against the cold cement wall and peeked around it.

And then I saw them.

My body went cold as death. I could practically hear the blood washing out of my head and waterfalling to my feet. My vision grayed out.

My parents.

I hadn't seen my mother and father since the night the golems broke down our door. That was almost eight years ago.

And yet here they were, strung up in chains and dangling like captives in some forgotten oubliette. Their bodies were mottled and pale, just like the cadavers in the morgue. Just like the stacks of paper. I could barely make out little tattoos on their arms.

In front of my parents stood a table with a carcass on it. That wicked surgeon hovered over it, screeching instructions at his nurses. He sliced and carved the body like a chef cutting into a roast. Rage and anguish burned away my common sense; I wanted to rush over to my parents.

"Mom!" I screamed across the room. "Dad!"

My feet walked themselves out into the open, taking me with them, exposing me to the hospital staff. I didn't care anymore. The golems had taken my parents from me once before. I wasn't going to let death take them too.

A huge pair of arms wrapped me up from behind and plucked me straight off the ground. My first thought was that a golem had snatched me, but when I felt the warm hands, I knew it was Trent.

Everything happened so fast. The surgeon wailed upon sighting me, spit frothing from his mouth like a rabid dog's as he ordered our capture. The nurses bolted toward us, slashing the air with deformed blades. My parents perked up and cried out my name, desperately reaching toward me with frail hands.

Every emotion I'd ever felt rushed over me in tidal waves. Trent flew down the hall, me in his arms, golems and nurses behind us. And behind them, getting smaller and smaller with each step, were my parents. Even if I made it out of this hospital alive, its monsters had ripped out my heart and thrown it into their precious grinder.

The golems cornered us at the end of the hall. Trent set me down and pulled out a knife, ready to die to protect me. A single, dim light swung back and forth between him and the three beings who meant to put me on that surgeon's table.

Suddenly, like a prayer answered, the locked door at our backs opened. There stood Dr. Farmer, veiled in shadow. He yanked us inside and slammed the door shut.

"Doctor, m-my parents," I sobbed. Tears drenched my face and neck. "My mom and dad, they're here..."

Dr. Farmer whispered something to Trent, then placed a firm hand on my shoulder and said in an unsympathetic voice,

"They're not your parents anymore, boy. We need to get you out."

The two men blocked the door with a large bed as the golems pounded against it. The smashing of the creatures' boots shook the entire room.

We stood in what appeared to be a recovery ward. Trent noticed something on one of the beds, but I couldn't see it. He stammered to himself, or to whatever he saw, as I ran to the far end of the room with the doctor. I took the opportunity to glance out the window.

I could see the woods far down below, and a little meadow. An orange moon cast the scene in ugly light, barely revealing a barn at the edge of the clearing. Outside the barn stood a man. He looked around like he was lost.

"Come," the doctor commanded from behind me.

I left the window and followed him through a door at the

end of the room.

Trent came after us, but paused at the window I'd been staring out of. I didn't wait around to find out what he saw, but when the doctor fetched him, his face was fiery red like a hot iron grill, and his eyes brimmed with sorrow. I wiped away the tears in my own eyes; the thought of my mother and father still gnawed at my mind.

We took a short elevator ride to some kind of torture chamber. The doctor hurried me through it so fast I didn't get a good look around, but I did see a huge stone table with a person lying on it. This man didn't look like one of the featureless bodies I'd seen before. He was dressed in a strange costume, like something I'd seen in an old book. A black bag covered his head.

Again, Trent stopped to examine the place. Dr. Farmer and I exited through a secret door that looked like part of the wall. We ended up in a huge ceremonial room with a long dining table at the center. Instead of a body, on this table there was food.

"Who was that?" I asked Dr. Farmer.

He sucked in a breath and leaned against the door, searching for words appropriate for a child.

"Have you ever wanted something so bad you dreamed of it?" he asked.

"Yes," I replied. "I dream of my parents."

"Trent dreams of someone too. Someone he lost."

"Who?" I asked.

"It's not really my place to say. Maybe someday you can ask him."

We stood there in silence for a few minutes. My thoughts wandered to Dietmar and his family.

"Will my parents be okay?" I asked.

Dr. Farmer didn't answer.

Trent came through the secret door, interrupting our conversation. He stared at the table, then up at a painting on the wall I hadn't noticed before. It was a pretty lady with green eyes. She reminded me a bit of Dietmar's daughter, but older. The detective's brow furrowed. His gaze fell to the floor and he brushed past us in silence.

We followed the doctor up a few flights of stairs to the medical wing's reception area. A receptionist caught sight of us and took off running down the hall, then alerted the entire prison of our whereabouts over the PA system.

The sound of doors crashing open and slamming echoed up from the hellish surgical ward. Boots clunked louder and louder, undoubtedly heading for us.

Dr. Farmer took off with surprising speed. We followed close behind him, dashing up halls and around corners. We spiraled up flights of dirty stairs and into a hall with prison cells on both sides. Pathetic, weak prisoners reached out at us, desperate for help we could not give. Their faceless heads turned as we zipped by, somehow watching us. My heart broke for them. I knew exactly what was going to happen to them.

The doctor led us into a little room that had been violently tossed. As he barricaded the door, the clamor of boots resounded from the stairwell.

"Trent," I said, watching him examine two windows on the wall, "I can't leave without my parents." I hoped Dr. Farmer would translate for me.

They both ignored my pleas. The doctor held the door against my pursuers while Trent gazed out one of the windows. It was the only one I'd seen in this place that didn't have metal bars on it. It was the only way out.

I ran over to see what Trent found so interesting, and instantly recognized the view.

A squeal of joy rushed up and nearly escaped my mouth.

"Trent!" I yelled, grabbing him by the jacket. "My house! It's my house!"

A cobblestone street led up to a quaint little house. Dusk had fallen, and the street light in front of my home had just come on. Someone moved behind the curtains inside; It looked like my father pacing in the living room as he usually did. My parents' faces appeared in my mind, and with them a mournful ache, the price I paid to keep their memory alive.

The golems crashed against the door, shattering my quiet reminiscence. The poor doctor braced himself against it, but he couldn't have been half their size. There was no way he could them back for long. The room darkened and the crashing grew louder. The office seemed to shrink down over me, becoming my tomb. Each boot against the door was a nail pounded into my coffin.

Even with these monsters at the gates, Trent remained mesmerized by something beyond the barred window. He shouted and screamed like a maniac, pounding his fists against the bars and trying to rip them off. His rage terrified me. He was so big I almost believed he would tear through the metal.

Alas, he failed, and whirled around to grab me just as the golems broke down the door. They trampled over Dr. Farmer, no doubt killing him as they came at me. Trent roared like a lion and blocked stepped between me and the golems.

It happened so fast the world blurred around me. The three beings lunged for us. Trent bashed a fist against the unbarred window. He lifted me up and heaved me out of it, holding my shirt collar just long enough for me to drop to the ground feet-first.

In that moment, I remembered the golem who saved my life — the one that had gently lowered me from my parents' bedroom window.

CHAPTER 58

I hit the pavement with a smack. It was slick with rain, and judging by the scent in the air, another storm was coming. It was after dark, and a thousand little moons reflected in the puddles that lined the streets. Warm yellow light seeped from the windows of my house. Behind me, the hospital had vanished, and Trent with it.

I picked myself up and wandered to the front door. Though I hadn't been home for the better part of a decade, it felt like only yesterday that I was here. Before I could knock, my mother opened the door and swept me up in her arms. I threw my hands around her and buried my face in her neck. She smelled just the way I remembered. I followed her inside.

My father was exactly where I expected him to be – in the living room with a newspaper and a cup of coffee. He was overdressed as usual. When he saw me, he pushed the little glasses up from the tip of his nose and smiled.

"Getting sleepy?" he asked.

I was unsure of how to respond.

"Uh...not yet."

"Well," he said, "go on into the kitchen. Your mother left some soup for you."

I nodded obediently and went for the kitchen. I wasn't sure if I was dreaming, or if I'd just woken up, and the past several years of my life had been an elaborate nightmare. My parents looked healthy, like nothing had ever happened to them. Like they were never taken.

As I stood in the kitchen, I could hear my parents bickering in the next room.

"Every day it gets worse," I heard my father say.

"We could go back home," my mother replied. "My parents would—"

"Your father would shoot me on sight," he interrupted. "You want to go back to that? It'd be the end of us!"

My mother joined me in the kitchen, not wanting to deal with my father any longer. He followed her, concealing his frustration with a warm smile.

"Eat up, my son," he said to me. "It's bed time soon."

As I reached for some bread on the table, the lights flickered.

New rain splattered on the kitchen window. Lightning set fire to the sky. A cloud rolled in front of the moon and darkened the view.

I held still. My stomach churned. The room went cold.

A deafening wooden crack erupted from the hallway, followed by the crash of a potted plant against the floor. I bolted to my mother's side and peered down the hall.

The closet had exploded from the inside. Pieces of the flimsy door were scattered across the ground. A dazed man lay slumped against the staircase, looking around in shock.

"Trent!" I shouted. My parents shrieked as I hugged him. Trent stood up and brushed himself off, saying things I couldn't understand.

My father stepped forward.

"David," he demanded, "who is this man?"

I didn't know where to begin.

"He's my friend," I explained. "He protected me. He saved my life, Dad."

"From what?" my mother asked, clutching my father's arm.

"The golems," I replied.

"The what?" they both asked in unison.

"What in God's name is he doing in our house?" my father said, his voice brimming with anger. "Hiding in the closet like some kind of rodent!"

That, I could not explain. Before I could think of anything, my father held his hand up to silence the room. He'd heard something outside.

Trent rushed over to the front door and flipped the lights off. The ominous sound of boots rose with the pummeling rain, and between cracks of thunder, I could hear shouting from outside.

It was happening. The golems had come for my parents. They'd come back to take everything from me. Again.

"Hide!" I screamed at my parents. As I'd done when I was four, I thought to run upstairs. "You have to hide, Mom! Don't let them find you!"

"What's going on?" my father asked, pulling my mother close to him. The sight of my proud father, bug-eyed and afraid, amplified my own terror.

"They've come for you, Dad," I said. The words stung me as they came out. My eyes went slick and blurred the room. "They've come to take you away."

Trent rushed at my parents, collecting them in his big arms, trying to shoo them to the back of the house. As he did, the front door burst open, shattered by the gigantic foot of a golem.

Four of them trampled in, barely giving us time to react. I hid at the top of the stairs while Trent bull-rushed at them. His bravery took the creatures by surprise.

A battle ensued. It was less a street fight and more like a gladiatorial mêlée. Trent evaded his enemies with lightning speed and landed attacks with martial expertise. The golems brawled like burly fools. They were merely thugs who'd been given weapons and a false sense of authority.

One of the beings ran up the stairs at me, but Trent pounced like a tiger, dragging the creature over the handrail. The detective's battle cry exploded from him like dynamite, and the two plummeted to the wood floor below. They recovered and squared off, but Trent snatched away the golem's weapon and delivered a merciless beating. At some point, Trent's whip-like speed caught one of his foes by surprise. He crushed the monster's faceplate with the club and sent it to its knees in agony. For a moment, time seemed to slow down, and the injured golem looked up at me.

Its mask crumbled away and revealed the face of an ordinary man. His eyes betrayed a profound sadness, and he looked up at me with an expression of remorse. In that moment, a million thoughts and emotions ignited in my mind. All four golems collapsed into piles of lifeless rock, which smoldered with the departure of the dark force that had animated them. Although I couldn't speak, let alone make sense of this revelation, I somehow knew that my nightmare was over.

Decades later, I began to collect pieces of the puzzle.

CHAPTER 59

"Puppets of a primitive ideology," my dad – well, Trent – used to say. I never understood what it meant until I was in my thirties. I suppose I should backtrack.

My birth parents were born in Poland and fell in love as members of the same *shtetl*, Yiddish for "Jewish community." My father, the son of a poor baker, and my mother, the daughter of a well-respected rabbi, eloped in Germany to escape the scrutiny of their class differences. My father knew he could find work there through the diaspora of Polish Jews in the country, and my mother was weary of her affluent and overbearing family.

I was born to them in the spring of 1934 in Bavaria. We lived in a sleepy, well-to-do little Dorf near a stream whose name escapes me. By this time, Adolf Hitler had become *Reichskanzler* of Germany, and was threatening to unmake the entire government. By the time I was a toddler, Jews had been stripped of many of their rights via the Nuremberg Laws. Anti-Semitism ran rampant throughout the country. I remember my father reading the paper each day with growing disgust.

Despite the frightening political state of Germany, the larger cities bore the brunt of Nazi zealotry, and my family experienced relatively little friction with the locals. My father, a secular rationalist, insisted to my mother that they do everything they could to hide or deny their Jewish heritage. But the idea was wishful thinking, both with respect to my mother's deep-seated faith, and more immediately the obviousness of our nationality. My father was the only one of us who spoke a word of German.

I was barely four when the Nazis came for us.

It was 1938, and the collective hatred of Jews had finally come to a head. A Jewish man named Herschel Grynszpan assassinated a Nazi diplomat in France, and Hitler's government used the incident to launch a full-scale race war against the Jews.

All of Germany exploded in violence that night. Tens of thousands of Jews were taken from their homes and sent to the infamous concentration camps. Jewish businesses and houses were destroyed. Scores of people were murdered. That night would be remembered as *Kristallnacht*, the "Night of Broken Glass."

When the Nazis finally came for us, my father was reading the paper, my mother was preparing me for bed, and I was thinking about which book I wanted to take to school the next morning. We could never have known what was coming.

The soldiers took my parents, but for some reason, one of them allowed me to escape. Perhaps the man felt pity for me. Perhaps he had a son my age. I'll never know for sure, but I like to think that he and I shared a deeper humanity, despite the rabid hatred with which he'd been indoctrinated.

I spent that night in a ditch in the nearby woods, suffering vivid nightmares. I think the stress was too much on my little brain, and it just disconnected from reality. The next morning, a Nazi soldier chased me into the arms of Dietmar. This man and his family were Germans, but they had all managed to resist the appeal of Nazism and the hypnotic charm of Adolf Hitler. When I look back on my fading memories, I see Dietmar's face. It's the thing I remember most clearly about my time in his care. He peered into my eyes with a concern I could never understand at that age, but today, it brings me to tears. I can't imagine the horror he must have felt, knowing what was being done to innocent people...to children. He knew what would have happened to the boy he'd found in the woods.

When the British police took me from Dietmar, they recognized me as a Polish Jew and shipped me back to Poland, where they believed I was from. Since I had no documentation or identity, my new caretakers couldn't prove I belonged with them. Furthermore, I imagine the Brits probably considered a German family to be monstrously unsuitable for raising a Jewish child.

In Poland, I was placed in an orphanage. I spent weeks asking about my parents, but no one had ever heard of them, or even our family name, Petri. Eventually, word spread to us that Germany had invaded Poland, and that we were all in serious danger. Each night we were told that things would settle down soon, but each day the planes got louder, the explosions got closer, and more people went missing. After a few weeks, a man named *Gzregorz* (in English, Gregor) rescued me from the orphanage and took me to his cabin in a snowy forest, far from the German border.

Gregor was a broken man. The Nazis had come to his home in the city while he was out buying food. They took his wife and his ten-year-old daughter, and executed them in the public square. Gregor fled with his brother to their cabin in the northern woods, but his brother too was killed by pursuing Nazis.

Why Gregor adopted me, he never said, but I got the sense that he felt it was his duty to protect other Jews after the loss of his family. He would often drink himself stupid and rant about genocide against all of Germany. He bellowed that Poland would rise up and ride warships to Berlin on rivers of German blood. He even talked about slaughtering their children in revenge. Later in my life, I would refuse alcohol because of what it did to Gregor.

Still, I understood his malice. Although I was unable to describe the men who'd taken my family, or why they would do such a terrible thing, Gregor knew exactly what had happened to me. He looked upon me like a father looks at his sick child, and despite his constant drunken rage, I knew he'd never let anything happen to me. Gregor *wanted* to die protecting me. He boasted about slaughtering Nazis with his axe if they ever came around. Maybe he believed it would absolve him of the guilt he felt for being unable to protect his daughter.

We spent five years living in that forest. I pestered him to tell me more about the war, but while he was sober, he refused to give details. Gregor repeatedly told me that he wanted me to have a normal life. He wanted me to be ignorant of Poland's surrender, and of the factories of death the Nazis were building for us. And because of Gregor's stubbornness, the Nazis remained faceless to me. They were mere shadows, bogeymen who came in the night to rip children from their beds. I couldn't even remember what they looked like.

Instead of educating me on the brutal state of things in Europe, Gregor taught me the pleasure of a simple life. By day we hunted, and by night we snuck into the nearby town, which had remained mostly unscathed by the war. Gregor had many friends, and was apparently a member of some sort of black market that smuggled food, weapons, and Jews in and out of the country.

In 1943, Gregor's masochistic lifestyle caught up with him, and his heart gave out in the living room of his cabin. I came in from gathering firewood to find him dead and cold. With the help of some of his associates, I buried him in the woods, and a rabbi presented a moving eulogy in Hebrew, a language I'd heard only a few times in my life. Had Gregor lived only a few more months, he'd have seen the Russians destroy the Nazis in Poland and throw them out of the country. He'd have seen his enemies cower and die, as they did in his dreams each night.

Over the next two years, Gregor's friends looked after me well enough. I moved around with them until the end of the war. Eventually, after much prodding, my protectors smuggled me into England, where I could resume my search for Dietmar and his family. They put me in the perfect hiding place: a simple orphanage. It was a life to which I'd already grown accustomed, and the war had caused such chaos in England that nobody had tried to make sense of my presence.

In the early years at Gregor's cabin, I suffered from occasional nightmares, most of them involving the wretched golems. At that age it never occurred to me what the golems really were, but in hindsight it was obvious that my young mind was coping the loss of my family. During my last year in Poland the dreams slowly faded away, and I finally believed I was rid of them. The nightmare in England that drove me to flee the orphanage came as a tremendous emotional setback.

While the monsters were clearly a figment of my imagination, the tumble down that staircase wasn't. My sleepwalking through Pine Rest earned me a life-threatening concussion, along with a handful of shattered bones. Luckily, Trent Cadler, a hero of a man, was in the same town. And by sheer coincidence, it was his very occupation to protect and serve people like me. Never in my life have I met a person so loyal to the ideal of defending the meek; I can only imagine what he was like as a soldier. Even now, as a grown man, I still recall Trent with a sort of superhuman quality to him. He is the example I aspire to follow, but also the bar I can never quite reach.

I, unlike Trent, am a coward.

CHAPTER 60

Smoking wasn't the only thing Trent gave up that day at the hospital. When we woke from the Nightmare, he began a new life with me and a police secretary named Francesca. He gave up the memories that had kept him alive up to this point. He gave up Anja.

Trent and Francesca married that year and adopted me shortly after. We picked up and left for the United States, far away from our unbearable pasts. We ended up in Oregon and bought a little house. Francesca got a job as an editor at a small publishing company, and Trent gave up police work to become a carpenter. He took great pride in woodworking, and on the side, he published a few novels through his wife's company.

Francesca reminded me of my birth mother in many ways. She loved to cook for me, and even taught me a few things in the kitchen. She spent every night reading stories to me in English to help me learn, and kept her eyes on me when I explored the forested edges of our property. For the first time in years, I felt at home.

Trent, on the other hand, was always an enigma.

He couldn't hide from me the fact that he'd been engaged in the past. He couldn't hide that a part of him had died with his lost love. I knew her name, but I didn't even know what she looked like. He never kept a single photo of his beloved Anja, and would rarely permit questions about her.

The only thing he ever kept was a simple letter. He couldn't bear to part with it. And how she died, he took that secret to his grave. Not a word was ever spoken that might explain why her loss was so tragic. I privately imagined she fell ill and slipped away in his arms. Trent made me promise never to ask my mother.

I wondered about Anja in secret, though.

I have long considered the possibility that Anja was the German girl with whom I traveled to Pine Rest. Trent and I once discussed the idea briefly, but he was always so hesitant to say anything about her. The very name "Anja" was a source of unfathomable pain for my dad. He wore her loss in his face, in his eyes. And although my mom assured me that he'd put that heartache to rest long ago, I could still see what Anja's death had done to him. It was a permanent scar that never faded.

I eventually let the idea go. There were so many immigrants to Britain during that time, and many of them had the same story: they'd lost someone, and had fled their war-torn homeland. Neither of us could be sure that Anja and I had ever met. But I secretly like to believe that it was Trent's beloved fiancée who'd brought me into his life.

I like to believe the three of us are connected.

Trent was a tight-lipped man, but he loved me like a son. I could feel it when he saw me reading out loud with my mother, or when I caught a baseball with his glove for the first time. He was proud of me, and expressed it the ways a father often did in those times: by giving me permission to try beer (I refused), by shaking my hand like I was a man, by letting me drive his truck on the back roads. As he aged, he became grizzled and bearded, barely recognizable as the clean-cut policeman from decades before. But the warmth in his eyes didn't fade. It grew with him through the years.

Trent Cadler died when I was twenty-eight years old. He was hit by a drunk driver one night after delivering a table he'd crafted. His loss devastated me and Francesca, and I remember realizing then that I was simply not meant to have a dad at all. I tell him when I visit his grave that he doesn't have to feel bad for me, or worry about us. I tell him that he saved my life, and that he showed me how to be a good man. I tell him I'll always look after Mom.

I tell him that I'll be as loyal to my wife as he was to Anja.

I must confess though, one of my life's greatest woes is that I have trouble remembering his face. For some reason, Trent is lost in the dark reaches of my mind, along with my birth parents, and the face of the Nazi who helped me escape. I have no idea why I block out the things I want to remember most. Everything that causes me pain gets sent there, to that foggy prison beyond the edge of memory.

CHAPTER 61

I finished my Ph.D. in 1965. I was thirty-one years old and full of energy, so I decided to travel before starting my career. I hadn't been to Europe since the end of the war, and I'd always wondered about my birth parents, so Germany seemed like the right place to start. After a few weeks, I found some leads and followed them through Germany's astounding network of war archives.

When I arrived in Munich, a German official and a few American soldiers led me into a nondescript building and sat me in a plain white room. It felt a bit like waiting for a doctor's appointment. After an excruciating fifteen minutes, a little old man in a bowtie led me down a hall and into a tiny office with a desk. He offered me a seat, and then poured me a glass of water.

I don't know what it was about that simple act, but watching him pour that water was like watching an executioner grind his axe. He offered me a few pleasantries about travel and sightseeing, just to bullshit me while we waited. His flimsy lightheartedness sickened me. My stomach lurched and folded on itself with each passing moment.

The door behind me opened, and in walked two men, apparently rabbis. They didn't make any eye contact with me. I'll never forget that moment, the clammy feeling of my socks against my sweaty feet, the taut-rope stiffness of my lower back, the ice in my blood.

The old man pulled out an unmarked brown file, opened it, and took a deep breath. He began to read. After only a few seconds, his words became meaningless, and dissipated like vapors before they reached my ears. His silence afterward felt like a crowbar to the jaw. The room spun. Hands found my shoulders, trying to console me.

My birth mother and father were taken from our home on *Kristallnacht* in 1938. I was a little boy. After a few weeks, they were processed and shipped off to central Germany, into the dark forest, to a concentration camp named *Buchenwald*. In its seven years of operation, fifty thousand people – Jews, gays, prisoners of war, Slavs, Soviets, religious minorities, gypsies, the physically and developmentally disabled – died there. And they didn't just die. They starved or succumbed to disease in the unspeakable filth of the place. Or they were executed: lined up and shot, experimented on, tortured, beaten.

According to recovered Nazi documents, my birth father died there in 1943. My birth mother was taken from the camp two years before that and forced into prostitution for Nazi soldiers. There is no further record of her. It is almost certain that she was executed at the end of the war. The Nazis had a penchant for clearing their tracks.

When I staggered out of that building and into the blinding sunlight, I felt like I'd just had my blood drained. I was cold and numb, and the world blazed around me at a thousand miles an hour. People laughed and talked and went about their lives while I sat there on the pavement, dead as leaves.

On the flight home, I kept thinking about the golem from my childhood dreams – the one whose face broke away to reveal a mere man. A man clearly remorseful for what he was doing. All those years ago, while looking down at him from that staircase, I began to understand.

On those stairs I realized that these golems weren't the otherworldly monsters I had believed them to be. They were just people, like Trent or myself, but they'd been given fancy costumes and a dark purpose. Beneath those masks, some of them still had consciences, and could still feel guilt for their actions. They could hide their faces from their victims, but they could not hide their feelings from themselves. They knew there would be no redemption for their atrocities.

When his mask came off – when I looked into that man's eyes – I was overwhelmed with pity and disgust, sickened at what these men had allowed themselves to become. I was no longer afraid of them, only revolted, for even a young child expects his fellow man to aspire to a certain level of human decency. Not even children, so often accused of ignorance of right and wrong, behave with such savage barbarism. In that moment, a glorified murderer of the innocent owed an explanation to me, and to himself. And he had none.

At that point the golems lost their power over me, and ceased to be the subject of my nightmares. And yet, in the decades after the war, as the world slowly became aware of the Holocaust, I began to better understand my dreams. For years I continued to put together the pieces of that moment on the staircase.

As an adult, I learned how the Nazi Party was obsessed with the concept of identity. Hitler took away individuality from the Germans and gave them a collective identity under the banner of Nazism. He redefined their social norms, making racial hatred a sign of virtue. He did the same thing to the Jews, and assigned them an identity that made them subhuman in the eyes of his followers. People began looking upon Jews as cattle: mindless, emotionless, incapable of human experience. By reassigning identity to groups of people, Hitler turned the murder of human beings into something so banal that it was merely a step between filing papers and going out for drinks. I now believe that my nightmares were a glimpse into this world of identity-obsession.

That long flight home inspired me to do two things. I decided to honor my birth parents by keeping the faith, and to be more mindful of my dreams.

CHAPTER 62

Life kept bending around blind corners. In 1972, while attending an academic conference in Colorado, I met a woman. We bumped into each other in the hotel lobby after she'd been out in a blizzard. Everything about her made me dizzy, the way she said hello, the way she walked, even the way she brushed the snow from her jet-black hair. We spent that whole night talking about books, recounting the best, the worst, and the saddest ones we'd read. We married a year later and bought a small house in Santa Cruz, California, where we planned to start a life beneath the quiet redwoods.

And it was a simple life, just like we'd imagined. We hiked a new trail every weekend. If there was a ray of sunlight left in the sky, we were outside. After dark, we'd sometimes go to the local pizza joint and then dash home for a horror flick. It was our disgustingly cute ritual, and we were devoted to the practice.

Several months ago, my wife and I were seated next to a rather distressed man in a business suit. He ate nothing; he simply drank cup after cup of coffee with a shaky hand and kept looking over his shoulder at us. He watched the door nervously whenever someone came into the diner, like he expected the reaper to stroll in.

As my wife and I chatted about our weekend plans, the man saw something outside and fixated on it for a long while. The waitress tried to get his attention but he ignored her, then suddenly jumped up and ran out of the restaurant without paying. A chubby fry cook chased him out, bill in hand, but lost him in the darkness.

The waitress looked pissed, so I snuck over and left a

crinkled five on the table on behalf of the strange man. And as I approached, I noticed that he'd left behind a book.

The thing looked ancient and was worn down to the spine. The cover was nearly bare. It must have been enthralling because it'd been read a thousand times. Small, elegant letters at the bottom read *Palingar's Prison*. On the spine, the author appeared simply, *Curre*.

Frothing with nerdy excitement, I palmed the book and took it home with us. I intended to read it as soon as I'd wrapped up a sci-fi I'd been tearing through. Alas, *Curre* ended up on my office desk, unread. When I finally opened it, my eyes stuck to the pages. I was like a twelve-year-old boy with his first porno magazine.

The story was about Ulric Palingar, the sickly ruler of the kingdom of Raos. By its flowery writing style and the antiquated language, I judged the book to be from the late 1500's, but it seemed to be a translation of something even older. Someone had scribbled detailed notes across every page, like the frantic scrawlings in texts I'd read in graduate school. But this handwriting was in a language that neither I nor any of my colleagues could identify.

In the story, old Palingar's son Daegan was growing impatient for his succession to the throne. The king grew paranoid that his son would murder him, so he had Daegan killed, and ordered his royal guards to discard the body into the sea. The next night a terrible storm came on, and out of the angry sea came a devil. The monster pursued the old king, haunting his every step and whispering promises of death into his ears.

The king ordered his guards to find the monster and kill it, but eventually he realized that it could never be found. It was always waiting in the darkness, and came for him only when he was alone.

I never found out what happened next. The book went missing when I was about a hundred pages deep. I searched everywhere, but it was as if the book had simply vanished into thin air, just like the monster itself.

Felix Blackwell

CHAPTER 63

Just when I thought things had settled down permanently, trouble found me once again. My marriage soured, I lost my job, and the nightmares returned. This time, however, it was not golems that haunted my dreams.

It was a creature of unspeakable evil...a demon. I know no other word for it. The first time it came to me, I dreamed I was at that diner with my wife, and it was watching me from the woods outside. On another occasion, it stood on the side of the road as I drove home from work. Each night the demon got closer to me, and each night I got less and less sleep.

Then things got worse. I began to see it while I was awake.

As I walked up the driveway to my house one night, I swear I saw the thing standing in the living room. It loomed over my wife, looking down at her as she watched TV. I nearly broke down the door coming in, but of course I found nothing out of the ordinary. A week later I got up in the middle of the night to get a drink, and a huge shadowy form stood in the hallway between me and the staircase. When I flipped on the light, it vanished.

I feared I was losing it. I stopped talking to friends, and even began withdrawing from my wife. She didn't seem to notice, as she and I had been fighting for months prior. I saw a few doctors and had some tests done, but we never figured out what was wrong. And the nightmares kept coming.

One night I came home to find my wife hunched over the fireplace. She had stacks and stacks of my books, even the ones my mom used to read to me, piled all around her.

She was burning them.

I was in such shock I couldn't let go of the doorknob. Not until I saw *Palingar's Prison*.

"What in God's name are you doing?!" I shouted at her.

My wife simply glanced over her shoulder and said, with a flick of her hair, "you spend too much time with these. You need to spend more time with me."

With that, she grabbed another pile, *Curre's* work on top, and tossed it into the flames. The fire roared with satisfaction.

This incident was one of many, each of them worse than the last. I'd never been so angry at someone I loved. I could feel that love mutating into hatred, and I cursed our marriage and the day I met her. I stormed upstairs, packed a bag, and left. I stayed in motels and with old friends. I told myself that this time, it's for good. But I've said that a few times before.

Now I'm sitting in a dingy airport bar, jotting down the last of these pages like a madman channeling voices from beyond. The bartender took special interest in me when I ordered a root beer, and he's been trying to make conversation ever since. He even had the nerve to crack a funny.

"Writin' your final wishes there, pal?"

When he caught my silent offense, he poured me another and placed it next to my notebook, then retreated to the other side of the bar.

I spared a moment to look up at him.

His nametag read *Mike F.*

I surprised him by sliding the drink down the bar and ordering a shot. Tonight seemed like a good night to make an exception. Tonight, there are no rules. There is no plan. For the first time in decades, I feel like I've lost everything. All I can do is sit here with my lonely suitcase, thinking about my childhood, about my dreams, about my wife, about Trent.

Ah, yes, my dad.

I wonder what he would say to me now, if he were to see me fighting with the love of my life.

"Wish I'd had the chance to fight with Anja," I imagined him saying through a grim chuckle.

Felix Blackwell

I still have the pocket watch he gave to me. He told me of how he counted down the miserable hours until he could return home to his beloved fiancée. To him, the watch was a symbol of the eternity he'd spent away from her during the war, and of the bittersweet forevermore he'd spend remembering her smile.

I hold it in my palm now, as my dad held it when Anja gave it to him. And yet I wonder what eternity will be like without my wife. She's the only one I've ever loved, and the only one who's ever loved me. I may not have lost her to an early death, but I'm certainly losing her to another sort of tragedy.

I don't know where I'll go. I don't know where I can run to escape my troubles, or to sort out this disaster. I don't know how to leave my wife. I only wish that she were beside me now. Instead, she's across the battlefield, returning my stare and awaiting my next move. They say you cannot truly hate a person you haven't truly loved, and now I understand why.

Though I've been considering it for weeks, I know that suicide isn't really the answer.

I know what Trent would say about it. He sure as hell thought about it for years after he lost Anja. But I just don't know if I'm as strong as he was.

Maybe I need to wait a few days before making any permanent decisions. I owe it to myself. And to Emily.

Maybe I'll head to Waldport.

Maybe I'll visit my mother, in her little house by the woods, near that cliff overlooking the sea.

ABOUT THE AUTHOR

Felix Blackwell emerged from the bowels of reddit during a botched summoning ritual. He writes novels and short stories in the horror and thriller genres, and draws most of his inspiration from his own nightmares.

For more creepy things to keep you awake, visit
www.felixblackwell.com

Connect with the author at
facebook.com/felixblackwellbooks

Printed in Great Britain
by Amazon

38104237R00182